FINAL TAKE

The guy was a major talent, I had to admit. The videotape had everything—sex, drama, violence, pathos. I wished I could have stayed for the whole thing, but I didn't know how long I had until Cairns returned and there were things to do. I rewound the tape and ejected it.

A studded black-leather thong was knotted on the brass crossbar of the headboard and disappeared in the space between the bed and the curtained wall. It was taut, as if there was a lot of weight pulling on it, and I stepped around the bed to take a look.

It was Cairns.

FAST FADE

BOOKS BY ARTHUR LYONS

OTHER JACOB ASCH NOVELS
All God's Children
The Dead Are Discreet
The Killing Floor
Dead Ringer
Castles Burning
Hard Trade
At the Hands of Another
Three With a Bullet

NONFICTION
Satan Wants You:
*The Cult of Devil Worship in America**

*Published by
THE MYSTERIOUS PRESS

FAST FADE

Arthur Lyons

THE MYSTERIOUS PRESS

New York • London • Tokyo

MYSTERIOUS PRESS EDITION

Cover design and illustration by Peter Thorpe

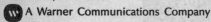 Mysterious Press books are published in association with
Warner Books, Inc.
666 Fifth Avenue
New York, N.Y. 10103

W A Warner Communications Company

Printed in the United States of America

Originally published in hardcover by The Mysterious Press.
First Mysterious Press Paperback Printing: July, 1988

10 9 8 7 6 5 4 3 2 1

FOR MARIE
The Love of My Life

ACKNOWLEDGMENTS

I would like to give special thanks to Norm Prescott, Mark Levinson, Charles Engel, Joel Schumacher, Ray Sackheim, and Rita Miller, whose advice and expertise were invaluable to the writing of this book.

FAST
FADE

1

It was one of those gray, wet, midwinter beach mornings when the fog rolls in during the night with the clear intention of spending the day, when the stiffening dampness bores into your bones and makes you feel old, the kind of day to stay in bed and watch reruns of *Leave It to Beaver* just to remember with vague fondness what *little* problems were like. But being the model of the mature, responsible adult Ward Cleaver would have wanted his Theodore to grow up to be, I dragged myself out of bed and down to the office to sift through the mail that had been accumulating for the past three days. The last thing I expected to find waiting for me there was a client. I could tell she was a client by the confused look on her face. All my clients have that look.

She was standing on the sidewalk, fog swirling around her, glancing uncertainly from the paper in her hand to the peeling, two-story stucco office building, as if she couldn't quite believe what she'd written down. She'd probably been expecting something from *Matt Houston*; Hollywood has done that to us. It was about to do a lot more, but I didn't know that as I walked up behind her and asked: "Can I help you?"

She turned, startled. She was in her late thirties, and the kind of innocuous-attractive you would notice in a crowd only if you made a point of it. Her small oval face ended in a small, sharp chin, and her short brown hair was shag-cut. She had brown eyes set far apart, a long nose with slightly flared nostrils, and a small turned-down mouth that looked as if it were used to frowning. She was color-coordinated in maroon and gray—a gray jacket over a gray-and-maroon-striped blouse, gray wool skirt, gray pumps, gray handbag, which she was clutching tightly now. I couldn't blame her; this wasn't the best neighborhood. "No, thank you," she said resolutely.

Her eyes took in the brown paper bag in my hand, then darted past me nervously, scanning the street for help, in case I tried to drag her back into the alley beside the building. It would make an interesting headline, anyway: WOMAN AS-SAULTED WITH CHEESE DANISH.

"My office is in this building, is the reason I asked," I offered, trying to put her at ease.

"Oh." Her eyes registered relief and she smiled uncertain-ly, as if trying to recall how that was done. "I'm looking for the office of Jacob Asch Investigations." She had been out west long enough to shake most of the magnolia blossoms out of her speech, but the Southern accent still popped up on certain words, lending a soft, lilting charm to her voice.

"Number five, second floor. I'm going up. I'll show you."

"You know him?"

"Only professionally. Personally, he's a complete enigma."

"I'm only interested in him professionally. Is he reliable?"

"The American Academy of Private Eyes gave him a 'ten' last year. That's their highest rating."

"I didn't know they were rated," she said, obviously impressed.

"The same people who do the Nielsens do it. The same people who made *The Dukes of Hazzard* number one."

I went ahead of her up the outside stairs before she had too much time to think about that one. I stopped in front of number five, the door that says JACOB ASCH INVESTIGATIONS on it, and put my key into the lock.

"You're him?" she asked.

I stepped back and gave her my Errol Flynn bow, and

opened the door. I hit the light switch and pulled open the venetian blinds to let in whatever meager light the day had to offer. She stepped inside slowly, misgiving growing in her eyes as they took in the soil marks on the threadbare green carpet, the smudge marks on the brown walls, the two battle-fatigued chairs and metal desk, the chipped enamel on the filing cabinets, and the small Diebold safe in the corner.

I felt annoyed to discover I was self-conscious. I only used the place as a mail drop and a repository for my case files, so consequently I'd never seen any reason to spend a lot of money on a big front. Eighty percent of my business is conducted through attorneys, and of the other twenty, nineteen will usually have the sense to call first, at which time I will arrange to meet them elsewhere—preferably a restaurant for lunch, where, if I was lucky, they would pick up the check. But no, this woman had to show up in person.

I motioned to one of the chairs and asked: "May I get you some coffee?"

"Thank you," she said, and sat down.

I put my bag down next to the Mr. Coffee on top of the safe, grabbed the glass coffeepot and excused myself to make a quick trip downstairs to the men's room for water. When I came back I found her staring at my one wall adornment, a four-by-four oil painting of the Midnight Skulker behind the desk. It had been a gift from an artist I used to date; she had painted it after I had jokingly told her one day that the Skulker was my role model. I said, "Do you read 'B.C.'?"

She looked at me, uncomprehending. "Pardon me?"

"The comic strip."

"Uh, no."

"The painting is a character from 'B.C.'"

"Oh." She smiled weakly. Very weakly. It was obvious that her confidence in me was growing by the minute.

I poured the water into the coffee maker, then sat down at the desk.

"Now, Miss . . . ?"

"Norris. Lori Norris."

On the third finger of her right hand there was a small diamond ring. Probably not a divorce case, then. "It is *Miss* Norris?"

"Yes."

I nodded. "What can I do for you, Miss Norris?"

She crossed her legs. They were nice legs; I was surprised I hadn't noticed how nice before this. She was the kind that looked better the longer you looked at her. Not exactly the steamy sexpot always waiting in the detective's outer office, but then I didn't have an outer office, so who was I to complain? "First of all, I'd like to know what you charge?"

"That depends on the job," I said, as Mr. Coffee began to gurgle and hiss. "My standard rate is $250 a day plus expenses, plus twenty cents a mile, if there's a lot of driving involved."

She looked surprised. "I didn't know it would be that much."

She looked around again, and I could tell by the skeptical look in her eyes what she was thinking. She was dividing $250 a day by the furniture and multiplying that by the number of my clients. Mr. Coffee continued to gurgle and hiss, audibilizing my irritation. To hell with her; if she was so shallow as to judge by appearances, I wouldn't want her as a client.

"What kind of a car do you drive, Miss Norris?"

She seemed surprised by the question. "A Toyota Celica. Why?"

At least she hadn't said a 1971 Monte Carlo. For a Celica driver, I was willing to put off my cheese Danish, at least for a while.

"You probably pay your mechanic $35 an hour to change your oil and never say a word about it."

She finally got my drift. Her tone turned apologetic: "I didn't mean to offend you. I'm sure you're worth what you charge."

"You didn't offend me. There are investigators around who charge less, some who charge more. May I ask how you got my name?"

"From the Yellow Pages."

"There are other detectives in the book. Why me?"

"I don't know. I guess I liked your name," she said, her cheeks flushing. "And it was convenient. I don't live far from here."

The scientific method. She picked detectives like some handicappers I knew picked horses. From their win-loss ratio, I supposed it was as good a method as any.

Mr. Coffee stopped gurgling and hissing and I got up and poured two Styrofoam cups, then pulled the half-pint of milk from the paper bag. She said she would have a little, and I put a splash into her coffee and handed it to her. The admiration in her eyes told me unmistakably that she knew now her scientific methodology had paid off. No powdered nondairy-creamer crap for this detective. You couldn't trust a man who would take those kinds of shortcuts; he'd short-change you every time.

I sat down and she opened her purse and took out a copy of *People* magazine. She opened it to a marked page and put it down on the desk in front of me, tapping a photograph with an unpainted nail. I picked it up and took a closer look. In the picture, Robert Wagner and Candy Bergen were yukking it up at a post-premiere party for some movie called *No Love Lost*.

"I want you to prove the man in that picture is my ex-husband," she said gravely.

Wonderful. Instead of a cheese Danish, I was starting my day with Fruit Loops. "You were married to Robert Wagner?"

"Of course not. The man standing *behind* Robert Wagner." The tall, gray-haired man she was talking about was turned partially away from the camera, holding a cocktail and talking to a smashing-looking blonde. The caption beneath the photograph identified him as film director Walter Cairns.

"His real name is William McVey," Lori Norris said. "He's an electronics engineer."

She took another photograph, this one color, out of her purse, and handed it to me. In it, a younger her and a tall, lean man with dark hair and a long ruggedly handsome face smiled happily in front of a white house. "That was taken sixteen years ago, in Atlanta. Just before he disappeared."

"Let me get this straight," I said, not because I really wanted to. "You and this man were married sixteen years ago and he disappeared—"

"That's right."

"And you had no idea what happened to him?"

"Not until I saw that picture in *People*."

I put both pictures side by side and studied them carefully. There was a resemblance, in body type and general shape of face, but even taking into account the differences in appearance sixteen years would make, it was impossible to say any more than that, from the quality of the magazine photograph. "I'm willing to admit there's a slight resemblance, Miss Norris, but frankly—"

"That *is* my ex-husband," she said stubbornly.

"How can you be so sure?"

"Because I talked to him."

That one stopped me. "When?"

"Last Saturday. He's shooting a movie in Palm Springs and I drove down there. I had to see for myself if it was him. It was."

"What did he have to say?"

She waved a hand in the air. "Oh, he denied everything. Said he didn't have the slightest idea what I was talking about, that he'd never heard of Bill McVey, and that if I didn't get off his set immediately, he was going to have me arrested."

"You left?"

"What else was I going to do?"

"But you're convinced Cairns is your ex."

She caught the doubt in my voice and said definitely: "There's no doubt in my mind. He could change some things about his appearance, but he couldn't change his voice."

"How long were you married?"

"Four years."

She proceeded to tell me about it from the beginning, lacing her narrative with the most minor details, down to the kind of drink she'd been having (a Yellow Cadillac, whatever that was) when the handsome McVey had approached her in the Skyroom bar of the Peachtree Hotel in Atlanta. He hailed from Baltimore, and had come to Atlanta four years before to accept a position at Dynotran, an outfit that made components for missile guidance systems, among other things. He was witty, intelligent, and charming, and she had been immediately smitten. They started dating regularly after that, and within two months were married. She was twenty-three, he was twenty-eight.

Eight months later, when she became pregnant with their daughter Melanie, McVey persuaded her to quit her job as a computer operator to become a full-time mother, arguing that his salary at Dynotran was sufficient enough to keep them comfortably in the new three-bedroom tract house they'd bought in Marietta, just outside Atlanta.

Everything had gone along Georgia-peachy for three years, an idyllic suburban dream, until the afternoon she'd come from shopping and found McVey's Camaro in the driveway, but no McVey.

When he didn't show up that night or for work the next morning, she'd called the police, fearing he'd been in some terrible accident, but a check of the hospitals and morgue turned up zilch. The thought hadn't even struck her to check the closet, and probably wouldn't have until the cops suggested it, and when she did, she found some of his clothes missing, about enough to fill one suitcase, which was also missing. A call to the bank had confirmed that McVey had withdrawn $5,000 from their savings account the morning of his disappearance, leaving a balance of $11,500. Eleven grand was not enough to keep all payments juggling for very long, and when the idea finally crystallized for her five months later that Wonderful Willy wasn't coming home, she sold the house and one of the cars, moved into a small apartment in Atlanta that took ankle-biters, and got a job as a computer operator at a large payroll company.

I interrupted her narrative to ask: "Did you ever try to find McVey?"

"How?" she asked, shrugging helplessly. "Where was I going to look?"

"Didn't he have any relatives? Family?"

She shook her head. "Everyone was dead. His parents were killed in an automobile accident two years before I met him. Or so he said. Anyway, I had enough to worry about, just trying to take care of myself and my daughter."

"You say he came from Baltimore. Is that where he was from?"

"Yes."

I got up and poured myself another cup of coffee. She hadn't touched hers, which was probably better for her. I sat back down and asked: "While you were living together, did your husband ever evince interest in the movie business?"

"No. He was a creative person, though. He wrote stories. He even submitted a few of them to magazines, but none were ever accepted."

I nodded and picked up a pencil and began doodling on my pad. "Go on."

She picked up her life from the time of the divorce. She began to suffer from lengthening periods of deep depression after her divorce, and began to see a psychiatrist. She put on weight. A lot of weight. To avoid dealing with her feelings of personal failure, she threw herself into her work, and her dedication made an impression on her supervisors. When the company opened a West Coast branch in Los Angeles and offered her the position of district supervisor, she'd jumped at it, thinking that a change of scenery might snap her out of her emotional doldrums. That had been seven years ago.

Whether it was the California sunshine, her new managerial position, or just the healing effects of time, she began to get better. She slimmed down to her old weight and began to date again. She got married again, this time to a stockbroker. She didn't quit her job, which was a good thing, because the marriage ended in divorce a year later, but she found that this time she was not shattered by the experience.

She had become a whole woman, able to cope with life's cruel vicissitudes. "It took me a while," she declared, almost defiantly, after her recitation, "but I'm finally happy with myself, with my life."

"Then why are you here?"

Her back straightened. "What do you mean?"

"Say, just for argument's sake, Cairns is McVey, and I prove it. What then?"

"I want him to admit it. I want him to acknowledge what he did to me and Melanie."

"That's all?"

Her face reddened. "Do you have any idea what kind of emotional scars being abandoned leaves on you, Mr. Asch? For a long time, you can't stop blaming yourself, you think there must be something terribly wrong with you, to cause the person you loved to leave you like that. Then, just to survive, you start to see that it wasn't you, it was him, and you start to get your self-confidence back, only at the expense of your confidence in others. You're afraid to get involved with anyone because you think, every time he goes to work in the morning, that you'll never see him again. You stop trusting. That's probably part of why my second marriage failed."

The anguish in her voice sounded real, her eyes brimmed with tears. "I've struggled for thirteen years to raise my daughter, Mr. Asch. I've scrimped and I've saved and I've denied myself and I've denied her. Who the hell is he to deny who he is and tell me he's going to have me *arrested?* Who is he to drive his Rolls-Royce and lounge around his Malibu house while I juggle my paycheck to meet the condo payment and buy Melanie school clothes?"

"You want him to pay?"

"Why shouldn't he?" she asked, angrily.

It had taken a recitation of *Gone With the Wind,* but she'd finally gotten down to it. "No reason, if he's who you say he. is. That part will be up to an attorney. Do you have one?"

"No."

I nodded, my mind working on that angle already. "I can recommend a few who are very good on this kind of thing, if it gets to that stage. But first things first."

I pulled a standard contract out of the desk drawer, filled in her vitals, along with the amount of $750.00 in the "Retainer" space, and handed it to her to look over.

She winced when she saw the amount, but said nothing about it. "How long do you think it will take?"

"If you're wrong, not long. If you're right, a little longer. Either way, I don't anticipate much more than the retainer."

She nodded curtly and signed the contract and a check for seven-fifty, and I slipped them both into the desk drawer. She might have gotten nervous seeing the check disappear in my coat pocket, although that was where it was going to wind up the minute she was out the door.

Once the important business was out of the way, I took down the information she had on Cairns—his address in

Malibu, the color of his Rolls Corniche (white), and the name of the movie he was directing in Palm Springs (*Death in the Desert*)—and told her I'd need to hold on to the photograph of her and Cairns for a while. "You were married in Atlanta?"

"Yes."

"Would you happen to have a copy of your marriage certificate somewhere?"

"I don't know. Why do you want that?"

"There is a wealth of information on those things. It might be very helpful."

"I'll see if I can find it."

I smiled and told her I would take care of everything, and she stood and held out her hand. "I feel as if I've made the right choice." Her glance caught the Midnight Skulker behind me and the confidence seemed to dim in her eyes. Before it vanished completely, I walked her to the door.

I pulled my cheese Danish from the bag, poured myself another cup of coffee, and looked up Lori Norris in the phone book. The Marina del Rey address and phone number matched the one she'd given me. I called the number and got no answer, then dialed Acutron Data Processing. A receptionist put me through to Lori Norris' extension, and the girl who answered said Miss Norris wouldn't be in until ten. I told her I would call back and hung up. On the surface, at least, the woman appeared to be who she said she was. I guess I should have been thankful. I'd once had a client—a hippie-type leftover from the sixties with stringy hair that reeked of incense—who told me she'd gotten my name throwing *I Ching* sticks. At least this one didn't smell like the inside of a Buddhist monastery.

It wasn't that I found her story particularly strange, or even uncommon. There were thousands of men out there with Walter Mitty dreams dancing in their heads, and every year, more than a few of them leave wives and kids to pursue them. Some of them even make them come true. If Cairns was one of them, he wasn't likely to be very understanding when I popped up threatening to turn his dream into a nightmare, and before I did that, I wanted to be sure Lori Norris and her check were bona fide. I stared at the check while I called Larry Bigelow.

Larry had been a film critic at the *Chronicle* while I was still a reporter there, and we had struck up a friendship almost immediately. He was a flaming queen, and a bitchy one at that, but I'd found his acerbic wit and sharp-tongued cynical observations about the human condition a perfect cure for the dreary boredom of slow news days. On those afternoons, we would drift down the street to Shaunessey's and he would fill me in on all the latest Glitter City dirt—which church-going, Moral Majority actress had the clap or which macho-man TV-series cop liked to slip into a silk dress when he took off that itchy old L.A.P.D. uniform—while we tippled a few at the bar.

I'd often told him that he should be doing a gossip column instead of futzing around with movie reviews, and shortly before my own newspaper career went down the crapper, he'd taken my advice and left the *Chronicle* to give it a try. Within four years, "Lawrence of Hollywood" was syndicated in 223 papers across the country and, although many whose names appeared in the column complained bitterly that Larry had managed to raise innuendo to a new art form, some even going so far as to call him a liar, few had dared go further than that. I only remember one man who had, in fact—a kiddie-show host who sued Larry for libel after he'd hinted in his column that the man's love for his kiddie audience might be more than paternal. The host had wound up being bounced ignominiously from the airwaves when Larry's attorneys produced two nine-year-old boys who testified in court that the man liked to watch them "do things" while he was dressed up as Big Bird.

I fed him a morsel every now and then, when I ran across something I thought the public should know, for which he always offered to pay, and which I always refused. I preferred to take it out in trade; in this business, you never can tell when you might need a morsel of information yourself.

Hugo, Larry's latest male secretary-squeeze, answered. He didn't know me, and refused at first to put Larry on, but finally I convinced him, and he summoned the Great One to the phone.

"Jacob! Where have you been keeping yourself? I haven't heard from you in months. I was beginning to think you'd been bumped off by one of those desperate criminals you intrepidly hunt down."

"The cops hunt down desperate criminals, Larry. I hunt down desperate deadbeats and alimony cheaters."

"Make my day," he said. "Tell me you're calling to give me a juicy morsel about one of them."

"No morsels today. In fact, I need some information from you."

"If you want to know who has AIDS, you're out of luck. You're just going to have to take your chances with the rest of us."

"Walter Cairns," I said.

"What about him?"

"Know him?"

"We've met a few times."

"What's his story?"

"Professionally or personally?"

"You can start with professionally."

"Writer-turned-director," he said as if reading from his column. "Turned out a string of semi-hits in the late seventies, early eighties, mostly medium- and low-budget suspense-mystery flicks in the *noir* style. Hasn't done much in the past couple of years. His last two movies bombed—badly. Since then, he's been one of the Untouchables."

"Just for doing two stiffs?"

"In Hollywood, money is the name of the game, booby. To a studio executive, a movie can't *possibly* be any good unless it *costs*. If a two-million-dollar movie happens to gross twenty mil, that's great, but it's a fluke. A guy like Cimino can make a *Heaven's Gate* for forty mil and bring down a studio and still get work, but a guy like Cairns has two flops in a row and everybody nods and says, 'See, we always knew he didn't have it. Otherwise he would've been doing *big* pictures.'"

"I hear he's working again in Palm Springs."

"For Marty Resnick. I was surprised when I heard. One of the bombs he made was for Triad, Resnick's company."

"So why did Resnick hire him again?"

"I don't know. From what I hear, he's sorry he did. The picture is apparently behind schedule and over budget."

"Cairns' fault?"

"I don't know. I'm supposed to be down in the Springs in the next couple of days to interview Marla McKinnon. I'll find out then."

"Marla McKinnon," I mused, conjuring up an image of that dark, sultry beauty. "I haven't heard that name in a while."

"Four years," Larry said.

Starting out as a model, she had a face and body that appeared on almost every magazine cover in the world before she had launched into a successful movie career. On the screen, directors deftly exploited the sexuality she exuded so effortlessly, and for three or four years Marla McKinnon was every American male's fantasy fuck. Then, at the height of her stardom, she suddenly dropped out of sight and went into seclusion at her isolated beach home in Big Sur. Rumors abounded about the reasons for her premature retirement, from drug problems to her broken romance with hunk-star Rock Mason, but she would not publicly confirm or deny any of them, refusing any interviews.

"This is her first film since her self-imposed exile," Larry said. "She had a complete nervous breakdown, you know."

"No. I knew she disappeared, but I didn't know why."

"The pressure got to her, poor thing. Her agent talked her into taking on too much work, and she started popping pills to go to sleep, and it started to show up in her work. She started to forget her lines. Then she got arrested for drunk driving. The finale came while she was working on *Call Girl*. She fell apart like a cheap suit and they had to replace her. That was it for her."

"She's all right now?"

"You can give me a report when you go to Palm Springs."

"Who says I'm going to Palm Springs?"

"The tea leaves never lie, my son."

"What bout Cairns' personal life?"

"A bit of mystery there. If you solve it, let me know. He keeps a low profile, although every once in a while a bubble does rise to the surface."

"How does it sound when it pops?"

"This is totally unconfirmed, just rumor."

"What's a little rumor between friends?"

"He's kinky."

"What kind of kinky?"

"Cairns is a dominating personality. He is into *control* on the set, and I hear that passion extends into his private life, too—if you get my drift."

"Not really," I said. "I long ago came to the conclusion that the only thing in life I have control over is my weight, and I'm losing that fast."

"Isn't it horrid?" he asked sympathetically. "I hate growing old."

"Cairns is into bondage?"

"It's only a rumor," Larry said. "What is your interest in Cairns, anyway? Something I should know about?"

"Sorry, Larry, but I can't go into it. Not now, anyway. Maybe later."

"Tease."

"You have a bio on Cairns in your files?"

"My dear, I have files on *everybody*."

"Can I get what you have?"

"When do you need it?"

"This afternoon."

"I won't be here. I have to run to Burbank to interview Bunny Baxter, but I'll have Hugo run off a copy for you."

"Thanks. And tell Hugo to include any photographs of Cairns he might run across."

"Sorry, but there aren't any in the file. Or anywhere else I know of, either. The man does not allow himself to be photographed."

"Why not?"

"The reason he gave me four years ago when I did a feature on him was that he didn't want the public to know his face, just his work. Said he'd seen too many people get caught up in the celebrity thing and he wanted to keep his private life private."

I wondered if there could be another reason the man did not want his picture in circulation, like an ex-wife and kid he'd left in Atlanta thirteen years ago.

I picked up the photograph and stared at it. "You know what they say: One picture is worth a thousand bucks."

"Words," he corrected me.

"In this case, bucks. By the way, you know where Cairns is staying in Palm Springs?"

"He's renting a condo for the duration of the shoot. I have the number. The rest of the cast and crew are staying at the International. They've set up production headquarters there. Not exactly the Ritz, but it isn't exactly a twenty-million-dollar extravaganza, either. I think the whole budget is about four mil."

He fetched Cairns' address and phone number and I thanked him and hung up.

I spent the next half hour throwing out junk mail and paying bills, then drove to my bank and deposited Lori Norris' check to keep the ones I'd written from bouncing. That done, I stopped into the Pico office of the Associated Credit Bureau and had printouts run of both Walter Cairns and my client.

Lori Norris did indeed own a Toyota Celica, or at least part of one—the bank being the majority shareholder—and was making regular payments on a condo at the Marina del Rey address she'd given me. As the information credit bureaus like Associated supply does not cross state lines, her credit went back only as far as 1983, which was probably when she'd moved to California. Aside from a few Slow Pay codes, she looked like a pretty good risk, no judicial actions and no collections. That made me feel at least a little more secure, just in case I had to put in some real time on this thing.

Cairns' printout went back to 1971, and from the look of things, his first few years in the glamour capital had been shaky—a couple of collections, one lawsuit, and a repo on a 1966 Dodge Dart—but by 1976 he had turned things around.

The sheet showed he owned a house in Malibu valued at $750,000, about two-thirds of which was paid off, a Rolls Corniche, and a boat. His birthdate was listed as 1–9–41, and the first three digits of his Social Security number were 525, which meant he had applied for the card in New Mexico. One item stirred my interest: One week ago, Cairns had taken out a second mortgage with the National Mortgage Company for $100,000.

I drove to the nearest DMV office, where for a $1.00 fee I obtained a copy of Cairns' driving history. Like his credit rating, the printout began in 1971, nothing unusual in itself. What *was* unusual was that the computer pulled up a big fat blank when I asked the clerk to scan for prior licenses. If Cairns had been driving in another state before moving to California, he would have been asked to turn in his old license when he applied for his California license, which would have been in the computer. If it was true that life began at forty, it was beginning to look more and more like Cairns had gotten a jump on things by about eight years.

Larry Bigelow worked out of his house in the hills above the Sunset Strip. It was a small but Spanish-style house of the variety that was in vogue in Hollywood in the thirties. Hugo, Larry's secretary, turned out to be a lithe, peroxide-blond young man with a sunlamp tan and a nut and bolt through his right earlobe, and he met me at the door with a manila envelope with my name on it and a smile I was sure would have driven Larry crazy had he been there.

I stopped at a coffee shop on the Strip and went through the contents of the envelope over a tuna sandwich. Cairns' bio was conveniently devoid of details that could be disputed or verified. The only son of itinerant farm workers, he'd been born on January 9, 1941, in Marshalltown, Iowa. As the family never settled in one place long enough to enroll the boy in school, he was totally self-educated. To escape the drudgery and boredom of the farm camps, Cairns read voraciously, however, and indulged his overactive imagination by "writing stories," a pastime for which he found he had both a talent and a passion. At the age of fourteen he left home and bummed around the country, surviving by "begging, stealing, and picking up odd jobs here and there," all the time keeping journals on the characters he met and the stories they told him—"mulch," as he called it, for his own future stories.

In 1971 he arrived in Hollywood, with the "crazy idea of breaking into movies." He worked as a night watchman, a parking attendant, and a waiter while writing his first screenplay, *Double Entry*, which he eventually sold to Columbia. The picture was a hit, and Cairns' movie career was launched.

There were half a dozen articles in the packet about Cairns and his work that had appeared in various newspapers, and one in particular intrigued me. In it, the writer called Cairns a "resurrector of the *noir* sensibility," and said that all of his films had a downbeat, dark, urban mood, populated by the "alienated and the obsessed, shell-shocked Vietnam vets and amnesiacs, fugitives from themselves and an uncaring universe." "We don't know who the villains are anymore," Cairns was quoted by the reporter. "We are all struggling with the dark night in our own souls."

That was certainly true about *Double Entry*. I'd seen the film a couple of times on late-night TV, the last time only a month or so ago. It was a strange film about a con man who murders his identical twin brother and assumes that successful businessman's life, only to be ironically shot to death in the end by a competitor his dead brother had ruthlessly forced into bankruptcy. I had to wonder if the imposter plot Cairns had used for his first script had come from autobiographical material. Maybe he had been struggling with the "dark night" in his own soul. That struck me as being a little too obvious, but then, I didn't know the size of the man's ego. Maybe he'd been telling the world what he'd done and was daring anybody to do anything about it.

I'd never been able to turn down a dare, ever since I was a kid, and I had the scars to prove it. I didn't figure one or two more mattered much.

2

It had been almost five years since I'd been in Palm Springs—since the Fleischer case. I was shocked by the changes in the place, although I probably shouldn't have been. Things had been moving inexorably in that direction ever since I'd first come down as a college kid during Easter break to party with long-legged girls and beer-swilling classmates.

The site had originally been settled by lungers and arthritics who had come to be healed by the dry desert heat and the mineral-rich water that bubbled out of the ground, but by the thirties it had been discovered by the movie crowd, who found the sandy serenity a haven from the frantic pace of Hollywood, and recreation and glamour were added to the list of Palm Springs' selling points. "Fun in the Sun" became the town's new motto, and it didn't take long for the snowbirds to begin to flock, figuring it was more pleasant to play tennis and golf in seventy-five-degree weather than in the middle of a blizzard in East Jesus, Illinois. Condos sprouted like toadstools. Village gradually became city.

Five years ago, the transformation was still in progress, but now it was nearly complete. The quaint village feel was all but gone, the small shops and theaters in the center of town had been squashed flat by a gargantuan five-story deluxe hotel and shopping mall that blotted out the view of the mountains behind the town and made me feel claustrophobic as I drove down Palm Canyon Drive.

There was no more kid stuff here, no more innocent horsey charm. The street had a slick, subdued, deadly intent to it and the intent was to take your money. Gucci, Saks, Bullocks—Palm Canyon Drive was a paradise for Beverly Hills housewives suffering from Rodeo Drive withdrawal.

The Ramada International was at the far end of town, and was definitely more Main Street than Rodeo Drive. It was one square block and three stories of cheap-looking stucco fortress surrounded by a moat of parking lot. I checked in, got my key and directions to the production office, and headed over there.

The entire bottom floor of the hotel's south wing had been taken over by the movie, and on all the doors, pieces of paper had been thumbtacked on which names had been crudely scribbled in pen: WARDROBE, CASTING, TRANSPORTATION. PRODUCTION was at the end of the hall, next to the Coke machine. It was a two-room suite and the beds had been moved out to accommodate the desks and other office equipment that cluttered it. A long girl was at one of the desks, working out on a Selectric. I told her I was from the studio and inquired where they were shooting today and she gave me an address on Country Club Drive, in Rancho Mirage.

As I headed out of town, the designer aspect of the buildings began to give way to used-car lots and fast-food drive-throughs and seedy-looking gay bars that made up Cathedral City, and memories surfaced of the last time I'd made this drive. I had been on a case then, too, only things hadn't worked out so well, which was probably why I hadn't been back here in five years. Aversion therapy. I'd seen too much here, too much money and what it couldn't buy, too many diseased souls, too much death, and it all came back to me as I drove out the highway.

At Country Club I made a left, and about a mile down I spotted a line of big trucks and trailers parked half a block down on a side street. I pulled up behind them and parked and followed the trail of electrical cables into what had once been a date grove, but was now just an area of charred, blackened stumps like giant, spent firecrackers somebody had stuck in the ground and ignited. The ground was black where the fire had scorched it, and dead fronds had been stacked in huge piles, a harvest done by skeletons.

The cables led to a clearing marked off by yellow police crime-scene tape, where half a dozen men stood around and on two dolly-mounted 35-millimeter Arriflex cameras. Several others fiddled with the baffles on the four big arc lights. Outside the taped area, fifty or sixty gofers and gaffers and technical people, along with assorted spectators and several uniformed Palm Springs cops, mulled about, talking and swigging from canned soft drinks procured from two giant ice chests on the ground.

I drifted through the crowd, trying to spot Cairns, and I must have been trying too hard, because I wound up walking squarely into somebody. When I turned to apologize, I was startled to find myself staring into the face of a week-old corpse. He had been young when he'd died, and possibly even handsome, but now his skin was gray and peeling off his face and neck in rotten chunks. Blood had oozed from the bullet hole above his right eye and dried in a black trail down his cheek. Standing next to him made me feel slightly uneasy, even though I knew it was just makeup; I'd seen a lot of his type in my time, but I wasn't used to them ambulatory.

"Sorry," I mumbled.

"That's okay," he said with alacrity, and took a swig from a bottle of Perrier. Even the dead had to have a sparkling-water break.

"That'll teach you to use sunscreen," I said.

"Huh?" Then he remembered the makeup. "Oh yeah. My fucking agent."

"Pardon?"

"My agent," he repeated cryptically. "He keeps getting me these gigs. You a director?" His voice sounded hopeful.

"No."

"Producer?"

Again I made a disclaimer. He sighed disappointedly, but that didn't keep him from going on. "You know, I never intended to be an actor. I wanted to go to med school."

I wondered what it was about me that made them want to give me their life's story. "As what? A cadaver?"

"No, honestly, I did, but my grades weren't good enough and everyone kept telling me I'm so handsome I should be an actor, so I took up drama. My agent tells me I'm a natural for romantic leads. Some romantic lead. In my last movie I was a zombie."

"Sounds like typecasting to me," I sympathized, and asked him if he'd seen Walter Cairns. He pointed to a tall, gray-haired man in a red T-shirt and jeans standing fifty feet away talking animatedly to a short woman with long hair as black as her evening dress. I had only seen Marla McKinnon on the screen, that was the totality of her reality for me, and seeing her down here with the rest of us flesh-and-blood mortals was strangely unreal. Her unreality was more real than her reality. I wondered what Immanuel Kant would have said about that.

"It's really frustrating," the corpse droned in my ear. "I could at least get my SAG card if I could get a part with some dialogue. I just wish I could show these producers my range as an actor. I mean, I can do classical, Shakespeare, you name it."

"Keep the faith," I said distractedly, keeping my eyes on Cairns as I moved away. "You'll get your romantic lead. All you have to do is find a leading lady who's into necrophilia."

I edged up to the taped-off area in which Marla McKinnon and Cairns were talking. From his hand motions, I guessed Cairns was telling her the way he wanted her to walk into the frame, and when he'd finished, she sat down in a canvas chair shaded by an umbrella and began going over some script pages.

"Scott!" Cairns shouted.

"Yo!" answered a husky man standing beside the camera holding a bullhorn.

"Where the hell is Adrianne?" Cairns asked, as the man trotted over.

"In her trailer."

"Well, send somebody over there and tell her to get out here. This location is costing ten thousand a day and we have to be out of here by five."

The man with the bullhorn shrugged sheepishly. "She says she's sick and can't come out."

Cairns' face reddened. "Sick? How in the fuck can she be sick? She just did a scene here twenty minutes ago."

"She says she stepped on an ant. She says she's allergic."

"Bullshit!" Cairns thundered. "Get her out here!"

The other man looked very uncomfortable. "She's locked the door. She won't open it. Maybe she'll talk to you. She wouldn't to Barry—"

"Is Suzanne in there with her?"

"She won't let her in, either."

"Jesus fucking Christ," Cairns said, and started toward me. The black letters on his red T-shirt read: IF I HAD ANY FRIENDS I WOULDN'T BE WITH THESE ASSHOLES. That I could believe. I took an angle to intercept him, but was beaten out by a short, slightly built man with very short black hair, who shouldered past me, frantically waving a sheaf of pink papers. He said with a noticeable British accent: "Walter, I have to talk to you—"

"Not now, Matthew," Cairns said in an irritated tone, and tried to step around, but the man was having none of it.

"The script needs to talk to you, Walter—"

Cairns' eyes rolled up. He put a hand on his hip and shifted his weight. "What is it *now*, Matthew?"

"*Now?*" The little Englishman sounded close to hysteria. "It's these pages, that's what's *now*."

"What about them?"

"They stink."

"We went through this already—"

"That's what *I* thought. We agreed that the ending had to be changed, but not changed for the *worse*."

"Look," Cairns said, starting to move off again, "I've got enough problems right now—"

The Englishman followed, waving the pink pages like an angry pennant. "That's right. And the main one is *this*. If this ending stays, you haven't got a movie!"

Cairns kept walking. "That's your opinion, Matthew. And to tell you the truth, I don't give a shit about it." He stopped suddenly and turned to the man with the bullhorn who was trailing behind. "Scott, from now on, Matthew is banned from the set. Get him out of here."

"You can't do that," the Englishman stammered.

Cairns stared straight at him, and his mouth twisted into a self-satisfied smirk. "Wanna bet?"

"I'll call Marty—"

"Call any-fucking-body you want. Just stay away from my movie."

"*Your* movie? You sonofabitch!" He started for Cairns, his right fist clenched, but the assistant director stepped in his way and put a hand on his chest, stopping him. The Englishman's face reddened and contorted in rage. He ripped the script pages in half and threw the pieces at Cairns, who stood impassively, not blinking. The A.D. grabbed the man's arm, but the small man wrenched his arm loose violently and stepped back. "Take your fucking hands off me," he said, in an attempt to regain some lost pride. He looked around, embarrassed, then glared hatefully at Cairns. "I'll get you for this," he said and stalked off.

Cairns watched him go, then started off again, and as he passed me, I took a closer look at his face. It was tanned and ruggedly lined, and with his prematurely gray hair and square jaw, he looked like one of those men on freeway billboards showing the robust, outdoorsy, healthiness all cigarette smokers share. He had pale blue eyes, a straight, long nose, and a thin-lipped mouth, and although it seemed as if he might have had a bit more cheekbone and chin than the man in the picture in my pocket, that could have been due to the quality of the picture. Or surgery. There was no doubt that there was a very strong resemblance.

I followed the small band that had congregated around him through the blackened date grove to one of the trailers, where a tall, slender blonde in white slacks and a blue silk blouse was knocking on the door. "Adrianne, honey, come on. Open up. It's Susanne—"

Cairns strode up to her. "What's going on, Susanne? What's all this bullshit about an ant?"

The woman was mid-thirtyish, not pretty or plain, but pleasant-looking, or at least would be when her face wasn't mapped with tension and there wasn't so much makeup gobbed around her hazel eyes. "She's allergic—"

"Don't give me 'allergic,' Susanne. It's about her close-up, isn't it?"

The woman shrugged and said pleadingly: "It's her best scene, Walter. She was *crying*. I mean, really *crying*—"

Cairns said, throwing up his hands, "We'll shoot it later,

as an insert, for shit's sake! Right now, we have to finish up. We don't have this location tomorrow. So get her out here."

"I've been trying," the woman said helplessly.

"You're her fucking agent, goddamn it!" Cairns' face reddened. "You're supposed to be able to control her. That's why you're down here, or have you forgotten?" He turned to the assistant director and said, "Get a crowbar and rip the door off."

The man ran off to find a crowbar and I stepped up to Cairns, knowing I might not get the opportunity again. "Mr. Cairns?" I took the photograph out of my pocket, pinching it carefully from one corner so as not to get any of my own prints on it, and held it out to him. He looked at me questioningly, then took it. I thought I saw something ripple across his blue eyes, like a breeze across the surface of a pond, but it was gone too fast to be sure. "What's this?"

I searched his face for scars. If he'd had cosmetic surgery, the doctor had been good.

"My client says it's you, taken a long time ago."

His eyebrows knotted above his nose and he looked at me with angry intensity. "Your client? Who the hell are you?"

"The name is Asch. I'm a private investigator." I took the picture out of his hand before it wound up like the pink pages scattered back in the grove. Emotions seemed to be running high around this set. I dropped the picture into the jacket pocket I'd lined with a Baggie, and he said, "Don't tell me: Your 'client' is that nut-case woman who was around here last week, right?"

"If you're talking about Lori Norris, yes."

"This is all I need." He looked up at the sky and threw his arms out dramatically, as if appealing to the gods. "Is the entire universe conspiring to keep me from finishing this movie."

"I guess some of us haven't heard of cinematic privilege," I said.

His eyes were filled with icy anger. "Listen, Whatever-yournameis, go tell your client she'd be better off spending her money on a shrink than a private detective. I don't know what you're trying to pull, some publicity stunt or what—"

"I'm not in the publicity business, Mr. Cairns," I told

him. "I'm just a working-class stiff trying to make a fairly honest buck. The way I make that buck is by investigating things other people want investigated. Right now, that's you. The woman claims you were married to her—"

"Look, you," he snarled, pointing a finger at me, "I have a movie to finish here. I have enough problems without dealing with some crazy woman suffering from menopausal delusions. I told her, and I'm telling you, time is money in this business and if her disruptions cost me one more fucking minute, she's going to find herself slapped with a big fat lawsuit. And you too. So I'd suggest you move your ass out of here—now."

I locked stares with him and didn't move. The crowd around us was very still, waiting to see what would happen, then a skinny gofer who looked about nineteen stepped forward. "You want me to get him out of here, Mr. Cairns?"

I looked at him and smiled. "You'd better stick to running for pastrami on rye, kid. I don't think this is your line."

He glanced uncertainly at Cairns, who shouted, "Marv!"

Whoever said "No man is an island" hadn't seen the black man who parted the crowd to get to us. He was at least six-six, with an ebony trunk for a neck and a chest and arms that were sorely testing the elastic limits of his yellow Gold's Gym T-shirt. Cairns said to him calmly: "Marv, escort this man off the set. And while you're doing it, study his face. I don't want to see it anywhere near me for the duration of the shoot."

Marv nodded and moved. He was deceptively fast for his size—apparently he hadn't heard of the theory of continental drift—and before I had a chance to step back, my right elbow was in his huge black mitt and I was being propelled efficiently through the crowd, which had stopped to watch the action.

Maybe it was the pain of his grip on my elbow or the fear of losing my hand because of a lack of circulation or the smug smirk on the face of the gofer or just the fact that I have a thing about being manhandled, especially in such an expert, humiliating fashion, but something activated my limbic system which shot off a message to my Foolish Gland, and before my Right Mind could countermand the order, I brought my foot back and smashed the heel as hard as I could into his shin.

He emitted a surprised "Motherfucker!" but the rest of the desired effect—i.e., his grip loosening enough on my elbow for me to get my arm free—didn't happen. What happened instead was, my right arm was bent painfully behind me in a hammerlock and I was spun around like a Ken Doll and thrown into the side of the trailer. A vise fastened onto the back of my neck and my skull reverberated as my face was slammed twice into the metal trailer body and then voices were shouting: "Okay, break it up! Break it up! What's going on here?"

My arm and neck were released and I stopped eating the trailer and turned around. Over the shoulders of the two cops who had finally decided to make an appearance, Marv glowered at me.

"This man was making a nuisance of himself," Cairns told them. "He was asked to leave, and when Marv tried to escort him from the set, he assaulted him. Marv was only defending himself."

I daubed at my nose with two fingers and they came away bloody.

"You want to press charges?" one of the cops asked Cairns.

"No," Cairns said. "Just get him out of here."

"What about me?" I asked. "Maybe *I* want to press charges—"

"You really like pushing your luck, don't you, buddy?" one of the cops asked. He took my arm and started leading me away.

I could have kicked him in the shins, but thought better of it. I'd kicked enough ass for one day. Anyway, there was more than one way to skin a director. "Be seeing you again, Cairns," I called over my shoulder. He was grinning at me.

The assistant director ran past us, crowbar in hand, heading for the trailer. The cops turned and watched him curiously and I pinched my nose to try to stop the bleeding. All that commotion and she still hadn't come out. Maybe if

Marv had pushed my head through the wall and I'd said in my crazy Jack Nicholson voice, "Here's Jakey!" it would have appealed to her sense of the dramatic.

"Don't believe what they say," I told my escort as we started off again. "Everything about it *isn't* appealing."

3

They had built the new Palm Springs Police Department right next to the old one, and from the outside it didn't look that much different, a low brownstone building capped off by a thick slab of white roof, with an attempt at a lawn out front. Inside, things were a little more impressive. The front doors opened into a high-ceilinged, white-tiled corridor with smoked-glass walls behind which brown-uniformed men and women worked on the latest high-tech computer consoles.

I asked the cop at the front desk for Ron McDonald and gave him my name and he picked up the phone and told me to wait. A minute or so later, a door buzzed on the other side of the hallway and McDonald stepped out. He was a little thinner on top and the buttons of his brown sports shirt looked as if they were taking a little more strain around the belly, but other than that, five years hadn't changed him much.

We shook hands and he said: "Jesus Christ, talk about exhumations."

"Who was talking about exhumations?"

"I was," he said, waving a set of papers in his left hand. "I have to go to one this afternoon."

I tried to look disappointed. "You get all the good jobs."

"You want it? You can have it."

"Normally I would, but I just got a manicure and all that digging would ruin it."

He noticed the blood spots on my shirt collar and said: "Remind me never to go to your manicurist. What did she do, get a little carried away and try to manicure your face?"

"You've seen those commercials on TV for the Universal Studios tour, the one where they have King Kong, and they say, 'This time *he* wins'?"

"Yeah?"

"He won."

"Who was it, some irate husband you caught cheating on his wife, or some construction worker catch you trying to repo his car?"

"It's a long story," I said. "I'll tell you about it."

"I was afraid you were going to say that," he sighed. "Come on back."

We went through the door he'd come out of and down a hallway and I asked: "So what's been happening with you?"

He shrugged. "Murder, arson, rape. That's the nice thing about this job. You never lose your wonder of the inventive spirit of humanity. Just when you think you've seen every possible way of doing it, some creep comes along with a new way."

"You know what they say: 'Build a better pooper scooper and the world will beat a less shitty path to your door.'"

He stopped at a door that said: DETECTIVE SERGEANT RON MCDONALD. The office was a tiny ten-by-ten cubicle with a smoked-glass window that looked out onto the street. He added the paper in his hand to the pile scattered over the top of the desk and sat down. I took the chair facing him and surveyed the place. A poster behind the desk said: SUPPORT YOUR LOCAL POLICE—BE A SNITCH. I sat down. Someone had made sure that the shrunken head on the desk would never be a snitch; its lips were sewn together.

He sat behind the desk, somehow managed to locate a pack of cigarettes among the rubble, and shook one out. I pointed at the shrunken head, which seemed to be staring at me, despite the fact that its eyes were shut. "That thing real?"

He lit up and shook his head. "Naw, just made of cowhide. A friend of mine just brought it back from Ecuador."

I nodded and waved at the office. "Looks like you're coming up in the world. Your own office and everything."

He smiled and ran two fingers along one side of his brown mustache. "I managed not to fuck up a couple of cases and they made me sergeant. What kind of trouble did you bring me?"

"No trouble."

"That's what you said the last time," he said, blowing smoke toward the ceiling.

"Whatever happened to Lainie Fleischer, anyway?"

He shrugged. "Simon Fleischer kicked off and she inherited and blew town. I don't know where she went." He paused. "Where's the justice, huh? A broad like that beats her own fucking kid to death and walks away with enough to keep her in caviar for the rest of her life and I struggle here, making barely enough to afford Burger King."

I shrugged. "No matter what the ad says, you can't always have it your own way."

"Ain't that the truth?" He tugged on his lip. "So this is just a social visit, right?"

"Not exactly."

"I didn't think so."

"You know an I.D. tech who might be interested in doing some moonlighting?"

"What kind of moonlighting?"

"Lifting and classifying some prints."

"What's the deal?"

"I'm trying to resolve a disputed identity. Marital abandonment case."

"Here we go again," he said, rolling his eyes up. "That's just how it started the last time—"

"This isn't anything like the Fleischer case," I said, trying to sound convincing, except I wasn't sure who I was trying to convince, him or myself.

I laid it out for him briefly and he asked: "Who's the alleged husband?"

"His name is Walter Cairns. He's directing a movie down here."

"*Death in the Desert*?" He waved the cigarette at the window. "Those people are a royal pain in the ass. They call every fifteen minutes wanting something—streets blocked off, squad cars, drivers—"

"He's the one responsible for this," I said, pointing to my nose. "I was just over at the set. Cairns ordered one of his scenery movers to move me. If a couple of your boys hadn't come along opportunely, I might have looked a lot worse."

"Sounds like you upset Mr. Cairns," he said thoughtfully.

"Not half as much as I'm going to upset him if I can prove he's who my client says he is. I can get the prints classified in L.A., but it would save me time if I could get them done here."

He stuck out his lower lip. "If the guy is available, he charges twenty-five dollars an hour."

"Fine."

"Where are they?"

I handed him the photo in the plastic baggie and he looked at it for a moment and put it down on his desk. "Any other prints on it?"

"It was wiped clean before Cairns handled it."

He nodded. "Leave it with me and I'll see what I can do. Where are you staying?"

I told him the International and he took out a business card from the desk drawer and wrote a phone number across the front. "That's my home number. Call me there about eight-thirty."

"Thanks," I told him and stood up. "Good luck with your exhumation."

"Right," he said as if he didn't believe in such a thing, then sighed heavily. "This will make the third time I've had to dig up this cocksucker. One more time, and I'm going to put a wing nut on his casket."

I waved good-bye and went out, laughing.

4

I went back to the International and lugged my garment bag up the outside stairs to the second floor. The room was small, with a wallboard partition separating the combination bathroom-closet from the queen-sized bed. It had a small writing table, a dresser, a color TV, and even a postage stamp of a balcony, complete with patio chair, which overlooked the large pool area. I hung up my bag and went down to the bar.

The place would have been chic—in Ponca City. The flower-print brown vinyl walls were adorned with wicker baskets and a silver fire extinguisher, which hung conspicuously by the bar like a piece of pop art sculpture. There were two pool tables overhung with LITE beer light fixtures, and in the middle of the room, a huge grand piano flanked by two Trivia consoles which constantly flashed categories in full color. Most of the Formica-topped tables were filled with young people, a couple of whom I recognized from the set.

I slid onto a stool between a red-faced man in a brown leisure suit and a heavyset woman with dyed black hair piled into a beehive. This looked like their kind of place. I ordered a vodka-soda from the bartender, and the red-faced man looked up from his rocks glass as if he were really happy I'd finally arrived. "Howdy."

It was against my religion to say "Howdy," so I just said "Hi," and he said: "John Willis is the name."

"Jake Asch."

"Glad to meetya, Jake," he said enthusiastically. He waved his glass at the woman with the beehive on the other side of me. "Say hello to the little lady, Jake. Emily."

I said hello to the "little lady," but she seemed more

interested in her drink. I didn't ask why they were sitting a stool apart, afraid there might be a story to the answer.

"Where you from, Jake?"

"L.A."

"We're from Omaha," Willis said. "How about this weather, huh? It was snowing in Omaha when I called there yesterday. Would you believe that? *Snowing?*"

I said I believed it.

"I'm in the fertilizer business," he went on. "Chemical fertilizer. We have the biggest manufacturing plant in Omaha. You know what our motto is? 'There's no bullshit in our fertilizer.'" He chuckled at that, as if it were the first time he'd said it. The "little lady" went on slurping her drink.

"What line you in, Jake?" he asked.

"I guess you might say I'm in the fertilizer business, too, John. Except mine is strictly bullshit. I'm a writer."

His eyes lit up. "You with this movie they're filming down here?"

"No."

"They're staying here, y'know. We met Marla McKinnon yesterday. Emily got a big thrill out of it."

I looked over at Emily, who didn't look as if she got a big thrill out of anything except bourbon. Willis said across me: "Honey, this guy is a writer. What've you written, Jake? Anything we'd have heard of?"

"*The Picture of Ed Jones.*"

He inventoried his memory and shook his head.

"It's a modern-day version of Dorian Gray, about a guy who never changes as long as he keeps wearing his leisure suit."

He was still trying to work that out in his mind when I excused myself and slid off the stool. As I did so, I spotted the man who had thrown the pages in Cairns' face, hunched over a table by one of the Trivia consoles. He was drinking by himself and looked as if he'd probably been doing it for a while. I went over and said: "You're a writer, aren't you?"

He looked up and tried to focus. "My accountant says so," he remarked in a slurred English accent. "Some others seem to doubt it."

He was in his mid-thirties, with a face like a worn hatchet with no chin to speak of. His lips were dark, almost red, and glistened with Scotch and spittle.

"Like Walter Cairns?"

He drained his glass savagely. "That prick."

"May I buy you a drink?" I offered.

He squinted one eye, measuring me belligerently. "You a friend of Walter's?"

"No."

He shrugged and slumped back in his chair. "Then sure, why not? After all, I have a reputation to uphold. You know what notorious drunks writers are supposed to be."

I signaled the waitress and ordered us two drinks.

"Matthew Dart," he said, offering his hand.

"Jake Asch."

"You with the movie, Jake?"

"No. I'm a private investigator."

"Yeah?" he said, his voice perking up a bit. "I write detective novels. Jason March is my character."

I tried to look astonished. "This is *really* a pleasure. I'm a big Jason March fan."

"Yeah?" He smiled for the first time. I smiled back, hoping he wouldn't ask me any questions about Jason March or his escapades; I'd never heard of him. To sidetrack him, I said quickly: "I saw what happened on the set today. I take it you and the director have some differences of opinion over the script."

His voice took on an edge. "Differences? Hell, no. We don't have any differences. I don't know how to write, that's all. I don't know what the fuck I'm doing. I've only written nine fucking detective novels but I don't know anything about it. I'm stupid enough to think that if you have a detective as your main character, *he's* gotta be the one who solves the crime, otherwise all you got is a schmuck for a hero."

I said that sounded reasonable to me. The waitress brought our drinks and Dart hoisted his in a toast. "Well, here's to our schmuck, Jason March." He took a good drink and his mood soured again. "Hell, I'm the schmuck. I actually believed all that horseshit they'd fed me for the past year and a half. 'We love your book, we love your screenplay, we're all in agreement about the kind of film we want.' It's all bullshit. The writer is the most important person on any movie—until the first draft screenplay is in. Then, they don't want to talk to you anymore." He shook his head. "You hear all the horror stories, but you don't think it'll happen to you."

"I take it Cairns did some rewriting."

"You take it right. Like the whole thing. What I don't understand is if they didn't want to do the book, why did they *buy* it? All Cairns keeps saying is, 'What works in books doesn't necessarily work on film.'" He leaned forward. "You know what doesn't work in either books *or* film? Bad lines, faulty characterization, and holes in plots. And we've got 'em all."

It was a common writer's lament, one that had driven dozens, from Faulkner to Wambaugh, tearing their hair out and running for home. "Can't the producer do anything about it?"

"Marty Resnick?" he asked disbelievingly. "That cigar-chewing gnome has about as much creativity as a Pet Rock. I called him today, after I was banned from the set, and all he said was, 'You're creating negative vibrations. Maybe you should divorce yourself from this project.' They're ruining my character and he wants me to divorce myself from this project."

His expression was childlike, an odd mixture of puzzlement and anger, as if he couldn't quite grasp what was happening to him, but knew he didn't like it. "Hollywood," he said disgustedly, and took a gulp of his drink. "It isn't a place, it's a mind-set. The people who work in it deal in fantasy all day long, until they can't tell the difference between fantasy and reality anymore. With one swipe of a pen, they put millions of dollars into motion to create a project, and half the time, they don't even have the faintest notion of what they're creating."

His forehead wrinkled, pressured by his thoughts. "The other day, I get a call from a big agent—I mean *big*. He tells me to meet him at the Cafe Casino in Beverly Hills at ten, he's got an idea for a series he wants me to write for James Coburn. So I drive all the way up there, two hours, thinking this guy *really* has an *idea*, and I get there, and he says to me, 'I want a series based on the battle between good and evil.'

"Now, I'm dumbfounded, trying to fathom what's in this asshole's mind, and I say, 'Fine. Who do you want as a main character? A cop? A priest? A doctor?' You know what he says? He says: 'I want a cross between Maurice Evans in *Rosemary's Baby* and Lee J. Cobb in *The Exorcist*.' I tell him I'll get right on it, that I know a police artist who can work up a composite sketch, and this guy doesn't even laugh. He just says, 'Maybe you're not the person for this project.' Then it hits me that this guy is *serious*, that he actually doesn't realize that there is no project, that there isn't even an *idea*."

He chuckled, trying to act blithe and push his rage below the surface, but it had too much buoyancy and kept bobbing up again. His voice turned suddenly sad: "I've wanted to be in film since I was eleven. Now, I just want to get as far away from it as I can."

Two tanned and blond young people who looked like they surfed for a living moved over and put some money in the Trivia game. The girl picked the subject—"Intimate Sex"— and the machine started booping and they started rattling off the names of porno stars.

"What were you doing around the set today?" Dart asked suddenly.

"I was just in the area and stopped by to watch," I lied.

"You on a job?"

I nodded. "Small-time stuff. Workman's-comp case."

He tried to look interested, but he was too drunk and too self-absorbed. His expression glazed and his eyes got a faraway look in them. "I'd like to kill the asshole. Like he's killed Jason. Like he's killed my dreams."

"You mean Cairns?"

He nodded.

Trivia booped and beeped and the girl giggled.

"Excuse me," Dart said politely, and stood up unsteadily. He picked up the glass ashtray from the table, tested the weight in his hand, and stepped behind the two contestants. He hid the ashtray behind his back and bent over and tapped the man on the shoulder and asked deferentially: "May I impose on you and your lovely date for a moment?"

The man looked up and said irritatedly: "We're in the middle of a game—"

"I realize that," Dart insisted. "It's rather important."

The girl recognized Dart and slugged her boyfriend on the arm. "You're Matthew Dart."

Dart leaned back, smiling. "Yes."

"You don't know us," she went on effusively. "We're with the production crew. It's really a pleasure to work on *Death in the Desert*. I love your books."

"Thank you so much," Dart said. "Could you two do me a favor? Could you step over here for a moment?"

The boy looked uncertainly at the girl, but she was already getting up. Dart waved them to a spot behind the computer console and brought the ashtray from behind his back and I knew immediately what he was going to do. I covered my ears as he sidestepped the machine and hurled the ashtray through the screen.

The customers in the bar must have thought they were being attacked by Moslem terrorists and dove for the floor as the vacuum tube exploded in a shower of glass. The bartender's head popped up from behind the bar, and he shouted, "Hey!" and started around the bar with rage in his eyes. The room buzzed as people resurfaced from below their tables.

Dart held up two hands, and said loudly: "It's all right. I'll pay any damages. Room 123."

"What are you? Some kind of nut case?!" the bartender screamed at him.

"*I*," Dart intoned like John Barrymore reciting a Hamlet soliloquy, "am a writer."

"Some kind of a fucking nut case," John Willis contradicted angrily.

Whatever else Dart was, he was trouble. I got away from him in a hurry before any of it rubbed off on me.

5

I went back up to my room and watched the news. There was another terrorist attack at the Athens airport, a rape and murder of a seventy-year-old woman in West L.A., an accident in Terre Haute involving a schoolbus which had overturned, spilling its contents of children all over the freeway, and a kicker about a man who raised jumping frogs. That was a firm newsroom rule: Always finish with an "up" story, to buoy the spirit and keep the viewer from taking cyanide. Polls have shown that audiences from Jonestown buy considerably fewer sponsors' products than viewers in other parts of the world.

I shaved and showered and went downstairs to the office shop where I took my time with a chef's salad. When the little hand finally made it to the eight, I paid my check and used the pay phone in the lobby to call McDonald. He told me he had something for me, and gave me directions to his place.

The road wound through a sandy wash, then began to climb steeply. On my left, the mountain rose in a sheer rock face and on its top, the floodlit houses of the very rich sat like Tibetan monasteries, aloof and remote from the rest of the world. I passed some houses, then the houses ended, along with the pavement, and I was on a narrow, potholed dirt road that made a horseshoe turn along the gully, before it began to descend.

The road dead-ended in a cluster of three or four small houses huddled together on the side of the rocky slope on the right. I pulled up behind a red Toyota truck parked in front of one of the houses and killed my engine.

The house sat in a thicket of mesquite and creosote below

the roadway, and stone steps led down to the front door, which was open. It was a small, primitive-looking structure made of odd-shaped rocks pasted together with cement and covered by a wooden roof. I started down the steps and McDonald stepped into the doorway with a drink in his hand. "I see you found it. Come in."

I followed him into the tiny living room and immediately felt as if I'd stepped into a set for *Death Valley Days*. The walls were unadorned rock, like the exterior, and Navajo rugs lay on the wood floor. The furniture was thrashed and mismatched, but it somehow went with the place. "Unusual house."

"These rock houses are the oldest in Palm Springs," he said, echoing my thoughts. "Nearly a hundred years old."

"You own it?"

"Just rent. The Indians won't sell. We have the richest Indian tribe in the world, did you know that?"

I told him I did, but he went on anyway. "Nobody ever thought this town would amount to shit, so when they settled it, they gave the Agua Calientes every other square mile of what they thought was worthless desert. The Indians have been getting even for Sand Creek ever since." He waved his glass at me. "How about a drink? You'll have to settle for Canadian whiskey. That's all I've got."

I told him Canadian whiskey would be fine and he nodded and stepped into the adjoining kitchen. "Ice?" he asked as he got a glass down from the cupboard.

"Don't bother. How'd your exhumation go?"

"Terrific. I love digging up old corpses. Especially that one. I must. I seem to be making a career out of it." He poured a couple of fingers of whiskey into both glasses. "Water?"

"Sure. This really the third time you've dug him up?"

"Yep."

"How come?"

"First time, on a tip from an informant. The last two times, because we ain't got Quincy. We don't even have his Nip assistant."

"The coroner fucked up?"

"I think you could safely say that. The guy was supposed to have died from an overdose of phenobarbital. The M.E.

ran a test on the bone marrow and found phenobarb traces, all right, but the dipshit pathologist forgot to also run a test on the brain, which we need to prove O.D. as the cause of death."

"So that's what you were doing today?"

He nodded and took a slug of his drink. "And they better get it right this time, because that was it for me. I've had it with this case. The scumbag was just a dope dealer. Who cares how he ate it?"

He stepped over to a scuffed maple coffee table in front of the couch, picked up a business-sized envelope, and handed it to me. "You owe me fifty bucks."

On the paper inside the envelope was a set of prints along with their Henry System classification, standing for how many whorls and loops and whatever else prints are composed of.

$$I \ 21—100 \ 12$$
$$M \ 27—000 \ 18$$

I took two twenties and a ten out of my wallet and as I handed them to him, I dropped a hint: "Thanks, Ron. Now all I need to do is dig up a set of prints or classification numbers for my client's ex and see if they match."

The subtlety must have been too much for him, for he didn't offer a comment, but only suggested that we sit outside.

We went out a back door onto a small stone porch and pulled up two vinyl-strapped patio chairs. The patio was on the side of the hill and the city lights below burned like a banked fire. The air was cold and sharp and the stars were close, just beyond the reach of my fingers.

"Listen," he said suddenly.

I listened. At first there was only silence, then the life-sounds began to come to me, the chirping of night birds, the faint, yipping cries of a coyote pack hunting in the hills. It was nice. You live in the city long enough, and you start to equate the sounds of life with car horns.

"I love it here," he said. "This is one of the last places left in this town that still feels like the desert." He pointed to a huge domed house on top of the mountain. "If it was up to him and his golf buddies, there wouldn't be any desert or any water table left. Just one big fucking golf course."

"Who?"

"Bob Hope."

"Bob Hopes lives in that thing?"

"Old Ski Nose himself."

I looked up at the monstrous structure. "It looks like a gymnasium. An *ugly* gymnasium."

He chuckled. "We got a trouble call from the guard of the gate up there the other night. When the car responds, they find this drunken Marine hanging around, so they ask him what he's doing there. He says he's waiting to see Bob Hope. They ask him if he knows Bob Hope, and he says, 'No, but I hear he digs service guys.' The cops offer to drive the jerk to his hotel, but he gets belligerent and tries to take a poke at one of them and takes off down the side of the mountain. They let him go, hoping he'll fall and break his neck, which he pretty nearly does. They picked him up at the bottom with assorted broken bones. That was one stupid fucking Marine who found out the hard way—you can't believe the image. No matter how well they sell it, you can't get sucked in. Those people aren't like us."

I wondered if there was going to be a point to his story, but apparently he had already made it, for he got up suddenly, took the glass out of my hand, and went inside. I sat and let the chilly air bite my cheek and looked at the banquet of stars. He returned with two full glasses and sat back down. After we had downed half of our drinks, I figured his mood was probably as expansive as it was going to get. "How about doing me one more favor?"

"What?"

"The man whose prints I want to compare Cairns' with used to work for an outfit in Atlanta called Dynotran. From what my client says, Dynotran handles a lot of government contracts, which means security clearances for key personnel, which means they'd probably keep prints on file."

He smiled tightly. "You want me to call Dynotran and get the guy's prints."

"I could call and try to scam them, but they'd probably be

a lot more cooperative about an inquiry from law enforcement. I have friends in L.A. who would do it for me, but I thought since I was here—"

"What happens if Cairns turns out to be your man?"

"My client has a big fat lawsuit."

"You going to approach him again?"

"If the prints match, I won't have to."

He sipped his drink thoughtfully. "You going to press assault charges?"

"And make a lot of unnecessary work for the Palm Springs P.D.?" I scoffed. "I think you dedicated social servants have enough to do chasing down dangerous felons, without having to be saddled with all the paperwork on some piddly-ass assault charge."

That seemed to be the right answer. He nodded and said: "Okay, I'll make a call for you, but whatever comes back, you didn't get it from me. I have to deal with enough political bullshit without having the mayor's office calling me up demanding to know why I'm hassling some asshole Hollywood director."

"No problem."

"I'm not about to make the mistake that dumb jarhead made. I *know* these people aren't like us."

We drank some more and swapped more bits from the missing years and by the time I got up to leave, I was a bit unsteady on my feet. I was a bit unsteady on the road, too, but managed to get back to the hotel without hitting any palm trees. I was sure my streak of luck had run out when I started to turn into the driveway of the International parking lot and was blinded by headlights.

I slammed on my brakes and yanked on the wheel and caught a glimpse of the white Le Baron convertible as it peeled rubber out of the driveway out into the street, missing the front of my car by a foot or two. The driver was a woman, but I was too busy trying to get out of her way to get a good look at her. I skidded to a stop and started letting her know how I felt about her, but she was already out of hearing range, sailing through the green light at the intersection.

The near-miss had sobered me, but it didn't take long for the adrenaline jolt to dissipate and for me to drunken again. I was not too drunk, however, to realize I was parked in the middle of the street. Lucky for me, the street was empty. I conjured up a parking space near my room and went up the stairs, still muttering.

I managed to get my pants off without falling down, and collapsed into bed. There was nobody there to tell me if I snored, but then, there rarely was.

6

I woke up with a splitting headache and then realized the axe that was doing the splitting was the telephone. I lunged for it, figuring any voice would be better than bells. "Hello?"

"Asch?" It was McDonald. He sounded fresh and alert, the sonofabitch.

"What time is it?"

"Eleven-thirty in Atlanta."

"I'm not in Atlanta."

"No, but Gilbert Davis is."

"Who in the hell is Gilbert Davis?"

"Chief of Security at Dynotran. He's sending your boy McVey's prints out. Looks like your client is in the chips. You've got a match."

I sat up. "You're sure?"

"He read the classification to me. Same numbers."

My headache was still there, but I didn't care about it anymore. "Fantastic. Thanks a million, Ron."

"You going to be leaving town now?" he asked, kind of hopefully, I thought.

"I have a few things to do yet."

"I was afraid of that."

"Fear is the policeman's constant companion."

"*Insanity* is the policeman's constant companion," he said. "Fear is one casual acquaintance."

Lori Norris was getting ready to go to work when I called and gave her the news. Her reaction was predictable: "I *knew* it! I knew it was him."

"I suggest you retain an attorney immediately," I advised. "The sooner you file suit on Cairns, the better. If you don't have anybody in mind, I'd recommend Herb Edelstein. He's good."

"Whatever you think."

I gave her Edelstein's number and told her I'd call him and tell him to expect her call. I turned on the tube and took a hot shower and when I came back out, a woman was saying that if I needed help with my future, Jeane Dixon could help. I probably should have taken down the phone number flashing on the screen. Instead, I got dressed and went downstairs.

Luckily, the bar was open, and after a Bloody Mary and three aspirins, I felt good enough to tackle a couple of eggs and toast. By that time, it was late enough to call Edelstein at his office.

I thought I could hear him drooling on the other end of the line as I laid it out for him. "I'll have to get a temporary restraining order to put a freeze on everything. We're going to have to find out what the guy owns."

"That's what you're retaining me for, right?"

"The woman hasn't even retained *me* yet," he said.

I told him to think positively and called the production number. The girl who answered told me it was a night shoot tonight and that she didn't expect Cairns in until later in the afternoon. I drove over to the address Bigelow had given me. I was not going to take any chances losing the Golden Goose, at least until he started to lay.

The street was just off Murray Canyon Drive, a narrow drive of densely packed duplexes that ran along the edge of the Canyon Country Club golf course. Whoever owned the one Cairns was renting had tried to give it a different look by fronting it with white ornamental wrought-iron grillwork, but it still looked like all the others on the block, rectangular and boxy. Cairns' white Rolls was parked out front and I pulled over across the street and killed my engine.

If my banged-up Plymouth had been painted pink, it would have been more conspicuous, but not much. Maybe Cairns would think it belonged to one of the Mexican gardeners. I thought about going downtown and picking up some khakis and a rake, but rejected the idea immediately. My luck, the foreman of the green crew would come by and put me to work. It was awfully soon to be thinking stupid thoughts like that. That always happened on a stakeout, but it usually took a couple of hours of boredom for them to crop up, not five minutes. Be a detective—sit around and listen to your IQ drop. No retirement plan, but you won't need one; by the time you're ready to retire, you'll be a total idiot and the state will have to take care of you.

A gray-haired crone strolled by wearing a white lace see-through cover-up over a one-piece black bathing suit and twenty thou worth of diamonds on her wrists. I wondered how many husbands she'd buried for the collection. She flashed me all her dentures and casually brushed back the cover-up so that I could get a tantalizing look at her sun-blackened skin, which hung on her skeleton like a worn-out jumpsuit. She seemed oblivious of the pathetically comic picture she cut, or maybe she just thought that the jewelry would buy off the audience's laughter. In a lot of cases, it probably did, but it would take a lot more than a few baubles to buy off Jacob Asch. I turned away and when she saw I was not responding, she stuck her beak of a nose haughtily in the air and sauntered on, a barnacled frigate passing in the night.

After that, the pace of the entertainment flagged. A hundred years of minutes went by. I cursed myself for not stopping on the way and picking up a paperback. Not only would it have helped to kill time, but I could have seen how a *real* detective, like Jason March, did his job.

At one-ten, a blue Mercedes 450 SLC pulled up in front of Cairns' Rolls and Marla McKinnon stepped out wearing a baggy navy-blue sweatshirt, tight-fitting jeans, and white tennies. A lot of her face was hidden behind round dark glasses, and her hair was tucked up under a Dodgers baseball cap, but there was no mistaking who it was. She went to the front door and rang the bell and stood there for a while. She rang it again, knocked, then went around the side of the house and disappeared. About three minutes later, she reappeared, walking very fast. When she hit the street, she glanced around nervously, then hurried to her car, jumped in, and took off. I got out of the car and retraced her steps.

The back of the house sat at the edge of a golf-course putting green surrounded by weepy elms and olive trees. A Mexican gardener circled the green on a lawnmower cart, filling the morning with noise and the fragrance of freshly-cut grass. His presence didn't seem to bother the two men putting the hole. The plaid clowns' pants they wore were deceptively frivolous; the expressions on their faces were of intense concentration. They took their golf seriously around here. A few years back, Sam Giancana, the Chicago mobster, was granted a court order in Palm Springs ordering the F.B.I. to play two holes behind him. The Mafia chieftain claimed their listening devices were screwing up his game, and the sympathetic judge, being an avid golfer himself, agreed. A slice on the fairway took precedence over a slice of the jugular, at least in Palm Springs.

I waited for them to play through, then stepped around the clutter of the patio furniture on Cairns' back porch to the sliding glass door that opened into the house. It was ajar about three inches. White drapes were pulled across it, blocking my view inside. I slid it open the rest of the way and stepped through the drapes.

The living room was roomy, with a high, slanting ceiling and a large white brick fireplace along one wall. The carpet was an industrial grade of beige, the walls white, the furniture all overstuffed and done in desert tones. There were a lot of potbellied white lamps and a large coffee table in front of the couch with a glass top and a chopped-off gnarled tree trunk for a base.

I stood and listened. "Anybody home?"

Nobody answered. Apparently Cairns had been picked up by someone and left his car here. I saw a chance to save myself a lot of work. Two hallways faced each other across the white-tiled entryway by the front door. As I went to the one on the left, I noticed a crescent-shaped ashtray on the carpet by the couch, along with its spilled contents of cigarette butts.

The hallway ran back about thirty feet. The two doors on the right side of it were a bathroom and a small bedroom, which showed no signs of recent habitation. The one on the left was a den which contained one wall of poorly stocked bookshelves, a desk and two chairs. A partially completed page of script was rolled up in the IBM Selectric on the desk, and there was a stack of pages beside the typewriter, with lines crossed out and added in pen. I pulled open the middle drawer of the desk and a gun jumped out at me.

It was an old .38 Smith and Wesson M & P, with a four-inch bull barrel. I picked it up and sniffed the barrel. It hadn't been cleaned lately and smelled faintly of cordite. I broke open the cylinder. Four cartridges. I wondered where the other two had gone. I was beginning to get that old uneasy feeling. I put the gun back and went through the rest of the drawer.

Cairns' checkbook was there, from the Westwood branch of B of A, and, looking back through the check record, two recent entries stood out. On November 9, eight days ago, he had deposited $80,000—probably the second mortgage check—then, five days later, he had written out a check to "Cash" for the amount, leaving a balance of $4,560.98. I wondered what someone would do with that kind of cash, and as I was sure Edelstein would want to ask that question in court, I took down the account number and transaction dates.

The only other curious items in the desk were two catalogues, one called *Centurions*, which included between its covers every known S-and-M and bondage device known to man, along with illustrations as to their use, and another that advertised nothing but women's shoes in men's sizes. It looked like Cairns or whoever he rented this place from had some major wrinkles in his personality.

The wastebasket beneath the desk was half full, and since I might not get the chance again, I pulled it out and went through it. Most of the contents were pages of discarded dialogue, but among them I found one sloppily handwritten note that had been crumpled into a tight ball.

"Butch"—

I thought we had an agreement, now you won't even return my calls. Is that any way to treat your old buddy? I'm at the Desert D'Or, Room 14, until tomorrow. 327-1423. Call me or drop by.

Hal

I pocketed the note and straightened up, coming eye-level to the bookshelf. I stood for a moment, wondering why I was staring at it, then realized it was the leather-bound, gilt-lettered copy of *Moby Dick* that was leaning anomalously against the twenty or so cheap paperbacks on the shelf. I pulled it down and opened it up.

The center of the book had been cut out, leaving just enough room to hold the VHS video cassette inside. It was labeled in blue felt pen "Marla M."

The living room had a television set, but no video recorder. I found one in the bedroom at the end of the opposite hallway. The room was large, with ceiling-to-floor curtains on the far wall next to the king-sized bed. The bed had an ornate brass headboard, and its salmon-colored sheets were rumpled and empty. A quilted mocha bedspread lay in a heap at the foot of the bed and the red T-shirt and jeans that Cairns had been wearing yesterday had been tossed on top of it.

I turned on the VHS machine on top of the 27-inch MGA TV, and put in that tape, and while waiting for it to start, looked over the half dozen other cassettes stacked on the antique dresser. There were a couple of Cairns' old movies, *Double Entry* and *Dark Mirror*, but the others bore more exotic and obscure titles—*Latex Slaves, Perils of Prunella*, and *Palace of Pain*. I doubted any of them had ever made it to theater screens around the country; still, they had to have better production values than the home movie I was watching now, of Walter Cairns, naked except for a studded leather harness, lightly scourging a naked Marla McKinnon with a cat-o'-nine tails. She was spread-eagled on a bed covered with a fur skin, her wrists and ankles secured to the legs by fur-lined leather straps. Her eyes had a glazed, drugged-out look as Cairns put a dog's choke-chain around her throat and stuffed his huge, rock-hard cock into her mouth. I fast-forwarded it a bit and Marla seemed a little more alert now. She was demanding in a slurred, whiny voice to be released. Cairns, who was now wearing a black leather executioner's mask, responded by gagging her with a leather strap and mounting her. On the next fast-forward, her arms were secured behind her, sheathed in one long black latex glove, and she was bent over the bed while Cairns penetrated her from the rear. He had removed the gag and she was complaining that he was hurting her, but that only seemed to inflame the Masked Marvel more, and he whipped her buttocks with a riding crop while he plunged into her savagely. The guy was a major talent, I had to admit. The film had everything—sex, drama, violence, pathos. I wished I could have stayed for the whole thing, but I didn't know how long I had until Cairns returned and there were things to do. I rewound the tape and ejected it.

I'd been too absorbed in the tape to notice it when I came in, but I did when I turned around. A studded black-leather thong was knotted on the brass crossbar of the headboard and disappeared in the space between the bed and the curtained wall. It was taut, as if there was a lot of weight pulling on it, and I stepped around the bed to take a look.

It was Cairns. He was looking at me from his supine position on the floor, sticking his tongue out, but I didn't take it personally. He couldn't help it any more than he could help the purple mottling on his face or his eyes, which bulged out of his head like a Boston bull's.

The thong was wound tightly around his throat and knotted on the left, just under the jawline, and his wrists were handcuffed in his lap in front of him. His ankles were bound together by a length of white rope, and another studded thong like the one around his neck was choking his limp penis, which was peeking through the crotchless woman's black silk panties he was wearing. Besides the panties and a black silk bra, he was stark naked, and either he or someone else had written all over his body with lipstick. From the gist of the words, I assumed the poet hadn't been a fan. Hooray for Hollyweird.

I took the tape out to my car and put it in the trunk, then came back in. After copying down the names and numbers on the note in my pocket, I put it back into the den wastebasket—it could be a clue—and called McDonald.

"Just an errant-hubby case, huh?" he said with rhetorical disgust. "What's the address?"

I gave it to him and went out back. I stretched out on a chaise longue and relaxed, watching a foursome golf through. They hadn't finished the hole when I heard the sirens in the distance.

7

He came in like royalty, with an imperial scowl on his face, and trailed by an entourage of uniformed and plainclothes cops.

"He's in the bedroom," I told him.

"Did you touch anything?"

I put a hand on my heart and tried to look shocked. *"Moi?"*

"Don't give me any of that *moi*-shit," he growled, his jaw hardening.

"A few things," I admitted. His face suffused with anger, but before he could shape it into words, I tried to short-circuit it. "I didn't know he was dead at the time. I'll give you a list."

His face looked like it had been dipped in resin. "What were you doing here?"

"Keeping an eye on Cairns until we could serve him papers. I was across the street in my car and I saw Marla McKinnon drive up. She rang the bell and went around back, then came out in a hurry. I went around back and saw the door open, so I came in."

He nodded, semi-placated, and turned to his troops. "Okay, you guys, I want every inch of this place gone over with a fine-tooth comb. This one is going to make the evening news and I don't want some asshole reporter saying later how we fucked up." To me: "Let's take a look."

I led him back to the bedroom, where an I.D. tech and photographer immediately went to work. McDonald took one look at the corpse and grinned sardonically. "See? I told you these people aren't like us."

The photographer popped off a flash. Even dead, Cairns didn't look as if he liked being photographed. "You think the McKinnon broad had something to do with this?"

"I don't know how. If she was inside, she was only in long enough to find Cairns and get out."

He turned to a uniformed cop standing in the doorway. "Get a unit over to the International right away to locate Marla McKinnon. Tell whoever finds her to keep her there until I get there."

"Take a look at this," the I.D. tech said, stepping out of the closet holding a small black suitcase in a gloved hand. He opened it up on the bed. It looked like it had been packed for a weekend at the Marquis de Sade's. Besides the cat-o'-nine-tails that I recognized from the tape, there was a dog's choke-chain, miscellaneous lengths of rope, a "hers" pair of handcuffs to match the "his" set Cairns was wearing, a ball-gag, and a leather mask with a zipper for a mouth.

"Like bondage, will travel," I said.

"Looks like the guy was into some first-class sick shit," McDonald remarked.

The I.D. tech began dusting the accoutrements for prints and the sandy-haired cop McDonald had sent out stuck his head in. "Marla McKinnon is in her room. Travers is making sure she stays there until you get there. Also, there's a pushy little jerk out here making a lot of noise. Says his name is Resnick."

"What does he want?" McDonald asked irritably.

"To talk to you."

"If it's Marty Resnick," I said, "he's the head of Triad Films."

"Bring him into the living room," McDonald told the cop, and we followed him out.

On the way down the hall, we were met by a short, roly-poly Mexican carrying a briefcase and whistling "King of the Road." He was casually dressed in a green golf shirt and slacks and his brown bowling-ball head was fringed with graying beard. He stopped whistling and greeted us cheerily: "Hi, Ron. Great day, huh?"

"Terrific, Jaime," McDonald answered. "How's the taco biz?"

"Good, real good," the man said, smiling broadly.

"I'll have to get by this week. I'm having withdrawals. I need an enchilada fix."

"We'll take care of it. Where's the stiff?"

McDonald jerked a thumb toward the bedroom and the man resumed whistling and disappeared into the bedroom.

"Who was that?" I asked.

"Coroner's investigator."

"Nice to see a man happy at his work. What was that about tacos?"

"He and his wife own a Mexican restaurant out in Indio—Jaime's. It's sort of a locals' place. Terrific soft-shell tacos."

"I won't ask what kind of meat he uses."

Resnick came into the living room with the confident, energetic strut of a man used to command. He wore a powder blue FILA sweater over a crisp white dress shirt, navy slacks, and blue alligator-skin loafers. He was late-fiftyish and short, with the slightly stout build of a man whose idea of exercise was morning walks in Sergio Tachini jumpsuits, or maybe an occasional steam at the Beverly Hills Health Club. His receding gray hairline was combed straight back from his prominent forehead, and his face was ruddy and plump-cheeked. He had a wide nose, a small mouth, and brown eyes that were slightly sunken but intently watchful, constantly appraising.

"Who's in charge here?" he asked.

"I am," McDonald told him and introduced himself.

"Nobody will tell me anything," Resnick said testily.

"What's going on here? Has something happened? Where's Walter?"

"In the bedroom."

"Tell him I want to see him."

"I can tell him," McDonald said casually, "but I don't think he'll care. He's dead."

Resnick looked stunned. "*Dead?* I just talked to him last night. How?"

"We don't know yet."

"Was he murdered?"

"That's for the coroner to determine."

Resnick blinked in disbelief. "You mean it's possible he *was* murdered?"

"It's possible," McDonald admitted.

Resnick shook his head and turned away. "This is terrible. Terrible." He sounded as if he meant it.

"What time last night did you talk to him?" McDonald asked.

"Huh?" Resnick asked, with a dazed expression. "Oh. About nine, I guess."

"What did you talk about?"

"The movie," he said in a preoccupied tone. "There were problems."

"What kind of problems?"

"The shooting is at least ten days behind schedule. Walter thought he could make some of that up if he could make some script changes and reshoot some scenes. I wanted to know what kinds of changes he was talking about. He'd already made major changes and any more could jeopardize the negative pick-up deal with Universal."

"You'll have to pardon me," McDonald broke in. "I'm just a dumb cop. What's a negative pick-up deal?"

"It's a standard financing agreement between an independent production company, like Triad, and a major studio," Resnick explained. "The studio guarantees the cost of the film up through the production of the negative in return for major distribution rights. Only that guarantee is contingent on the film being a 'reasonable facsimile' of the script the studio approved. Too many changes, the studio can reject the film. Walter didn't feel we would have a problem. He was convinced that he could sell me on the changes and that I could sell Universal. I was supposed to meet him here this afternoon to talk about it.''

Resnick turned away and rubbed his forehead. "Dead. This is terrible. I took a chance on Walter. Now look what he's done to me. Where in the hell am I supposed to find a director who can step in and save this picture now?"

McDonald asked Resnick where he was staying in Palm Springs and the producer told him he had a home here, and gave him the address and phone number. As the little mogul scuttled out the door, stepping aside for the gurney being rolled in, McDonald said: "There goes a real humanitarian. When he said, 'This is terrible,' I thought he meant Cairns. He was talking about his fucking movie."

One of the men wheeling the gurney asked where the body was, and McDonald waved for them to follow him.

Jaime the Happy Taco Vendor was bent over the corpse when we came in, taking fingernail parings from the corpse's right hand. He deposited the parings into a zip-lock bag, secured a paper bag over the hand with a rubber band, then snipped off a sample of the dead man's hair with a pair of scissors and bagged that. He dropped the bags into his briefcase, snapped it shut, and stood up. "I'm through," he told the men from the removal service.

"What do you think?" McDonald asked him.

"Died around midnight, or not long after. Not much doubt about the cause of death. Asphyxia caused by hanging. That groove on his neck matches the position in which he was found and the black-and-blue marks along the lower edge indicate he was alive when that thong went around his neck. My guess is accident or suicide, and I'd lean toward accident."

"Hard-on hanging?" McDonald asked.

Jaime nodded. "They even have a fancy name for it— autoerotic asphyxia."

"What about the lipstick writing? 'I Eat Shit. Pig.'"

"Not uncommon, either. Fits in with the bondage and women's clothing. This guy had a lot of self-loathing. Show business has a way of bringing that out in people. When I was working L.A., I had a case once, a starlet. Her career didn't take off like she'd hoped, so one night she piled all her press clippings and reviews in the middle of her living room floor, set fire to them, and jumped on top."

"Made her own P-R pyre," I mused. "Speaking of lipstick, where is it?"

McDonald's brow furrowed. "Huh?"

"If he wrote on himself, what'd he do with the lipstick?"

"Don't worry," he said testily. "We'll find it."

"There is one curious thing," Jaime broke in. "There are some deep indentations on his lower back, as if he was lying on something for a long time. Only there was nothing underneath him when I rolled him over."

McDonald grumbled at that, but Jaime smiled and clapped him on the shoulder. "Don't worry, Ron. I don't think you're going to have to work too hard on this one."

"Famous last words," he said deprecatingly. "Tell Maria to keep an enchilada warm for me."

Jaime went out and I asked McDonald if I could tag along when he talked to Marla McKinnon.

"Why?"

"I'm a fan," I said, shrugging.

He seemed to see the logic in that. "Okay, but I do all the talking."

"Right. By the way, while you're there, you might want to talk to Matthew Dart, the writer on the movie."

I told him about Dart's run-in with Cairns the day before and his subsequent remarks about wanting to kill the man and about the incident with the Trivia game.

He frowned. "You're just getting around to telling me this?"

"He was shit-faced. He probably doesn't even remember making any threats."

"He sounds like a whacko. And a violent one at that."

"Throwing an ashtray through a TV screen isn't in the same league as murder. Many a time I've wanted to throw something at one of those goddamned machines. They're irritating. Anyway, your buddy Jaime says it was 'autoerotic asphyxia,' remember?"

McDonald grunted. "I'm going to want to talk to him, anyway."

"I figured you would. That's why I mentioned him."

"I also want your client's name and number."

"Why?"

He stuck out his chin. "Because I said so."

He sounded like a parent telling his six-year-old to go to bed, but since I couldn't think of a reason *not* to give them to him, I did. We went outside.

A crowd of golfers had gathered behind the police tape, and McDonald stopped on the front doorstep and surveyed the gawkers, who were dressed in blue plaid slacks and lime-green sweaters and bright yellow shirts and white golf shoes with tassles on them. "Look at 'em," he said disdainfully. "That's why God invented golf—so white people can dress like niggers once a week."

He turned to the uniformed cop guarding the door. "Get these rubbernecks out of here. Send them back to their homes or their putting greens or wherever they came from before they can fuck up whatever evidence we have here."

We pushed through the crowd and I told McDonald I'd follow him over. I didn't want to leave my car there, not with what I had in it.

8

McDonald told the mustachioed cop stationed in the hallway outside Marla McKinnon's room he could go, and rapped on the door. She opened it, wearing the same sweatshirt and jeans, but without the cap and dark glasses. She was much shorter than she appeared on the screen—only five-one or -two—and without makeup and the proper lighting, her face looked familiar, yet different. The eyes were smaller and not quite as green and tiny age lines were visible at their corners and at the corners of the full, pouty mouth. Her upturned nose and high cheekbones were dotted with childlike freckles, but there was nothing else childlike about her. At thirty-three, the dark heat was still there, but it smoldered now instead of blazed, and I could see where it would soon cool down to a faint glow, then go out altogether. She could see it too. The fear in her eyes was not just because she was being visited by the police.

McDonald identified himself and asked to come in, but she did not immediately relinquish the doorway. "What's all this about?" she asked, trying to sound assertive, but it didn't come off. She knew what it was about, and it only took McDonald to say, "Walter Cairns," for her to say, "Oh," and let us in.

The room was a duplicate of mine, except for the clutter of makeup, face creams, and hair sprays on the bathroom sink and the colored pages of script all over the bed. She and McDonald sat at the small table in front of the sliding glass door and I sat on the edge of the bed. I eyed the VHS machine on top of the television set. I wondered if she had her own copy of her bondage scene with Cairns.

"Mr. Asch is a private detective," McDonald told her. "He saw you at Walter Cairns' place this afternoon."

She glanced at me, then raked her lower lip with her teeth, but didn't say anything.

"Did you go inside?"

She hesitated, then nodded.

"You saw Cairns' body?"

She shivered and made a face. "It was horrible." Her green eyes widened. "Did . . . did somebody *do* that to him?"

"We don't know yet," McDonald said, stroking his mustache, "but for the time being, we are investigating it as a homicide. Why didn't you report finding the body to the police, Miss McKinnon?"

"I was scared," she said. "I didn't want to get involved. The publicity—"

She stopped and McDonald let her, at least for the time being. "What were you doing over there?"

"I wanted to talk to Walter about the scene tonight. I

thought I knew a way it would play better and I wanted his opinion."

"When was the last time you saw or talked to Cairns?"

"Last night."

"What time?"

"About seven-thirty, I guess."

"What did you talk about?"

"The same thing. The movie."

"How long were you there?"

"I don't know. Half an hour, maybe."

"Anybody else there?"

She thought about it. "Sam Fields was just leaving as I pulled up."

"Who's Sam Fields?"

"The editor of the movie."

McDonald nodded. "Was Cairns into S and M?"

"How would I know?" she asked, her voice acquiring an edge of indignation. She was good, but that was how actresses made their living, by telling lies and making people believe them.

"What kind of mood was Cairns in when you saw him? Despondent? Happy?"

She thought a moment. "Restless. Edgy. I think he was expecting someone."

"Why do you think that?"

"I don't know exactly. It was just the impression I got. He kept looking at his watch and he seemed anxious for me to leave."

"You don't know who it could have been?"

"No."

"One more question, Miss McKinnon," McDonald said, studying her face intently. "Where were you between eleven last night and two this morning?"

"In bed, asleep," she said.

"Alone?"

"Yes, alone," she said irritably.

McDonald's expression remained placid. He stood up and said: "I guess that's all for now. I may have some questions for you later, Miss McKinnon."

"Of course." She stood up and touched his arm. "Lieutenant, is there any reason the media has to know I was there? You know how they can distort things—"

"I'm not a lieutenant," he said, "but I think we can keep your name out of it at this stage."

She smiled gratefully. "Thank you." She kept her eyes on him, ignoring me, as we went out. She didn't know it now, but she wouldn't be grateful for long.

In the hallway, McDonald said: "Okay, let's go talk to this Dart guy."

Dart opened the door of his room looking ill. His face was yellow and sweaty, like a cheese blintz that had been left out of the refrigerator too long. He was wearing blue swimming trunks and a yellow T-shirt that said: PALM SPRINGS—ANOTHER SHITTY DAY IN PARADISE. I could relate to that.

McDonald showed him his badge and said: "I believe you know Mr. Asch."

Dart squinted at me. "Oh yeah. The detective."

"May we come in?"

Dart shrugged and pulled open the door. The room was messy. The bed was unmade and the floor by the window was littered with crumpled pieces of paper. On the ubiquitous table by the glass door sat a typewriter and a stack of blank paper, along with a nearly empty fifth of Dewar's and a plastic glass. It looked like Dart was trying to find the Lost Weekend.

McDonald picked up the bottle of Scotch and while pretending to look at it, asked casually: "Where were you last night, Mr. Dart, between eleven P.M. and two A.M.?"

Dart waved a hand at the bathroom. "Praying to the porcelain god. I drank a bit too much in the afternoon, I'm afraid."

"Here?"

"Yes."

"Alone?"

"I don't usually invite guests over to watch me throw up," he answered snidely. "What's the big interest about where I was, anyway?"

McDonald put the bottle down and looked at the writer levelly. "The big interest is that that was when Walter Cairns died."

Dart's mouth dropped. *"Died?"*

"That's right."

His color came back for a moment and he couldn't suppress a grin. I thought he might break into a chorus of "Ding, Dong, the Witch Is Dead," but another thought squelched that: "Are you telling me Walter was murdered?"

"Why do you ask that?"

"Why else would you want to know where I was?" Dart asked belligerently.

"You and Cairns had a heated argument yesterday, after which you made certain comments to Mr. Asch about wanting to kill the man—"

"I was drunk, for chrissakes," he said, throwing out his hand in frustration. "I don't fucking believe this. Any time anything goes wrong, it's always the writer's fault. Look, I didn't have any use for Walter, I'll admit, but I had nothing to do with his death."

"Would you be willing to say that on a polygraph?"

"A lie-detector test?" He thought about it, then sneered: "Why not? You never said how Walter died, by the way."

"No," McDonald replied. "I didn't. We'll wait outside while you get on some clothes."

In the hallway, McDonald asked: "What do you think?"

"It isn't easy to hang someone. Especially as drunk as Dart was."

He took out a pack of cigarettes and fired one up with his lighter. "He could have sobered up by midnight."

"Maybe," I said. "The machine will soon tell you."

"Maybe not. All it'll tell me is if Dart *thinks* he did it. If he was *really* drunk, he might not remember."

"You're been reading too much Cornell Woolrich," I guessed.

"Who's that?"

"A guy who used to write stories about alcoholic amnesiacs killing other people while in drunken blackouts."

"It has happened," he said gruffly. "I've handled a few."

I told him, "Except Dart remembers what he was doing last night."

"I'll be interested to know exactly what he does remember."

I wished him luck and went down to the production office, where the secretary I'd talked to yesterday sat at her desk, daubing her eyes with tissue. She'd obviously gotten the news about Cairns. At least he had one mourner.

Through the closed inner door of the suite, I could hear Resnick's raised voice: "That's ridiculous, Myron. He's just trying to hold me up because he knows we've got trouble—"

I asked the girl where I could find Sam Fields and she stopped sniffling long enough to tell me I might try the editing room down the hall.

Behind the closed door marked EDITING I could hear voices. I knocked, but the argument kept up and nobody told me to come in. I knocked again, then pushed the door open and peeked in.

A thin man with gray hair and a gray-trimmed beard stood hunched over an upright Moviola editing machine, looking intently into the small screen. The voices were coming from the squawk box next to him.

The furniture in the room was mostly tables stacked with film cans marked with masking tape and littered with glue, scissors, razor blades, and other tools of the trade. The machine was noisy and I had to almost shout to be heard over it: "Mr. Fields?"

"What?" he asked irritably without looking up.

I stepped closer. "My name is Asch. I'm a detective. I assume you've heard about Walter Cairns?"

That broke his concentration. His head came up, then he looked back and realized he'd lost his place. "Shit." He turned off the machine and turned to face me.

He had watery gray eyes under dark bushy brows, and a red drinker's nose. The cheeks above the beard were lumpy and crisscrossed with lines of broken capillaries. His short-sleeved shirt had pink flamingos all over it and his baggy brown slacks and scuffed loafers looked like thrift-shop specials. The only thing new in his entire ensemble were the white cotton gloves on his hands.

"Marty just told me twenty minutes ago," he said, sorrowfully. "It's a shocker. Is it true he was murdered?"

"That's a possibility, but a remote one. Right now, it looks like either an accident or suicide."

"Suicide?" He shook his head. "I knew Walter was stressed-out, but I didn't realize it went that deep."

He pulled up a bar stool behind him and sat down to a plastic-lined-trash bin with a wooden rack above it. From hooks on the rack strips of film hung, marked with yellow grease pencil.

"I understand there have been problems with the movie—"

He nodded. "Since we started getting behind, Walter had been keeping a brutal schedule. We all have. He'd been up until two every night, looking at dailies, then up at five every morning to shoot. I don't think he'd slept more than three hours a night in the past three weeks."

"How did he act when you were at his house last night?"

He threw me a curious glance. "How did you know I was over there?"

"Marla McKinnon."

"Ah," he said, and pursed his lips. "He told me he was going to quit."

"Cairns? You mean, quit the movie?"

"That's what he said. He said he'd had it with executives breathing down the back of his neck and putting up with the temper tantrums of freaked-out, no-talent movie stars and he was walking. At first, I didn't think he was serious. I told him he couldn't do that, that not only would he be blowing the rest of the money on his contract, but Marty Resnick would make sure he'd never work on another film again in his life. I should know—I was blacklisted for seven years. But Walter just said not to worry, he'd get his money—all of it. And as far as working in Hollywood again, he didn't intend to, he was through."

"Did Resnick know that?"

"Apparently not. Marty was surprised this morning when I made my pitch."

"Pitch?"

"To take over as director," he said. "It was Walter's idea. That's basically what he wanted to talk to me about last night. I doubted Marty would go for it, but Walter thought he would. There are only a handful of specialists capable of stepping into a shit-storm like we have and pull it out, and they don't come cheap. Besides, he needs somebody to take over *right now*. *Death in the Desert* is scheduled for May release, and if Marty doesn't deliver on time, he forfeits big points, maybe everything. Technically, they can tell him to shove the film up his ass."

"Have you directed before?"

"No, but I've forgotten more than most directors today will ever learn. Ever see *Darkness at Dawn*? *Sunday, Sunday*? *Goodbye, Mr. Smith*?"

"About six times each."

"I cut all those," he said proudly.

"Those are all classics," I said, looking at him with a new respect. "How did you wind up blacklisted?"

"I got a swelled head and pissed some people off," he said casually. "They made sure I didn't work. *Death in the Desert* is the first cutting job I've had in seven years."

"So did Resnick give you the nod?"

"He seemed to like the idea, but he hasn't decided yet. He has to do something pretty quick, though."

I wondered whether suspicious-detective-type thinking was left- or right-brain. Not that it mattered; I was stuck with it, no matter what lobe produced it. "Nabbing that job would be a big break for you."

He frowned. "Yeah, but I'd hate to think I got it this way. Walter was a friend. He hired me when nobody else would."

He sounded sincere enough. "Resnick says he talked to Cairns early last night about script changes Cairns wanted to make. That doesn't sound much as if he intended to quit."

"He had changes in mind all right," he replied. "We talked about them. The main one was Adrianne Covert."

"Little Miss Crowbar?"

"You heard about that, huh?"

"I was there."

"Yeah, well, that's just a sample. Walter wanted to fire her and reshoot her scenes with somebody else, or write her part out entirely."

"Wouldn't that cost a bundle?"

"No more than the way we've been going," he said, shrugging. "She's the main reason we're so far behind. Half the time, she shows up late or so stoned-out on drugs that she blows her lines. The other half, she doesn't show up at all."

"Didn't anybody know she was going to be a problem before she was hired?"

"Susanne Capasco, Adrianne's agent, sold her to Walter on the basis of a couple of TV bit parts the girl had done," Fields said. "Walter thought she'd be perfect for the role of Gabrielle. Nobody she'd worked for popped up to say she was trouble, and Susanne claims she didn't know anything about a drug problem, although I'd hardly expect her to say anything else." He paused reflectively, and scratched his beard. "Then, part of her problem could have been Walter."

"Why is that?"

"Walter could be a difficult man to work with, even for the most case-hardened actor, which Adrianne definitely is not. He didn't like actors. To him, they were a necessary evil. He would feign toleration of their feelings or opinions only if they were producing what he wanted. With Adrianne, all pretense of toleration was off by the second week of shooting. Whenever she'd blow a line, Walter would stop everything and do his best to make her feel like an idiot, from throwing out little barbs to full-blown rages. But that only made her fuck up worse.

"The fact is, the girl already feels like an idiot, which is probably why she takes drugs. This business is littered with the bodies of people who blew it on the way up, a lot of them on purpose. Stardom is a shining beacon that draws them, but when they get close to it, they find it's too hot to handle."

"You think Adrianne Covert thinks it's too hot to handle?"

"She has no real belief in herself," he said. "You have to in this business, if you're going to succeed. I've seen a lot like her. They don't believe they have *real* talent, and that every step they take up is a fluke. The more visible they are as actors, the more certain they become their terrible secret will be found out—that they're nothing."

"So they blow it."

"Mediocrity has its attractions. It's a hell of a lot less demanding than success."

"You seem ready for the challenge," I commented.

He smiled sardonically and rubbed the back of his neck.

"After eight years of sitting on my ass, I'm ready for anything."

I wished him luck on his directorial bid and left, thinking about what he'd said about failure and success, and a Fred Allen comment popped into my mind. "Success," he'd said, "is like dealing with your kids or teaching your wife how to drive. Sooner or later, you wind up in the police station."

Maybe I was lucky to have avoided it all these years.

9

She had changed into short shorts and a halter top. Her legs were dancer's legs, slender, but with good muscle tone. The sight of those shapely thighs short-circuited the wiring from the brain to the tongue and I stood there in the doorway for a moment without saying anything. "What is it?" she asked annoyed.

The sharpness of her voice sparked the connections. "We have to talk, Miss McKinnon."

"About what?"

I pulled the VHS cassette out of my jacket pocket. "This."

A flame of fear flickered in her eyes before she could smother it. "What is it?"

"An exercise tape. 'Jane Bonda's Bizarre Workout,' starring you and Walter Cairns."

She tried to assume an innocent look. That must have been hard for someone who had been practicing looking like a vamp for ten years. "I don't know what you're talking about."

"In that case, you really should take a look at it," I said, pushing open the door and walking past her. "May I come in? Thank you."

"Who in the hell do you think you are?" she asked angrily.

"Just a simple guy trying to make a living."

She pulled the door open wide. "Get the hell out of here."

"Sure. Right after the sneak preview." I slipped the tape into the recorder and fast-forwarded it, then turned on the television. She watched me silently from the still-open doorway. "I found this at Cairns' place after you left. The cops don't know about it, by the way."

I hit the PLAY button. As soon as she heard her voice, she quickly shut the door, and came toward me, her face distorted with rage. I ejected the tape and held it away from her and held up my hand. She stopped and glared at me, her pupils pinpoints dipped in poison. "What do you want?"

When I didn't say anything, she picked up her purse from the bureau and from it pulled a fat, business-sized envelope. "There's ten thousand dollars in here," she said contemptuously. "First and last payment. Now give me that and get out of here. The room is starting to smell."

Being the magnanimous soul that I was, I ignored that last remark and pointed at the envelope. "You were taking that to Cairns this afternoon."

One corner of her mouth turned up nastily. "You're bright for a detective."

My eye caught a flash of pearl in her purse. "I have my moments."

I stepped up and held out the tape and as she reached for it, I grabbed up her purse behind her and turned it upside down.

A nickel-plated, pearl-handled .32 automatic thudded onto the dresser top along with the usual assortment of junk women carry in their purses, and I snatched it up. "What do you know," I said in wonderment. "A designer gun."

"Give me that!" she said angrily, and grabbed for it.

I pulled it out of her reach, stepped back, and ejected the clip. "What were you going to do, wave it in Cairns' face if he didn't come across with the tape?"

"Don't be an ass. I always carry that."

"Why?"

"Protection."

"Of course you have a license to carry it concealed," I said doubtingly. She didn't answer. "You *do* know how to use it?"

"Probably better than you," she said sullenly. "I happen to be an expert marksman."

"Really? Who taught you how to shoot?"

"My father, if you must know. That was about the only thing he did teach me."

I pulled back the slide to make sure there was no bullet in the chamber, and handed it to her. "And my clip?"

She looked as if she would have liked to use a few on me. "When I leave," I said, just in case she had any thoughts along those lines.

She stuck the gun back in her purse. "Which is now. Take your fucking money and get out."

"I don't want your money."

"No?" Her expression hardened even more, if that were possible. "What *do* you want?"

I shrugged. "Answers to some questions, that's all. I think I deserve that much. After all, I put my own ass in a sling taking this tape. The only reason I did is because I know how these things have a tendency to get leaked to the media, no matter how careful everybody is. I figured whatever you and Cairns had going together is your own business."

"Whatever we had *going?*" she blurted out in disbelief. "Walter Cairns was a pervert. I mean, the man had serious problems. Our relationship was strictly professional."

"Don't tell me. This was an audition tape for the lead in *Justine.*"

She eyed the tape, then me, trying to determine what my game was. "Not that it matters what you think, but that tape is of a rape. I went to Walter's house in Malibu that night for a so-called 'story conference' about *Death in the Desert*. We had a drink. He must have put something in it, because the next thing I knew, I was tied up. I only remember pieces from then on."

"If you were raped, why didn't you press charges?"

Her face flushed angrily. "Who would've believed me? He denied he slipped me anything. Everybody knows how decadent movie stars are. Anyway, I *needed* this part. I was flat broke. Walter apologized for the incident and I chalked it up to my own stupidity. I thought the whole thing was over and done with. Until I saw that tape."

"When was that?"

"Last night. Walter called me up around seven and asked me to come over to his condo. He said he had something urgent to show me. He wouldn't say what it was, but he assured me I had nothing to worry about, that other people would be there, in case I didn't feel safe with him alone. When I got there, Sam was just leaving."

"Does Fields know about the tape?"

"I don't think so. Walter claimed nobody knew about it but us. He told me he had a camera hidden behind a two-way mirror in the bedroom, which was how he taped us without me knowing."

"And he wanted money."

"'A loan,' he called it. He said he hated to ask me for it, but an emergency had come up and he needed the cash immediately—ten thousand bucks. He said he intended to repay the money with interest and would sign a promissory note for it."

I had to admit, his approach was different. "If you believed that one, leave thirty-two of your teeth under your pillow tonight for the Tooth Fairy."

"Right," she said scoffingly. "I told him it was blackmail, plain and simple, and why didn't he just call it by its name, but he insisted it was nothing of the kind. He said he could have sold it to a scandal sheet for a hell of a lot more than that, but he wanted me to have it as a token of goodwill."

"He couldn't have sold it without hurting himself."

"You'd be surprised what you can do with editing."

I remembered then that Cairns had been wearing a mask part of the time.

I held out the tape to her. She looked at me suspiciously, then reached out slowly, keeping her distance between us. When she had it in her hand, her eyes registered relief, and she clutched it immediately to her chest. That was one lucky cassette.

Her eyes scanned the room and lighted on the metal wastebasket under the table by the window, and in one quick move she was standing over it, pulling the tape out of the cassette. The more she pulled, the more frantic her tugging became, until it took on a manic intensity. When the tape finally reached the end, she dropped the cassette into the basket, picked it up, along with a book of matches from the table, and slid open the patio door.

Bent over the wastebasket, swearing as she struck match after match the gusts of desert wind kept blowing out, she looked like a vision of some crazed Camp Fire Girl, but then one stayed lit and the tape caught and she rocked back on her haunches and smiled, mesmerized by the black smoke coming up from the blaze.

"Feel better?" I asked, watching her from the doorway.

She breathed a sigh of relief. "You have no idea." She smiled up at me and her eyes softened. "I'm sorry, but I've forgotten your name."

"Jake Asch."

"Thanks, Jake Asch. I'm sorry I flew off the handle—"

"That's okay," I told her with mock seriousness. "Considering the present state of the human race, your suspicions are understandable. Very few are as noble as I."

She smiled and I asked her if she knew if Cairns had taped anyone else.

"I don't know," she said, "but I assume he didn't rig up his little setup just for me."

The breeze shifted, blowing the black, smelly smoke toward us, and we went inside and closed the glass door.

"Fields told me Cairns was walking off the picture," I said. "He mention anything like that to you?"

Her eyes seemed to register genuine surprise. "No."

"He claims Cairns wanted him to take over as director, and was going to make that recommendation to Resnick."

"That's hard to believe," she said.

"Why?"

"Because just a few days ago, Walter threatened to fire Fields."

A sudden gust of wind shook the sliding glass door. "Why?"

She shrugged. "Sam made a comment, I'm not sure to who, that Walter was directing like a second-year film student—master shot, close-up, reverse shot, close-up—that there was nothing interesting going on, no camera movement, nothing. He said it was just lucky Walter was shooting enough film, so that it could possibly be pulled out in the editing. I don't know how it got back to Walter, but he called Sam down for it in front of the entire crew. He told him that if he wanted advice from a recycled drunk of a cutter, he'd ask for it, and that if he didn't want to be out of work for another seven years, he'd better stick to his Moviola and keep his mouth shut."

I gave that a little thought before filing it away, and said: "You probably won't be shooting for a couple of days, huh?"

Her face fell. "If at all. Marty may just decide to fold the production rather than risk another two million trying to save it."

"In the meantime, no matter what happens, you'll be free for dinner tonight."

"Jesus Christ," she said in disbelief. "I'm talking major catastrophe here, one man dead and millions of dollars teetering on the rim of the toilet, and you're talking about dinner?"

"The millions aren't mine, my starving myself isn't going to bring anyone back to life, and I hate to eat alone."

She considered for a moment, then glanced at the smoldering smudge pot and smiled. "How could I refuse an invitation from anyone so noble?"

I told her I would pick her up at seven, and went out.

10

Down the hallway, heated female voices spilled through the partially cracked door of 216. As I passed, I heard Resnick's name mentioned and stopped to eavesdrop. "I've arranged for you to meet with Marty Resnick at four." It was the voice of the blonde agent outside the trailer at the date grove.

"What kind of meeting?"

"He wants to talk to you about the movie. He wants to get things straightened out."

"There's no way I can finish this picture now. Not after what's happened."

"You *have* to," the woman insisted. "Your career is at stake. Marty Resnick carries a lot of weight in this town. If you quit now, you can kiss everything we've worked for good-bye."

"I don't care! I can't go on!" The voice was close to hysteria. "Everywhere I turn, I see Walter's face—"

"Stop it! You have to put Walter out of your mind."

"How *can* I?"

The woman's voice turned firm, almost steely: "I don't know about you, sweetheart, but I haven't busted my ass for all these years to have it flushed down a toilet like this. I taught you how to walk, how to talk, and this is how you intend to repay me? By fucking up everything I've built up for you? You've been trying to do that for the past year. I can't take this shit anymore. I can't handle it. Get yourself another agent."

"No!" the girl wailed desperately. "Please. You can't leave me alone! Not now."

"Why not? You want to drag me down too? Thanks, but no thanks."

The girl began to cry and I could hear footsteps pacing. "This was going to be your big break. This is what we've been waiting for for six years. You know how hard I had to work to get you this part? You know how I've suffered with your neuroses and your obsessive habits? This is the end."

"No, please!" the girl sobbed.

Nobody spoke for a few minutes, and the girl's sobbing slowly subsided.

"You'll do everything I tell you from now on?" the woman asked.

"Yes."

"That's a good girl." The woman's voice was soothing now, motherly. "Have I ever let you down before?"

"No."

"Susanne knows best."

"Yes."

"You'll go see Marty at four and you'll ask—beg, if you have to—for another chance. You're going to tell him you'll be good—no more drugs, no more shooting delays."

"Yes."

Since I was already a sneak and an eavesdropper, I figured I might as well add Peeping Tom to the list, and pushed on the door gently.

The blonde from the trailer was sitting on the edge of the bed, gently stroking the hair of a young redheaded girl sitting next to her and cooing soothingly into her ear. "Shhhhh. There no—"

The redhead looked up and saw me and gasped. She was very young, no more than twenty-two, with a pale, heart-shaped face highlighted by big blue eyes. It was a very pretty face, despite the streaks of mascara that ran down it like rust stains beneath the window screens of an old apartment building. The blonde's head snapped around. "What the fuck do you want?" she demanded belligerently. "Get out of here!"

"Sorry," I muttered, backing out the door. "I must have the wrong room."

I started off, and halfway down the hall, the door slammed shut.

I caught Lori Norris at work. She expressed shock at the news of Cairns' death, but didn't sound particularly upset by it, for which I couldn't really blame her. She seemed more concerned with how his untimely demise would affect her case, which Edelstein was now officially handling for her. I told her that was something I wanted to talk to him about, too, and that I would try to get together with her when I returned to L.A. tomorrow.

Edelstein was in a good humor when I called, but that soon faded when he heard the news. "This means probate," he said unhappily. "Has a will been found?"

"Not that I know of."

"If he left one, and Lori isn't in it, we're going to have to contest it."

I didn't particularly want to ruin his day totally, but there was no way around it, so I told him about the case of the missing eighty grand. He took that about like I thought he would—not calmly. "What the fuck would he do with eighty grand in cash?"

"I asked myself the same question."

"It has to be somewhere," he said. "In a safe-deposit box, *somewhere*."

I agreed it was likely.

"*Find it*," he ordered. "And find out if he left a will. I want to know if there are any heirs."

I said I'd try, then asked: "Would a little publicity hurt our case?"

"Why? What have you got in mind?"

If I gave Larry a jump on things now, I was pretty sure we could use his column later to garner some sympathy for the cause in case we needed it. I told him that, and he said: "I don't see how we're going to get hurt by it. It might even help. I want to clear it with Lori first, though."

I told him not to worry, that I didn't intend to leak it for a day or two, and said good-bye. A thought flitted across my mind, and I looked up the number I'd jotted down in my notebook before burying the original back in Cairns' waste-basket. A woman's voice answered on the third ring: "Desert D'Or."

I asked for Room 14 and was connected. No answer. Outside the window, the dying daylight seemed to be begging to be used, so I hung up and used it.

The Desert D'Or was on Mel Avenue, a narrow, seedy street that ran off Indian Avenue, in the shadow of the bell tower of the old El Mirador, Palm Springs' first luxury hotel. The pointed tiled tower was now merely a ghostly relic of a bygone era, the hotel having long ago been sold off to Desert Hospital, and rooms which once housed glamorous stars from Hollywood's Golden Years were now filled with the bent and ravaged bodies of the lame, the halt, and the terminal. But at least the El Mirador had had its day; Mel Avenue's selection of old, small, rundown hotels were not graced with even the memories of glamour.

The Desert D'Or was fifteen rooms of cracked white stucco wrapped around a swimming pool the size of a large Jacuzzi. Several consumptive-looking old men sat around the pool in deck chairs, soaking up the last diluted rays of afternoon sun, as I knocked on the door to 14.

My knock was answered by a fifty-year-old woman whose one-piece bathing suit had not been made to accommodate her bulk. Pale white flesh popped out everywhere, like uncooked bread dough squeezed through the fingers of a fist. She told me her name was Latimer and she and her husband had had the room for the past two days and she'd never heard of anyone named Hal.

A game show blared through the curtained doorway behind the desk in the office. I rang the bell on the counter and waited for what seemed like a long time, the minutes counted off for me by a shellacked-wood clock on the wall with Jesus' face painted on it. Maybe this was a message. Maybe God had sent this Jew to this place to meet His Son, The Clock.

After I pondered the significance of that for a while, the manager finally made an appearance. She was a small, sour-faced woman wearing a purple shift that needed ironing and a gray head full of curlers.

An extravaganza song-and-dance number worthy of Busby Berkeley did nothing for her, but a twenty did. "Hal" was Harold Sarto, 1356½ St. Anthony Place, L.A. Another ten got me that he'd left five days ago in a 1974 Honda Civic after a two-night stay, but when I asked if he'd had any visitors while he was here, she replied indignantly that she wouldn't know, she didn't "snoop on the guests."

The message light was on when I got back to my room. The message turned out to be from Larry Bigelow requesting that I call him immediately.

"What's going on down there?" he asked semihysterically when I did. "Here I thought we were supposed to be friends, Jacob, and I have to get the news from *strangers*."

"Don't bust your corset, Larry. I was going to call you."

"When? Next week? That'll make a great scoop. That and Chernobyl."

"*Today*, Larry, I was going to call you today. I've been a little busy."

I told him about the condition in which I'd found Cairns, and he said in a revelatory tone: "Dr. Cyclops."

That probably should have meant something to me, but it didn't, and I told him so.

"*Dr. Cyclops*," he said impatiently, "the *movie*. 1940. Albert Dekker. He died the same way."

"Dr. Cyclops?"

"No, no," he replied snippily. "Albert Dekker. In real life. He died the same way. You would think Walter would have thought up something a little more original."

"This is Hollywood," I said.

He sighed disappointedly. "I suppose you're right."

The Peg Entwistle Syndrome. In the 1930s, a bit player named Peg Entwistle, unable to cope with her failure to achieve stardom, sought a faster and more direct route, by climbing to the top of the thirteenth letter of the now-famous HOLLYWOOD sign on the hills overlooking Tinseltown (the sign originally had had a few extra letters, spelling out HOLLYWOODLAND, an unsuccessful real-estate subdivision of silent-movie director Mack Sennett's) and leaping to her death. The craze caught on, and soon, other depressed and disenchanted starlets were doing sequels to Entwistle's act. In Hollywood, even the style of suicide is derivative.

"There's something else. And this *is* an exclusive."

His voice perked up. "What are you trying to do, take Hitchcock's place as the master of suspense? Let's have it."

"You have to promise to sit on it until I give you the word."

"All right, all right, I promise. Now *give*."

I told him about Cairns being McVey, withholding only the name of my client, and he asked excitedly: "You're sure nobody else has this?"

"I don't see how anyone could. The woman is my client."

"I can see the headline now: 'Nothing is what it seems in Hollywood.' This is good stuff, Jake. How long do you expect me to hold off on it?"

"A day or two, max," I assured him. "Tell me something, Larry, are productions like *Death in the Desert* insured in case something like this happens?"

"Usually. Most productions with budgets of over half a million are insured in the event the director or one of the principal actors dies or can't continue because of sickness or injury."

"What if the director quit? Walked off in the middle of shooting?"

"There's no coverage for that. The producer would have to try to find another director to take over."

"What if he was operating under a time limit from the studio, and he couldn't find one fast enough?"

"He'd be in serious trouble. Why?"

"Just idle curiosity."

"Don't bullshit me, Jacob Asch. Something is going on down there. What is it?"

"If something is going on and I find out about it, you'll be the first to know, Larry—"

"I believed you when you told me that before, and look what happened," he said, sounding hurt. "You smell something, don't you?"

This was why I'd put off calling him. "Larry—"

"You have to stay on this one for me, Jake. I can't get down there until Thursday. I'll pay you, of course—"

"I already have a client, Larry."

"So now you have two clients."

"There might be a conflict of interest."

"If there's a conflict, I'll defer to your other client," he said, insistently. "All I'm asking is for you to keep tabs on things until I can get there on Thursday."

"*If* it doesn't interfere with my duties to my client—"

"You're an absolute jewel," he said, not letting me finish. "I knew I could count on you."

I hung up feeling like a jewel, all right; one of those $19.95 ten-carat "diamelles" they sold on TV to schmucks from Rube City. If the rest of the schmucks knew who I had a date with tonight, they would have voted me in as Mayor.

11

Marla McKinnon opened the door looking wantonly spectacular in a red silk blouse, black leather pants, and boots. I asked if she liked Italian and she said that sounded perfect, which turned out well because I'd already made reservations at a small place downtown highly touted by an L.A. food critic friend of mine I'd called earlier.

When she saw the new silver BMW 635, she said admiringly: "The private-eye biz must be lucrative."

"It can be." For some reason, I felt like a complete phony. "But this isn't my car. It's a rental."

She didn't ask what kind of a car I normally drove, and my guilt was assuaged enough that I didn't feel compelled to point out the thrashed '67 Plymouth with the coat-hanger antenna parked a few stalls away. That car and I had been through the wars together, it was a nostalgic symbol of my own survival, and I'd drive it until it had to be junked, but I had to admit rather traitorously that it felt good driving downtown in the BMW with a sexy movie star at my side. Maybe it was time to adopt a new image, one with a little more glamour. Jacob Asch, Eye of the Stars. I made a mental note to start watching "Matt Houston" reruns, to get some ideas how to dress.

The restaurant was small, dark, and fairly crowded. The owner/maître d', a gray-haired man with a voice like a gravel grater, fell all over us when he saw Marla, and at her request whisked us into a quiet booth in the back.

I ordered a bottle of California Chardonnay while she signed cocktail napkins for several autograph hounds, then the owner returned with his recommendations. She decided

76

on the veal chop and I ordered tortellini, with Caesar salads to start. We sipped wine and made small talk.

She was witty and well informed and unashamed to express her feelings about any subject. Her husky voice was pleasant and relaxing and rubbed my body down like baby oil. The candlelight played on her features, hardening some, softening others, making her look even more exotic, and I felt myself responding to her in real life as I had in theaters. Whatever constituted the sexuality she projected, the reality of it could not be denied. It was not the product of fashion designers and makeup artists and cameramen, it was *real*, an animal emanation she gave off without trying, as other people give off body odor, causing a tightening in my stomach and gonads.

My friend, to my delight, had been right about the food; it was delicious. At least mine was. She only took a few bites of hers before putting her fork down. "You don't like it?"

She smiled. "I love it, that's the problem. There aren't many parts around for an aging sex symbol, but there aren't any for a *fat* aging sex symbol."

I watched as she took one more bite, poured salt all over the cannelloni, and pushed it away.

"When you said that you needed this part because you were flat broke, you weren't serious, were you?"

"Dead serious."

"But all those pictures you made—"

"I lived beyond my means. You think it'll never end, so you spend. Clothes, cars, dope." A self-amused smile crossed her lips. "I was seeing a shrink for a while. One day he asked me to square up my bill—about ten thousand dollars worth. I said to him, 'You don't really expect me to *pay* you? Just tell people you're treating me and your practice will triple.' The funny thing is, I believed it."

"Sounds like he was doing a terrific job."

"Nothing about the movie business is real, so it's easy to lose touch with reality. While you're on top, you think people are reacting to *you*, but they're not. They're reacting to something you project, and that something doesn't last forever. How does the saying go? 'Stars come and stars go, only agents last forever'? Only I wasn't satisfied to wait around for my career to start its downward slide. I had to speed things along."

"How?"

"I acquired a reputation for being unreliable. I went through two disastrous marriages and I'd begun to doubt my own self-worth. The pictures I was doing were hits, but they were stupid pictures. I realized I was playing the same one-dimensional character over and over. I tried to get other parts, but nobody would take a chance on me. They wanted Marla McKinnon, sex bomb. I started taking uppers and downers to get through the day, and after a while, I couldn't get through the day anymore. I cost the studio quite a bit of money on my last two pictures. When they didn't do so well at the box office, the offers stopped coming in. I wound up selling off everything I owned and buying a little place up in Big Sur. I became a recluse and tried to find some peace within myself."

"Did you?"

"Some. Peace isn't something that happens all at once. At least not for me. It's a continuing struggle."

I found the juxtaposition of the two words strange. "You've obviously found enough to work again."

She smiled over her glass of wine. "It was either that or learn how to type. Actually, when Walter sent me the script, I knew right away I wanted to do the picture. It wasn't just the money—God knows, I'm working cheap enough—I knew the role was for me. The woman is a real character with a range of emotion, not just a pair of tits that talk. Walter offered me the role because he knew I can act. That was another reason I didn't do anything when he pulled that stunt in his house. I saw this role as pivotal in my career. It was going to show people finally what I can do. Not too many actresses who have played my kind of roles can make the transition to character parts. I can."

I believed she could, but then, what did I know? I was smitten. "How did you get into acting in the first place?"

She sipped her wine. "The same reason every actor gets into it, whether they want to admit it or not—I wanted to feel loved."

"You didn't?"

Her eyes suddenly looked melancholy. "Believe it or not, I was a very shy little girl. I had a hard time making friends, and my parents were always too busy fighting to pay much attention to me. I don't know if it was an attempt to escape them and their arguing or from myself, but I tried out for a part in a high-school production, and for the first time, I felt love. The audience loved me." She smiled sheepishly. "Never underestimate the insecurity of a star."

I knew what she meant. I'd dated one actress, and had nearly been eaten alive by her insecurities. The girl was so nuts, she used to carry Valium around in a Pez dispenser. But Marla seemed different to me, less desperate and more real, maybe because she'd stepped back and grappled with that loneliness she talked about. Or stepped forward and embraced it. Those were the only two ways to deal with it; any other way, and you get beaten to death.

"How about you?" she asked curiously. "What makes one become a private detective?"

"Not the search for love," I said. "Most are ex-cops trying to supplement their retirement checks, or ex-insurance investigators. Most of the time, it's just something you wind up doing, not something you set out to do."

"What were you?"

"A reporter."

"What happened?"

"A judge wanted me to name my source for a story I wrote, and I refused. He found me in contempt and sent me to jail for a while. When I got out, I had no job and no prospects of finding one. I'd gotten a reputation too, one for being insubordinate and a troublemaker. It didn't take me long to discover there was something very basic missing in my life—food—so when a lawyer friend of mine offered me some investigative work, I took it."

"You must like it. You've stuck with it."

"Sometimes," I admitted. "Most of the time, it's boring. But every once in a while, you get a case that makes you feel alive. There's something very heady in collecting facts and making sense of them when nobody else can. It's a feeling of power, I guess."

She shook her head. "It seems to me it would sour you.

You must only see the worst parts of people, all the smutty, secret little parts. Like that tape."

I shrugged. "We *all* have bad parts, but that doesn't make us all bad. Expecting too much is the only thing that can sour you. I gave up expecting too much from people long before I got into this line of work."

She ran a fingernail around the rim of her glass. "What were you doing over at Walter's this afternoon, anyway?"

I told her about Cairns' previous life and she said: "I can't say I'm too surprised. Walter was schizoid."

"How do you mean?"

She turned up a palm and said: "He could be kind one moment, then incredibly cruel the next. He treated the cast and crew like that. The set was like choreographed schizophrenia. You could never tell what he was thinking, but he was a master of anticipating what everyone else was thinking. He'd play terrible practical jokes on people—especially Sam Fields—then dote on them later. It was like a game with him, keeping everyone off balance."

"What kind of practical jokes?"

"Oh, things like putting a snake in Sam's duffel bag one day on the set. Sam went nuts. He's terrified of snakes. He was furious and talked about quitting, but the next day, Walter sent him a new gold watch and told him what a good editor he was and how he needed him, and he stayed." This was the man to whom Fields had sworn his undying loyalty? Either the editor was the "M" side of Cairns' "S" or he was a liar.

"Did he do anything like that to you?"

"Only once, at the start of shooting. We were shooting a scene in the Whitewater wash over by Windy Point, where I fall into the river. The water was freezing, and luckily we got a good take the first time, but Walter said maybe we could do it better, and made me do it again. Six takes later, when I realized what he was doing, I told him to shove it and went to my trailer. He apologized later, but I told him if he ever did anything like that to me again, I'd quit, and he knew I meant it, so he laid off. Adrianne wasn't so lucky."

"How so?"

"The kid is spooked. She's terrified. That's why she takes

drugs. We've all been frustrated by her screw-ups, but instead of being supportive and trying to help her overcome her fear, Walter terrorized her from day one. And the more demanding and dictatorial he became, the worse she got, until she had to be pried out of her dressing room with a crowbar."

"I saw. So what do you think will happen?"

She shrugged. "I don't know. I talked to Marty this afternoon and put in my two cents for Sam. I think he can finish the picture. I hope Marty does too. It's too late to learn how to type."

On the way back to the hotel, she told me to turn right onto South Palm Canyon and we began to leave the city lights behind. We wound up on a potholed road close to the mountain, past clumps of creosote and gray sagebrush that floated like ghosts hovering above the landscape. The road dead-ended in a toll gate, and she told me to stop and got out of the car. I killed the engine and was almost knocked over by the quiet. The city smoldered against the dark backdrop of the mountains only a mile or so away, but it could have been in another galaxy. The only sounds were the breeze and the chirpings of an occasional night bird.

I walked over to where she was standing a few yards away, staring up at the stars. "I come here sometimes for hours. It's so peaceful. I can understand why mystics come out to the desert to find God. There's something cosmic in the solitude and the stars. It's like a place where heaven comes down and meets the earth."

The metaphor was wasted on me; my vision had been tainted years ago. The desert was not a mystical place; it was a hostile and unforgiving wasteland, a fact that the rich people who lived here forgot all too easily. They got up in the morning and shot their eighteen holes of golf and never looked beyond the edge of the green where a sidewinder sat coiled in the shade. It was a place where mistakes were not permitted and where I'd seen a few made. But I didn't tell her any of that. Instead, I pulled her into me and kissed her hard, on the mouth.

The move surprised her and she started to pull away, but then relaxed and melted into me and her mouth opened and her tongue probed mine. Her breath was sweet between perfect teeth. I felt myself stiffening against her and she felt it, too, and leaned back. She looked at me strangely. "Why did you do that?"

I shrugged. "It seemed like a good idea at the time. And because I've fantasized about it for years."

"Careful," she warned. "Fantasies can't disappoint. Only reality can."

"I'll take the chance." I started to pull her toward me, but she put her hands on my chest, holding me at elbow length. "We'd better get back."

I could tell by the tone of her voice that she was serious. The moment was lost, and with it, the fantasy. We drove back to the International in silence and I walked her up to her room, trailing behind a step or two so I could watch the supple ripplings that were alive beneath her skin-tight leather pants.

At her door, she turned and licked her lips provocatively, like I'd seen her do in half a dozen movies. I'd seen her do the next move in one or two, also, but I hardly expected it as she stepped closer and cupped my crotch gently in her hand. She lifted one eyebrow and grinned. "You're sure you want to risk being disappointed?"

It all seemed so contrived, her expression, the sultry tone of her voice, the patented moves, but I didn't care. I stepped inside and shut the door and she began unbuttoning her blouse, slowly. Her breasts were perfect—firm and round, with pale-pink nipples, which she began to tease erect with her fingertip. She smiled coyly, then took me by the hand and led me to the bed. She sat down and unzipped my pants and pulled out my cock. She put it in her mouth and began to suck it, her excitement picking up as she watched me watch her.

She stopped suddenly and said: "Fuck me, lover. Hurt me."

She made love with an almost desperate hunger, slamming her hips into me with hard, driving thrusts, telling me to go deeper, to make it hurt, and I had begun to wonder whether that scene with Cairns had been totally unpleasurable for her. I wondered a lot of things, which was what was wrong with it. I kept remembering who she was and who I was, and it was almost like an out-of-body experience with me floating above the bed, watching me fuck her, and then I came and she made sounds like she did, and we lay there, listening to our breath return to normal.

"I want you to know I only made love to you because I like you and I wanted to," she said after a while.

"What other reason could there be?"

She put her head on my chest. I must have drifted off because when I woke up, she was sitting up rigidly in bed.

"What's the matter?" I asked her back.

She didn't turn around, but asked in a voice full of hopelessness. "What am I going to do now?"

"Sleep seems like a good idea."

"I don't mean *now*," she said irritably. "I mean if this picture gets scrapped."

"There are other parts."

She shook her head. "You don't understand. They'll think it was my fault the picture was behind schedule. They'll say, 'See, Resnick took a chance on her, and look what happened.'"

"No, they won't," I tried to reassure her. She'd said it: Never underestimate the insecurity of a star.

She wouldn't look at me. "You know what Marilyn Monroe said when she signed her first big studio contract? 'That's the last cock I'll have to suck.' The funny thing is, toward the end, when she was slipping, she probably wished she still had that kind of leverage. She couldn't even find a cock to suck."

She got up and went into the bathroom and I heard her rummaging around and some pills being shaken out of a bottle. Water ran and she came back to bed and huddled next to me in a fetal position, shivering. "Just hold me tight. Please. Just hold me."

I wondered if she had picked up that line from one of the forty-two bad movies in which it had been intoned, but she sounded serious enough, so I did and she made little sad whimpering sounds and after half an hour or so, whatever she'd taken began to take effect, and she began to snore softly.

12

I slipped out of bed and dressed without waking her and went down to my room and found an old Mark Stevens film *noir* on the tube which was interrupted every six and a half minutes by Cal Worthington trying to sell me a used car by riding pigs and camels and zebras around his car lot. F. Scott Fitzgerald *almost* had it right: "In the dark night of the soul, it's always three o'clock in the morning—and Cal Worthington."

Neither the movie nor Cal Worthington could shut out the dissonant refrains of this case which kept running through my head, and by four-thirty I realized sleep was futile.

I jumped in the shower and threw on some clothes and went down to the car. There was no particular hurry; the wheels of justice ground slowly and I knew it would be at least late afternoon before McDonald could get a warrant for Cairns' Malibu house, but I thought I might as well give myself extra time, in case I needed it.

It was still dark when I went down to the parking lot. The rental place wouldn't be open for hours yet, which meant I would be paying for the BMW another day, anyway, so I decided I might as well go in style. On the way out of town, I stopped at Denny's for a large coffee to go, then turned on the car stereo and settled back into the cushy seat as I left the oasis of still-spotlighted palm trees in my rearview mirror and headed into a desert overloaded with a plum-colored sky.

The sun was just beginning to peak over the eastern rim of the mountains and San Jacinto was a pale pink in the dawn light. Those mountains were a perfect backdrop for the town, I thought, illusory, chameleonic, changing color with changes in the light. Pink, then orange in the morning, brown in the afternoon, blue to violet at dusk, their appearance and mood was dependent on the eye of the beholder. I wasn't sure what my mood was as the BMW purred along at an effortless eighty. My mind was cluttered with thoughts and images from the past two days, and I was too tired from lack of sleep to try to sort them out.

The dawn sky turned blue, then gray, and the closer I got to L.A., the grayer it became. By seven, I was driving along the Coast Highway, through a chalky fog, past deserted beaches and a sea the color of dirty asphalt. Dawn was only a dim hint through the fog, but somewhere beyond the soup, I knew the sky was orange-streaked and beautiful and I longed to be there. I wound up settling for Malibu, which appeared ahead in all its resplendent beauty.

The name "Malibu" has taken on a certain glamorous mystique because of TV and a lot of epic movies starring Shakespearean actors like Frankie Avalon and Annette Funicello. In reality, it is one long, boring strip of outrageously overpriced and undersized matchbox houses and cloned, fake-weathered-wood seafood restaurants jammed together between the beach and crumbling mud cliffs that continually teased with previews of what was going to happen when the Big One hit and Phoenix became a beach town. Only after you get beyond Malibu do the houses start to acquire any size and style. Cairns' address was two miles past Malibu, on a three-house cul-de-sac that ran along the beach off the highway. His was the last one on the street, hidden behind a six-foot hydrangea hedge.

It looked as if the local residents were fugitives from the fog. The windows of the houses were all dark, the only car on the street was a brown Mercury Cougar with an Alamo Rent-a-Car sticker on its bumper, parked in front of the house next to Cairns'. That was just fine with me; the fewer prying eyes around, the better.

The driveway dipped down to the front door and I pulled up and killed my engine. I slipped on the pair of black leather gloves I'd packed for the occasion, and got out of the car. The house was typical for the beach, with a weathered-wood exterior and an overhanging second story topped by a sharply angled shingle roof. There were no alarm-company signs posted out front and no evidence of any kind of security system. That didn't mean there wasn't one. I rang the bell, just in case Cairns had someone house-sitting, and when nobody answered, I went around back.

My shoes sunk into the soft sand and annoyingly began to fill up with the stuff. Behind the house was an elevated wood-plank patio occupied by some rope furniture. The entire back of the house was glass, covered inside by wood shutters. I went up the stairs onto the patio and, after emptying my shoes, tried the sliding door that led into the house. It was locked, as I expected.

I was stopped by the sound of a dog barking and turned to see a gray-haired man in a yellow sweatsuit jog out of the fog accompanied by a big German shepherd. The shepherd seemed to be mocking the man as it loped around him in noisy circles, giving him a demonstration of the superiority of quadrupedal motion.

I waited for the fog to swallow them up, then sat down on the damp planking facing away from the door lock and gave the frame a kick. Two more hard kicks derailed the door and I stood up and slid it open. No alarms went off, nobody screamed. I lifted the door back onto its tracks and locked it.

The gray daylight seeped weakly through the shutters, making the room seem even colder and damper than it was. The downstairs was one large, open room filled with rattan furniture and lots of healthy-looking potted plants. The redwood walls were covered with colorful lithos, among which I recognized two Lindners. There was a sunken bar along one wall with a mirrored backbar and next to it was a big-screen television and shelving loaded with sophisticated-looking stereo equipment. Along the opposite wall, a redwood staircase led up to a second-floor landing that ran around the perimeter of the house. On my way to the stairs, I spied a man watching me from the mirror behind the bar, and stopped. He definitely had the sneaky, shifty-eyed look of a housebreaker. I saluted him and went on my way.

There were three doors off the landing, and when I stepped

through the first one, I immediately recognized the room. The king-sized bed was covered with the same fur spread, and for a split-second I saw Marla there, chained to the legs, a leather gag in her mouth. Maybe next time I'd bring my handcuffs and see how she responded. My mother always used to say: Any girl who likes whips and chains can't be all bad.

There was a framed mirror above the Deco dresser alongside the bed. I went to it and ran my fingers around the edge of the frame. It was hinged and it swung open when I pressed on it.

The hole was two by two by two, with plenty of space to accommodate the bracket-mounted Panasonic Nighthawk. The power cord was plugged into a socket on the inside of the cabinet, and another thicker cord led from the back of the camera into a hole in the wall. The hole was about the same height as the stereo shelf unit next to the bureau that held a combination tuner-tape unit, two amps, and a pre-amp. On closer inspection, one of the amps turned out to be a CCU unit, to control the camera's iris opening and the white-and-color balance. Cairns had taken care with the setup to ensure quality control, and I doubted he had done it all just for Marla.

I closed up the cabinet and pulled open the top drawer of the bureau. The clothes in it—socks, underwear, and T-shirts—were unfolded and messy. All the other drawers were the same, clothes pushed to one side and rumpled, as if someone had gone through them looking for something. I stood very quietly and listened to the house, but it said nothing to me. The walk-in closet on the other side of the room did, however, when I opened its door. Somebody had left the light on.

Cairns had a lot of clothes, all good labels, and it took me a little time to go through them without coming up with anything. I moved the clothes and tapped the cedar-paneled walls, but they were solid. I turned out the light and adjourned to the bathroom.

It was done in dark green tile, and stepping into it made me feel as if I'd wandered into a dark forest thicket. A quick toss of the medicine cabinet came up with one interesting item—a half-empty prescription bottle for liquid Demerol. That could have been what Cairns had slipped into Marla's drink to make her more pliable. I put the bottle back and went through the drawers below the sink.

Funny the things you can find in bathroom drawers, among packages of double-edged blades and half-squeezed tubes of toothpaste. Like an opened envelope containing a statement from Shearson Lehman Brothers showing that between November 3 and November 5, Cairns had sold off four stocks totaling $37,567.90. With the money he had gotten from his second mortgage, that made almost $120,000 that was somewhere other than in the checking account I knew about. I pocketed the envelope and went out of the bedroom to the next door down, feeling like a privileged contestant on *Let's Make a Deal* who was allowed to see what was behind *all* the doors.

If I'd known what was behind Door Number Two, I would have gladly traded it for any other, including a doggie door, but I didn't, so I stepped through it. It was a small den lined with ceiling-to-floor shelves, crammed with books. That was all I had time to see. Something moved behind the door and I turned and was instantly blinded by the fire that engulfed my face.

I screamed and fell to the floor, clawing at my cheeks that felt as if they were being eaten away by acid. Mace. Footsteps went by my head and I made a grab for them, but wound up with a handful of air. I could have used a lungful, instead; my throat was constricting and I couldn't breathe.

I wrestled with the panic as the tightness spread to my chest, and somehow managed to get to my feet. I tried to open my eyes, but only my eyebrows moved; the lids were sealed with Duco cement. I put my hands out and located a wall, then felt around it until I got to the door. That took about eight years. My nose was running like a faucet and I knew my face would melt before I found the bathroom. I felt my way down the landing, to the bedroom door, and barked my shins on the corner of the bed. I would have sworn, but I didn't have the breath.

Somehow, I managed to get to the bathroom, and I turned on the cold water in the sink and splashed it in my face until the stinging abated a little and the steel bands around my throat began to loosen. After five minutes of splashing, the worst was over and I could open my eyes. I ripped off some toilet paper and wiped my nose. I might as well have used my shirt; the front of it was covered with snot.

The front door was wide open when I went downstairs, and I went out it and up the driveway. The Cougar was gone. I cursed myself for not taking down its license number, but I was hurting enough without adding self-recrimination to it, so I walked back to the house.

Three of the set of Great Books had been pulled off the shelf in the den and stacked on top of the Macintosh word processor on the desk. Two of them contained videotapes labeled like Marla's, with a female first name and last initial. The third—*The Scarlet Letter*—was hollowed out, but empty. It looked as if whoever had Maced me had gotten what they'd come for. I started pulling down the rest of the thirty books in the set to see if they'd had time to get *everything* they'd come for.

Ten contained tapes. I made a list of the names and put all the books back, except the three on the desk, which I left for McDonald. I thought about running the tapes, just to see if I could match up faces to the names, but decided to let McDonald do it.

I'd played Galahad once and gotten away with it, but the Jacob Asch Chivalric Code, Section One, Sub-section A, specifically prohibited me from pressing my luck, limiting me to "one-gratitude-fuck per month, no matter how sexy the wench or famous the actress." Besides, I had to protect what fantasies I had left.

I turned my attention to the desk, which contained nothing of particular interest, and the filing cabinet next to it, which did. The "did" was a file of bank statements from a money-market account at Columbia Savings under Cairns' name. The last one was a month old and showed a balance of $69,598.67. I wrote down the account number and went down the hall to Door Number Three.

It was a guest bedroom, and, like the guest bedroom in Palm Springs, did not appear to have been recently lived in. The walk-in closet, however, turned out to be a repository of the stuff that kinky dreams are made of. There was a pillory, a kind of swing complete with ligatures and chain for easy ceiling attachment, several pairs of very large women's dagger-heeled boots, latex masks and body suits, and a selection of gags and restraints for every party occasion. I left the stuff alone—most of it would probably wind up in the bedroom closets of the cops that searched the place, anyway—and began my wall-tapping routine. There would be nothing so mundane as a wall-safe-behind-the-picture for Cairns. Oh, no. His tastes ran to the more exotic, like hollowed-out books and two-way mirrored cabinets. When I saw the crack at the top of the doorjamb, I smiled and knew I'd hit the Grand Prize. Door Number Three was the one.

The jamb was held by a magnet at the top and anchored into three drilled holes in the floor by nails. I lifted it off and set it to one side. Three hidey-holes had been hollowed out in the wall, each about a foot deep. Mr. or Mrs. Mace hadn't found them. The top one contained crisp, new one-hundred-dollar bills, neatly packaged in two five-thousand-dollar bundles.

I thought about what I could buy with the money, but only for a moment. What would it profit a man who gaineth a BMW, but loseth his Plymouth *and* his soul? Anyway, ten grand wouldn't cover the down payment on a silver beast like the one out front. I put the money back and pulled the stash of papers from the second hole.

There was no last will and testament among them, but there were some other interesting items, including Cairns' birth certificate, showing he had been born in Albuquerque, New Mexico, on January 9, 1941; another birth certificate for a Timothy Oglansky, born March 14, 1942, in Los Angeles, and a death certificate, also for a Timothy Oglansky, who, at age four, had been killed in an automobile accident on August 17, 1946, in Riverside, California. Little Timmy must have been an enterprising young man—either that, or his parents hadn't heard of child-labor laws—because by the time he had died at age four, he already had a Social Security card, which was in with the other documentation of his short life.

The last and most curious item was a computer printout, across the top of which was printed "Picture Cost Report," and written in longhand, "Black Thursday." Columns of numbers and dates ran down the page, and under one headed "Acct Number" five entries coded with the number "222" had been circled. The entries were dated from December 12 through December 26, and there were money amounts for each entry, all apparently for checks made out to a Canyon Camera for "Equipment Rental." The amounts varied between $2,500 and $3,500, and totaled some $14,000. Alongside the name there was another number, 000004281, which I guessed was a bank account number. Farther down the page, under the heading "Set Construction," another item, this one with an "815" code number, had been circled, an amount of $8,070.98, which had been paid to a Carl Green.

I pocketed the papers and replaced the jamb, then went downstairs. I left the front door unlocked in Malibu, found a place open that did photocopying, and ran off triplicates of everything. There were no cop cars outside the house when I got back, just the fog and the sea lisping on the sand. I went in cautiously, but nobody jumped out from behind the furniture with a can of Mace. I redeposited the originals in the upstairs hidey-hole, leaving the jamb cracked about an inch at the top so McDonald couldn't miss it, then locked the place up and drove down the coast.

My eyes were still stinging when I stopped at one of the cloned restaurants that served breakfast, but they'd stopped watering enough for me to read, so I bought a *Times* and scanned it over a meal of greasy perch, hard scrambled egg, cold toast, and coffee.

The story on Cairns' death was on page three, and it spared the more lurid details, other than the fact that he had been found by "Palm Springs police" naked and hanged by a rope attached to the bedpost. My name was not mentioned. McDonald was quoted as saying that there was "no evidence of second-party involvement," but that investigators were looking into "every possibility." Resnick called Cairns a "major talent," termed the death a "shocking tragedy," and vowed to finish *Death in the Desert* as a monument to his memory. He termed "ridiculous" allegations by unnamed sources "close to" Cairns that he'd been "deeply depressed recently about career setbacks," and said that Cairns had expressed the optimistic opinion that *Death in the Desert* was going to be his best work. The article went on to list some of Cairns' credits, and I breathed easier when I got to the end of it without reading anything about Bill McVey or Cairns' former life, because Larry had kept his word. His column this morning was about rumors that Linda Evans was leaving *Dynasty*.

I used the pay phone in the back of the restaurant to call Troy Wilcox at L.A. First Federal. Troy was chief loan officer at the downtown branch and we'd swapped favors over the years to our mutual benefit; he supplied me with confidential bank information and I supplied him with the whereabouts of loan skips when I ran across them, which since the advent of Reaganomics seemed to be more and more frequently. I gave Troy the bank names and numbers of the two accounts I had for Cairns and asked if he could get me a list of transactions for the past month for both accounts, especially any checks written or transfers made to accounts at other banks, and whether he had a safe-deposit box at either location. He told me to call him back in a couple of hours.

Information had listings for both a Harold Sarto on St. Anthony Place, and Canyon Camera Rentals, but no address listed for Canyon Camera, which struck me as a bit odd. I tried the latter first and a recorded female voice told me that everyone was out of the office right now, but if I cared to leave a message, someone would get back to me. Since I had no message to leave, I tried Sarto's number. I took the busy signal I got as an omen and made the drive in thirty minutes.

13

St. Anthony Place was below Santa Monica, on the southern edge of Hollywood, and it was a microcosm of the world—a street in uneasy transition. Small, older houses and new, big, blocky apartment complexes glared hostilely at each other from opposite sides of the street like members of two rival gangs getting ready to engage in mortal combat. The address I had for Sarto was on the side destined to lose, a chocolate-colored, wood, prairie-style house with a shingle roof and fronted by a sheltered porch. A maroon Honda Civic was parked at the end of the weed-cracked cement driveway that ran alongside the house, and when I couldn't raise anyone ringing the front doorbell, I walked down to it.

The driveway opened into a large parking area out back, and there was a small stucco guesthouse there that had the converted look of a onetime garage. The window by the door was covered by faded green curtains. I knocked on the door. A lot of nothing happened very fast. I knocked again. The sound of canned laughter erupted from a television set inside. I'd teach them to laugh at me. The handle turned when I tried it and I pushed the door open a crack. That was all it took. The stench rushed out and gored me in the stomach like a charging rhino and I reeled backward, gagging.

I ran behind the Honda and took some deep breaths to get control of the nausea. My heart was pounding and my stomach felt like a clenched fist. I stood there for a minute or so, trying to work my courage up and practicing breathing through my mouth, then started reluctantly toward the door.

The door creaked appropriately, like a door from a horror movie, and I left it wide open, in case I wanted to get out of

93

there fast. The laughter had come from a rerun of *I Love Lucy*, which was playing on the 15-inch television that sat on rollers in the corner of the tiny living room. The walls were covered with cheap wood paneling and the furniture looked as if it had been picked out by Ray Charles at six different swap meets. There was a sagging red velveteen couch, a bright orange vinyl chair, a scarred Formica-topped coffee table, a glass-and-brass end table on which sat a purple potbellied ceramic lamp, and in one corner, a small refrigerator and table with a hotplate on it. The worn carpet was olive-green and covered with piles of dogshit, which lay all over like coiled brown snakes.

If it was a dead dog I'd smelled, it had to be a goddamned mastiff. A door on the other side of the room stood partially open, and since there were no dead mastiffs or people in here, I went toward it, tiptoeing through the dogshit as if negotiating a minefield. The trip was only twenty feet, but by the time I'd made it, I was sweating profusely. The air was thick and tepid and I tried not to think about the smell, but I could feel it entering my mouth, an oily, foul film. I hesitated at the door and listened to Lucy whine to Ethel how Ricky wasn't paying enough attention to her. We all had our little crosses to bear. I bore mine and pushed on the door.

It opened about a foot, wide enough for me to see the man's legs where he had fallen in front of the bed, blocking the door. A telephone lay at his feet, off the hook. I poked my head through to get a look at the rest of him and then I heard it, the low, throaty growl of a dog.

A brown dachshund stood behind the body, looking like a bloated blood sausage doing an ad for a credit dentist. Its upper lip was curled back, giving me a glimpse of all its nice white teeth as it warned me away from its din-din. This was no longer man's best friend; hunger had taken it back to a place in time when its dwarfed, misshapen legs were still long and it hunted in packs.

What was left of the body was lying on its stomach, surrounded by a large, dark stain where the blood had soaked into the carpet. The back of the white shirt was shredded and large hunks of flesh had been torn out of the back and neck. The right arm was shorter than the left by a forearm. The little Kraut canine obviously hadn't heard that he wasn't supposed to bite off the hand that fed him.

The growling picked up in intensity and I took the hint and pulled the door shut, just in case he decided he wanted a more varied menu. As I stepped back my heel hit something, and I looked down at a six-inch piece of PVC pipe sticking out from under the end of the coffee table. I bent down and picked up one end of it with my ballpoint pen.

The pipe was stuffed with bottle caps through which a hole had been bored and there was a hose clamp on one end. A notch had been cut out for the sight. All in all, a neat little disposable silencer. It looked like whoever had done Sarto was a real cutie.

I put the pipe back and stood up. There was an open box of Wheatsworth crackers and a can of Bud on the coffee table, along with a copy of the *Racing Form* and an issue of the *National Enquirer*, the headline on the front of which said: COUPLE FLEES TALKING BEAR. I was tempted to read the article, just to see what the bear could have said to make two people run away like that, but was distracted by the ashes in the large ceramic ashtray next to the Wheatsworths.

They were not cigarette ashes, but looked like the remnants of a piece of paper that had been shredded and burned. Poking through them, I found one singed particle that had not burned completely. It was from a newspaper and all I could make out was part of a name and a date—*ook*, and below that *14, 1955*. I jotted it down on the back of my breakfast receipt, then used my handkerchief to wipe off the knobs of the bedroom and front doors before shutting the place up again.

Only when I hit the street did I dare breathe through my nose. I stopped at the first bar I passed on Santa Monica and had a double vodka on the rocks. If the three other morning drinkers at the bar picked up the smell of death on me, they were polite enough not to mention it, but I could still smell it. I looked at my watch, said to hell with it, it had to be five o'clock somewhere, and ordered another, then went into the back and used the pay phone to call the L.A.P.D. I gave the cop who answered Sarto's address and hung up before he could ask me my name, then tried Canyon Camera again. I got the same recording as before.

I took the smell outside, hoping the new-leather smell of the BMW would override it, and drove downtown. I didn't know what was going on at Canyon Camera, but whatever it was, the fact that Cairns had thought it important enough to hide with his new identity was enough to make me want to find out.

The business license Canyon Camera had taken out with the city of Los Angeles gave a business address on Vermont and listed the principle owner as CCR, Inc., with corporate headquarters at the same address. Before driving over there, I stopped at the County Corporation Commission and found that CCR, Inc., was a sub-S corporation that had been incorporated nine years ago. There was only one officer listed—Shirley Magill, 2367 Playmor Drive, Bel Air. I took down the information, along with the phone number listed there, and drove over to Vermont.

The address was below Wilshire, an area where the names on the storefronts and the derelicts were racially mixed, and I went half a block beyond it before realizing I'd passed it. I parked the car and walked back.

The reason I'd missed it was because there was no name on the front of the building and two of the numbers had fallen off the address. It was a tiny sliver of soot-blackened storefront wedged between a Korean market and a used-clothing store, and one look through the dirt-streaked windows told me Canyon Camera had been out of business, at least at this location, for a long time. The interior was gutted and empty except for some pages of old crumpled newspaper that littered the filthy linoleum floor.

I hiked back to the car and was pleasantly surprised to find it still had all its tires; they worked fast in neighborhoods like this. I drove up to Wilshire and pulled into the first gas station I spotted with a phone booth and called Troy.

He gave me the bad news first. Six days ago, Cairns had closed out his money-market account at Columbia, withdrawing the $70,000 in cash—hundred-dollar bills, to be precise. The good news was that he had a safe-deposit box at B of A in Santa Monica, and had visited it on the same day he'd cleaned out his Columbia account. That was the last recorded entry into the box and nobody else had access to it.

I called Edelstein's office. He was out, so I left the news update with his secretary, then tried Larry, but Hugo informed me that he'd left for Palm Springs this morning and that he could be reached down there at Maxim's. I hung up, stared at the phone for a moment, and dialed the Bel Air number I had for Shirley Magill. The woman's voice had a Spanish accent. "Resnick residence."

I didn't say anything for a moment. "Pardon me?"

"Resnick residence."

"Marty Resnick?"

"I sorry, Mr. Resnick no ees home."

"Thank you," I said, and hung up.

This was starting to turn into a real potboiler; I wondered who I could call for a plot synopsis to find out how it ended.

As I drove home, my mind continually leaked thoughts of the case like the fine, steady mist that leaked from the gray sky. And like the mist on the windshield that refused to be cleaned up by my wipers, the thoughts stubbornly returned, no matter how hard I tried to blot them out. For a case without a murder, it sure had a lot of suspects.

I stopped off at Mama Lucinda's rib joint and picked up a couple of slabs of ribs, some slaw, and an order of baked beans to go, and inhaled the aroma on the way to my apartment.

The mess I'd left in the living room looked only vaguely familiar when I opened the door. A lot had happened in the past two days, and it seemed as if I'd been gone a lot longer than that. I turned on the heat to get the chill out of the place and put the ribs in the oven to warm. I was pouring myself a double Wild Turkey when I was rudely interrupted by the sound of knuckles on wood.

McDonald stood on my front doorstep, looking like one of Napoleon's soldiers in the Moscow campaign. His hands were thrust deeply into the pockets of his flimsy blue windbreaker and his nose was red and his eyes were watery. He didn't wait to be asked inside, but charged past me dragging fog behind him like the train of a wedding dress. "Fucking beach weather," he muttered.

I closed the door. "You've been in the desert too long. Your blood has thinned."

He rubbed his hands together and blew on them. "I won't be back there any too soon, believe me. Eight hours in this burg is eight hours too many. How in the hell can you live here? I'd have to be tanked to drive in that fucking traffic every day."

I'd often felt the same way, but said: "You get used to it."

He caught the scent in the air and sniffed. "Something smells good."

"Mama Lucinda's ribs. Want some? I have plenty."

Temptation flashed on his face for an instant, then he shook his head. "Thanks, anyway, but I can't stay. I have things to do."

"You do have time to join me in a little delicious cocktail?" I asked. "No Canadian, but I have Wild Turkey."

"Wild Turkey is fine."

I went into the kitchen and he looked the place over while I made the drinks. "Not bad," he said approvingly. "A little messy, but not bad."

"I had a girl come over once a week to clean up, but Immigration got her," I explained. "It might be another week or two before she can sneak back across the border."

I handed him his drink and we sat in a couple of chairs facing each other. "So don't tell me, you just happened to be in the neighborhood and decided to drop in."

"I was doing a warrant on Cairns' house in Malibu. Is that close enough to be considered in the neighborhood?"

"Not really, but I'll be magnanimous and let it slide." I took a swallow of my drink. The bourbon burned all the way down and landed warmly in my stomach. "Find anything interesting?"

"Quite a bit." He took out a cigarette, tapped the tobacco end twice on the coffee table, then flipped it over deftly and stuck the filter end in his mouth. He asked slyly: "How about you? How'd you spend your day? You left the Springs awful early."

He was playing cat-and-mouse games with me. I didn't mind that; it was "Hangman" I didn't care for. "I've been trying to trace down Cairns' bank accounts. It seems for the past two weeks, Cairns had been converting everything he owned into cash. Now the cash is missing. Nearly two hundred grand." That got his interest. "You wouldn't have happened to have run across it at the house, would you?"

He shook his head. "We did find ten grand in hundred-dollar bills, stashed in a hole in the wall, but that was it. Maybe we should take another look." He unzipped his jacket and pulled out some Xeroxed sheets and tossed them to me. "We also found those, in the same place."

I looked the stuff over, pretending like I'd never seen it before. There was no way I could tell him about being Maced without admitting I was in the house, and I didn't somehow think he'd be that understanding about it. I'd gotten away with it in Palm Springs, but twice would definitely be pushing things. "Looks like McVey was getting ready to start a new life again."

"He went through the old obits from the San Bernardino paper, found a kid who'd been born approximately the same time he had and who'd died young, and in different counties, so that the birth and death records weren't cross-referenced. Once he had a copy of a valid birth certificate, he could build a whole new I.D.—passport, Social Security number, the works."

I nodded. "He probably did the same thing in Atlanta, although we'll never be able to prove it. We know Walter Cairns was born in Albuquerque, but who knows where he died? California? Tuskegee, Alabama? Trying to find a death certificate would be like trying to find a cotton ball in a marshmallow factory."

"What do you think spooked him and made him decide to rabbit? Your client?"

I shook my head. "He started preparing for this two weeks ago. That's when he took out a second mortgage on the house. Lori Norris contacted him only last week."

"Why, then?"

I shrugged. "Your guess is as good as mine."

He said seriously: "A funny thing happened while we were going through Cairns' house. L.A.P.D. got a call from an anonymous tipster about a dead body at a house on St. Anthony Place. They went over and sure enough, there's a dead guy there, all right. Been dead at least four days. Harold Sarto. Ever hear of him?"

I tried to look surprised. "The same Harold Sarto who was in Palm Springs five days ago?"

He nodded sadly. "You don't know how disillusioned I was when the manager of the Desert D'Or described you. You wouldn't happen to be the anonymous caller, would you?" The unlighted cigarette between his lips bobbed up and down as he talked, and I wondered if it was some new hypnotic technique. Not that I was worried; I've always been a lousy hypnotic subject.

"Me? No."

"How did you come up with Sarto's name? The note in the wastebasket?"

I nodded.

"Maybe my memory is going bad, but I don't seem to remember that note on the list of things you touched in the condo—"

"Really? I could have sworn it was on there."

"I'll bet." He lighted his cigarette with a lighter and exhaled noisily. "You run across anything else there that you forgot to write down? Like a set of keys, maybe?"

"Keys? Keys to what?"

"Cairns' Malibu house. We couldn't find any. I had to pick the front door lock to get in."

"No," I said, then, in response to the dubious look in his eyes: "Honestly."

He took a swig from his drink and said in a hurt tone: "I thought we were supposed to be friends. I really didn't think you'd hold out on me like this."

"I didn't think Sarto was that important—"

"You thought he was important enough to follow up yourself."

"I saw that note and figured Sarto might know something about Cairns' past in Atlanta. It never occurred to me he might have had anything to do with your case." I hesitated. "How did he die?"

He stroked his mustache and grumbled: "Somebody shot him. Twice in the chest, point-blank range, although they won't know for sure that that's what killed him until they get the results from the P.M. From what I hear, there were . . . complications."

"What kind of complications?"

He shrugged casually. "Sarto had a pet dachshund named Heinz. After being trapped in the house for a couple of days without a can opener, Heinz sort of mistook his master for Alpo. There are some pieces missing."

"There were two bullets missing from the gun in Cairns' desk," I said, trying to get him off the subject of animal nutrition.

"I told them." The knots of muscle under his ears belied his offhanded tone.

"What did they say?"

"They didn't seem too impressed. They're looking for Sarto's girlfriend. I guess the two of them beefed pretty regular. They arrested her once for ADW when she stuck him with a kitchen knife, but he dropped the charges."

"They *are* going to run a ballistics test?"

He nodded. "I offered to have it done, but they said not to worry about it, that they'd send somebody down for the gun in a day or so. They said they realized how hard it must be to take care of tiresome investigative details and guard all those movie stars' homes at the same time."

I grinned. "They have a point."

"Fuck you," he snapped defensively.

"I was only kidding."

He scratched behind his ear and his eyes relaxed. "Sorry. I'm just rubbed a little raw. I get that kind of condescending bullshit from these L.A.P.D. hotshots all the time. I should be used to it by now, but it still frosts me." He took another pull from his drink. "You ask your client whether Cairns ever went by the name 'Butch'?"

"Yeah. She never heard the name."

He nodded, as if that made sense. "If Sarto did know Cairns, it wasn't from Atlanta. He was a California boy, born and bred."

That perked my interest. "Where?"

"Fallbrook."

"Toward San Diego?"

"Yep. His parents still live there." He pulled a spiral

notebook out of his pocket and flipped it open. "Gordon Sarto, 481 Alvarado, Fallbrook."

So that was what it was all about, why he was being so informative. He definitely believed there was some connection between Cairns and the death of Harold Sarto, and he wanted to rub the noses of the L.A.P.D. in it. He couldn't meddle in their investigation without repercussions, but I wasn't hampered by jurisdictions. So he'd just wandered by and casually dropped a few tidbits, hoping I wouldn't be able to resist looking into the matter. I had to smile; he knew me pretty well. "Who *was* Sarto, anyway?"

He shrugged. "A loser. Had a record. Petty larceny, shoplifting. For the past year, he'd been working as a bellman at the Ambassador. Before that, I don't know." He put out his cigarette in the glass ashtray on the coffee table. "What do you make of that computer printout?"

I pretended to scrutinize it, then said: "Looks like part of a movie budget."

"That's what it is. That and maybe something else. Cairns thought it valuable enough to hide with that other stuff."

I shook my head and handed him back the pages. "I don't know. Find anything else interesting at the house?"

He put the pages back inside his jacket and looked away. "A closet full of bondage stuff."

"That's all?"

"Yeah." He rubbed his mustache and looked at me curiously. "Why? What else were we supposed to find?"

"I don't know."

He had found the tapes; there was no way he couldn't have. I didn't feel so badly about holding back on him now.

"You still think Cairns' death was accidental?"

He rubbed his chin. "I should be getting a preliminary report from the coroner tomorrow. One thing for sure: Things are looking curiouser and curiouser. Dart flunked on the lie box, by the way."

"What do you mean, he flunked?"

"The test results were inconclusive. Another thing: The night before Cairns died, a Westec patrol was cruising the neighborhood and noticed a car parked across the street from Cairns' place. They stopped to check it out and found Dart in the car, drunker than six Indians. He told them who he was and said he was waiting for Cairns to come home. The security cops told him he couldn't wait there and offered to drive him back to the hotel, but he refused. They told him they'd be back in twenty minutes and if he wasn't gone, they'd have to call the cops. When they got back, he was gone."

"What was he doing there?"

"He says he had some script changes he wanted to talk over with Cairns, but even that tested out inconclusive. The poly operator says it could be because of all the alcohol in his system. We're going to wait until he's sober and test him again."

"You holding him?"

"What for? As far as we know, there has been no crime. Anyway, I know where to find him if I want him."

He drained his drink and stood up. "If you want to find me, I'm at the Holiday Inn in Santa Monica, Room 319." He hesitated at the door, and zipped up his jacket, frowning at the prospect of facing the fog again.

"I'll call you tomorrow," I said. "And think positive. Maybe Heinz ate the bullets and those L.A.P.D. jerk-offs will have to sift through four days of dogshit to find them."

That thought seemed to cheer him up a little. He smiled and went down the stairs and was swallowed up by the mist.

14

My fox terrier Asta was killed by a gigantic, ugly, spotted mongrel with slavering jaws, and I woke up very upset, until I realized I'd been dreaming and didn't have a fox terrier named Asta. While I made coffee, I pondered what Freud would have made of *that* dream—I wanted to be Bill Powell, so I could have Myrna Loy?—and after coming up with no answer I felt would be convoluted enough for Herr Doktor, I put it down to a Mama-Lucinda's-rib nightmare and got dressed. Three cups of strong coffee jump-started my motor and I was ready for the road. Luckily, the BMW only needed a key.

Traffic on the San Diego freeway was light, and I made it to the Highway 76 cutoff in less than an hour and a half. I drove through the outskirts of Oceanside, past a seemingly endless procession of tile-roofed pseudo-Spanish shopping centers and fast-food joints, past development after flag-waving development of regimented stucco-box tract homes (it was beyond me how they could want to duplicate anything that was singularly so ugly) squeezed between rolling hills patchily covered with grassy stubble. Gradually, the grass became more even and lush, the hills dotted with eucalyptus and sycamore and zigzagged with the white wood fences of horse training farms. After twenty minutes of winding road, the grass became thick groves of avocado and row after manicured row of citrus, and then a sign welcomed me to Fallbrook, the "Friendly Village."

The beginnings of Fallbrook looked like the outskirts of Oceanside, but in the center of town, the architectural style changed from Jack-in-the-Box Moderne to Contrived Quaint. The buildings were all covered with false wood-shingle fronts and fake balconies held up by balustrades and hand-painted wood signs, to convey the atmosphere of the turn-of-the-century Midwest. If the image was a bit forced, it didn't altogether fail, and one authentic touch I decided I really liked was the absence of parking meters. A friendly man in the Chamber of Commerce looked up the Sartos' address and gave me directions how to get there and to the office of the *Sentinel*, the local paper.

The *Sentinel* building was one story of white brick, and looked a hell of a lot more sturdy than the wood-shingle bank it stood next to. The gray-haired matron at the front desk confirmed that the paper had been in existence in 1954, and that they did have copies that far back, but said that I would have to look at it here, because they weren't on microfiche.

If she thought it odd when I asked for issues from the fourteenth of every month of that year, she didn't mention it, and five minutes later returned with a stack. I found what I was looking for in April; and I didn't have to dig through the issue to find it; it was the headline on page one.

TEENAGER SOUGHT FOR QUESTIONING
IN ARSON DEATHS

County Sheriff/Coroner Orrin Scruggs confirmed today that Terence Bailey, 14, of Fallbrook, is being sought for questioning about the April 10 deaths of Willard Sawyer, 41, his wife Eunice, 39, and their son, Edward, 14, all of Fallbrook. Sawyer, a local avocado grower, and his family died when their house at 222 Alvarado Street burned to the ground. Fire investigators say the fire was deliberately set.

"We're pretty sure the point of origin was the upstairs bedroom where Mr. and Mrs. Sawyer were found," said Fire Chief Dale Garretson. "We have found traces of accelerants there, probably gasoline. The place went up real fast."

Bailey, who was a classmate of the younger Sawyer at Potter High School, has been missing since the day of the fire. "We don't know where he is," Bailey's mother, Elizabeth Bailey, said yesterday. "He didn't leave a note or anything." She confirmed that the boy has a history of problems with the law, including one incidence of arson, but said she was sure her son could not be responsible for "anything so horrible."

Mrs. Bailey disclaimed knowledge of any animosity between her son and Ed Sawyer, but several schoolmates of the two boys have confirmed a history of ill-feeling between them, and Bailey had been admonished several times by teachers for "pushing and taunting" Sawyer on the school grounds.

Sheriff Scruggs has called the disappearance of Bailey a "possibly significant coincidence," but is not ruling out other possible suspects. "We're going through the Sawyers' background with a fine-tooth comb, looking for a motive for this crime," Sheriff Scruggs said.

I asked the lady for copies of the seven days following the fire and she graciously obliged. Murder was big news in Fallbrook, especially in 1955, and the *Sentinel* milked it for everything it was worth. Articles every day recapped the event, the only new development being the finding of a key chain and rabbit's foot identified as the Bailey boy's in the bushes behind the Sawyer house. Then, on day six, the headline screamed:

DEVELOPMENTS IN SAWYER CASE
LEAD TO MURDER WARRANT

The article stated that the warrant had been issued for Bailey after X-rays had turned up bullets embedded in the charred remains of Willard and Edward Sawyer, leading the coroner to conclude that both had been "shot to death" before the fire. The bullets had been extracted and found to be .38 caliber. No bullets were found in the body of Mrs. Sawyer, and from the elevated carbon monoxide levels in blood samples taken from her remains, it seemed likely she had died after the fire had started. Dr. Fenner, the examining pathologist, stated that he was continuing to examine a "suspicious fracture on the right side of the woman's skull," to determine whether it had been caused by heat or a blunt instrument. The latter possibility was made more plausible by evidence that the younger Sawyer's teeth had been knocked out, "indicating that blunt force had been used against him before the fire."

The lady behind the desk hadn't been in Fallbrook in 1955 and didn't remember the case, but she said the editor had been and she was sure he would know the answer to my question. She disappeared into the back room, then came out and said: "The Bailey boy was never caught. At least not that he knows about."

Ashes to ashes. It was appropriate that Bailey had burned

the article linking him to the fire and the deaths of three people, but he'd been in too big a hurry to get rid of the evidence. He should have taken it with him and burned it later. Not that it mattered now.

I thanked her for her time and paid her two dollars for Xerox copies of the series, and got directions to the Sarto house.

Alvarado bisected the town and narrowed as it wound up into the green sun-drenched hills. The homes that lined both sides of it were small, ranch-style affairs, and 222 was a typical representative. The sign on the mailbox out front, *Casa Feliz*—"Happy House"— said that no horrible ghostly vestige of the past remained.

The Sartos' address, 481, was just up the hill. It was a wood-sided barn-red ranch-style house, with white trim around the roof and windows, and surrounded by a white picket fence. Two large eucalyptuses flanked each side of the house and immaculately tended flower beds, filled with riotously colored snapdragons and zinnias and deep purple pansies, lined the walkway to the front door.

I stepped out of the car, and a breeze came up suddenly, making the eucalyptuses hiss like a thousand angry snakes. I felt like one ringing the doorbell; it was too soon to be intruding into their grief, but I had no choice. I just hoped it was new enough that they would be numbed by the shock, that the terrible reality had not sunk in yet. I hated that feeling of helplessness when people fell apart on me.

The woman who answered the door was a small and frail-looking sixty-odd. Her pale, thin face was heavily lined and liver-spotted and her hair was a thinning tangle of white. She wore a green wool sweater and baggy yellow slacks and white terrycloth house slippers. She didn't need to wear black; there was mourning enough in her red-rimmed eyes.

"Mrs. Sarto?"

"Yes?" Her voice was listless.

"My name is Jacob Asch." I handed her a card. She took it in an arthritic hand that looked like a deformed claw from an albino crab and held the card close to her eyes to read. "I'm sorry to disturb you at a time like this, but I have some information I believe to be pertinent to your son's death, and

I'd like to ask you a few questions, if you feel up to it. Is Mr. Sarto home?"

"No," she said. "He's over at the funeral home, making arrangements."

That was all right by me; I have always had better luck with grief-stricken women than men. Women needed to talk it out more, whereas men, socialized not to emote, usually converted their grief into rage and suspicion. I almost had to reappraise that theory when her tone grew firmer and suspicious. "What kind of questions?"

"About Terence Bailey."

The name didn't register at first, then it did, and the floodgates of memory opened. "Sakes alive. Terence Bailey. I haven't heard that name in thirty years."

"Nobody has. That's why I think your son died. I think he recognized Bailey and Bailey killed him to protect himself. There is no statute of limitations on murder."

Her mouth dropped open, and she looked stunned. "My God, that can't be true—"

"You can help me determine whether it is or not," I said. "May I come in?"

She vacillated, then pulled the door open weakly. The living room had knotty-pine walls and was furnished with heavy wood furniture. She asked if I would like some refreshment, some coffee perhaps, but I declined, wanted to get this finished up before Mr. Sarto returned and threw a monkey wrench in the works. We sat down on the couch. A Bible was open, face down on the oak coffee table. I got right to it: "Does the name 'Butch' mean anything to you, Mrs. Sarto?"

"Butch?" Her eyes misted over, thinking back, then suddenly they widened. "Wait. Yes. I think Harold used to call the Bailey boy 'Butch.' It was a nickname he used because he didn't like his own name. Why?"

I told her about the note her son wrote to Cairns and about the burned newspaper article in the ashtray. She shook her head unbelievingly. "You're saying this man Cairns is Terence Bailey?"

"Was. Cairns is dead. He died two days ago."

"How?"

"He hung himself."

She put her arthritic hand to her throat and her eyes wandered away to someplace in the distant past. "My God, can it really be true? It's like a ghost coming back to haunt us. That monster was the beginning of all Harold's problems. He was a curse in our lives. Now, to think that after all this time . . ."

Her voice broke and she pulled two pieces of wrinkled tissue from her pants pocket and daubed at her eyes.

"How was he the beginning of Harold's problems?"

She sniffled, and said: "Harold was a good boy until that fire. Always well behaved, went to church every Sunday, helped his father at the store. Gordon owned the Rexall downtown before he retired. After the fire, Harold began to change. He was devastated by Ed's death. He had terrible nightmares about the fire. He turned sullen and moody. He seemed to stop caring about anything. Gordon and I tried to reach him, but he wouldn't let us. That was when he started to get into trouble."

"Your son and the Sawyer boy were good friends?"

"They were inseparable. The Sawyers lived just down the street, you know. Ed used to spend a lot of time over here. He liked it here." She paused and looked down at the tissues she was twisting in her lap. "Maybe more than he should have."

"Why is that?"

"It became a bone of contention between Mr. Sawyer and us," she said. "It was sad, but Ed's home life wasn't very happy. Ed was a very sensitive child, very gentle and extremely bright. Unfortunately, his father mistook gentleness for effeminacy. Maybe he got that from the military, I don't know. He was a retired Army sergeant and he treated Ed like one of his recruits. He would constantly humiliate him in front of the other kids, calling him a sissy, things like that. It broke my heart to see it. I tried speaking to Ed's mother about it, but she just said there was nothing she could do about it. She always struck me as a very cold woman, but Ed worshipped her. She must have told her husband because he came storming over here and told me to mind my own business and that he didn't want Ed coming over here anymore. That was only about a month before the fire."

"Tell me about the fire," I said, picking up the cue. "The paper said something about a grudge between Bailey and Sawyer—"

"Terence Bailey was a no-good, hateful bully," she said sharply. "He was always beating up on the smaller children at school, just to show how tough he was. He was the reason Harold and Ed became such close friends. Bailey was picking on Harold one day and Ed stepped in and tried to stop him. Ed was a tall boy, almost as tall as Bailey, but he wasn't as husky and he wasn't used to fighting. Bailey wound up beating him up, but he'd saved Harold and Harold worshipped him after that. Unfortunately, after that, Bailey would go out of his way to make life miserable for Ed."

"That was the grudge?"

She shook her head. "One night a car was stolen from Murphy's Garage, on Main Street. They found the car in a ditch the next morning, about two miles away. Ed told the police he'd seen Bailey steal the car, and although Bailey denied it, Ed's testimony sent him to a juvenile work camp for six months. He swore in front of witnesses he'd get even when he got out. Four days after he was released, the Sawyer house burned down and he disappeared."

"Are his parents still around here?"

"No. They moved out of town right after the fire." A thought struck her suddenly. "Maybe that's why he wanted the book."

I leaned forward. "Who? What book?"

"Harold," she said. "Two weeks ago he came by, which was strange, because he rarely came home or called. The only times he did was usually during the holidays, and he always seemed so depressed. But this time, he seemed like a different Harold. He was so excited, said he was going to be rich. He didn't stay long, just long enough to get the book. That's what he said was going to make him rich, the book."

"What book?" I asked, as gently as I could.

"His high school yearbook."

I took out Lori Norris' picture of Cairns and showed it to her. "Is this Terence Bailey?"

She held the picture up to her nose, squinted at it for a moment, and shook her head.

"Are you sure?"

"This isn't Terence Bailey," she said positively. She looked at me, her eyes clouded with confusion. "Is this the man you say murdered my Harold?"

"Yes."

"This man looks like Ed Sawyer," she said.

15

I'd passed the turnoff for the high school on the way into town. It was a string of low, sleek brick buildings flanked by tennis courts and a football field. It was lunchtime and the quad was filled with kids sitting on walls, eating and talking, working off all the jaw-energy they had pent up for three and a half hours of sitting quietly in class. They were a pretty clean-cut bunch, and even the punker or two that stood out in the crowd were toned-down versions. Full-scale rebellion obviously hadn't reached Fallbrook yet. I asked one of the kids where the library was and he pointed to a building with double glass doors.

The librarian, Mrs. Spencer, was a short woman in her mid-thirties with curly brown hair and thick horn-rimmed glasses, and she was graciously and uncuriously helpful when I asked to see a copy of the 1955 high school yearbook.

The book was called *The Moccasin*, and in it the freshman class had been photographed in three alphabetical groups, three rows per group. Ed Sawyer was in the back row of the third picture, fourth from the end, his hair neatly combed, and smiling. The photograph had been taken from a distance and people do change in thirty years. All I could say was that there was a resemblance between the boy in the picture and

Cairns—in the shape of the head, the planes of the face, and particularly, in the eyes.

If Terence Bailey had grown up to be Cairns, on the other hand, he must have gone through some sort of larval-like metamorphosis. He was tall, like Sawyer, but thicker through the neck and shoulders, his face was too round and had an overall brutish look to it, with small eyes too close together and a thick-lipped, sullen mouth.

Mrs. Spencer, it turned out, had lived in Fallbrook all her life, and she told me that the only doctor she could think of who had been practicing in the fifties and was still around was Dr. Tabor, although he was retired now. She got me his home phone number and graciously let me use her phone to call. My luck was running a streak—Tabor was home and when I told him I was a detective investigating new evidence in the Sawyer case, he confirmed that he had been the Sawyers' doctor and agreed to see me.

His house was on a hill overlooking the town, an old, two-story wood house with a screened-in sun porch on the second story and a lot of prickly-pear cacti out front. Dr. Tabor was standing on the front steps waiting for me as I pulled up. He was a small, wiry man of seventy or so, with gray hair and a gray pencil-thin mustache. He wore a yellow shirt and a maroon bow tie, and his gray slacks were held up by suspenders.

He came spryly down the stairs and offered his hand. His grip was surprisingly firm and his gray eyes were bright and clear. I gave him a card and he asked: "Now what's this about new evidence in the Sawyer murders?" His dentures clicked when he talked.

"I'm working on another case that I think might tie into it," I said. "You say you treated Ed Sawyer?"

"Ever since he was a boy."

"How about Terence Bailey?"

He rubbed his chin. "There were only three G.P.'s in town then. Yes, he and his mother were both patients of mine. Why?"

"Do you remember if either of the boys had any identifying marks or scars?"

He brows bristled. "You realize you're talking about thirty years ago."

"Do you still have their medical records?"

He looked at me suspiciously. "In storage."

"This could be crucial to the case I'm working on, Doctor. Would it be possible to dig them out?"

"Before we go any further, maybe you'd better tell me what this is all about."

I pulled out the photo of Cairns and handed it to him. "Does this man look familiar?"

He shook his head. "There's a slight resemblance . . . Wait a minute. You're not trying to say this man is Ed Sawyer?"

"That's just what I'm saying."

"But that's impossible. The coroner identified the body positively—"

"From what? Not from dental charts. The teeth had been knocked out. The body was about the same height as Ed Sawyer, but Terence Bailey was also that tall. Bailey was heavier, but as you know, there's no way to even approximate weight when a body is that badly burned. The coroner identified the body as Ed Sawyer because it was logical to assume it was."

"Hold on, young fella," he said, shaking his head. "This is fantastic. You're trying to tell me that it was Terence Bailey in that house? What would he be doing in the Sawyer house?"

"I think he was shot and dragged in there. By Ed Sawyer. And if you get me those medical records, I think I can prove it."

"How?"

"I believe Ed Sawyer became a man named Walter Cairns. Cairns recently died in Palm Springs. If Sawyer had any identifying marks, Cairns would have had them."

Tabor gave it some thought and said: "I don't need to look up the records. My memory is still good, one of the few things that is still functioning in this old body. Ed Sawyer had a three-inch scar on the instep of his foot. He stepped on a broken bottle when he was twelve or so and I had to sew it up. I remember it well. I don't remember whether it was the right or the left foot, though."

I grabbed his hand and pumped it. "That's enough to go on for now, Doctor, thanks. And if you can find those records at your leisure, I'd greatly appreciate it."

He was still standing there, scratching his gray head, when I drove down the hill.

16

The sight of all those fast-food places made me realize I hadn't eaten all day, and I grabbed a cheeseburger and a vanilla shake at a Carl's Jr. on the way out of town and lunched on the highway.

I was finally beginning to get a handle on Walter Cairns. No matter how many times he changed his name or his Social Security number or his profession, he would have always been Ed and Eunice Sawyer's little boy. Feeling abandoned by his parents, he since abandoned others before they could abandon him, shedding entire lives like other people shed worn-out suits. The sadomasochism, the fetishistic urges to punish and be punished, were the rage he still felt toward his parents, toward his father's cruel machoism and his mother's refusal to defend him, and the guilt he'd felt for killing them. That fire had swept through his soul, permanently blackening it.

It was three-thirty and the sun was finally trying to make an appearance when I got back to my apartment and called the answering service. There were two messages, one from McDonald and one from Lori Norris. The number McDonald had left was the Holiday Inn and I called it first.

"I'm back," I announced when he answered.

"I'm thrilled."

"You should be. I brought enough crow with me to choke your detective friends down at Hollywood division."

He listened silently while I laid it out for him, then asked: "You're sure Cairns was this Sawyer kid?"

"If he has a scar on his foot, he is."

"So after he ran away, he went to Atlanta and became Bill McVey—"

"Who knows? He could have been a couple of people in between."

"You think Sarto was trying to run a little extortion scheme on his old buddy Sawyer?"

"It all fits. The yearbook, him telling his mother he was going to make a big score—"

"They were such good friends, you'd think he'd have been happy to see Cairns alive."

"Sawyer's death was a major trauma in Sarto's life. He turned into an embittered loser becaue of it. He probably would have anyway, but the fire sped up the process. When he saw his old buddy not only alive but a successful director, while he was working as a bellman, the unfairness of it must have hit him. He wanted a payback, only he found out payback can be a bitch. He forgot why Sawyer was still alive—he was a killer. You trace the gun in Cairns' desk yet?"

"California had nothing on it. A friend of mine in ATF is trying to run it down now, but he's not real happy about it. ATF wasn't even in existence when that museum piece was made. It was ATTU then—Alcohol, Tobacco, and Tax Unit—and it was part of the IRS."

"Ed Sawyer was a retired Army sergeant and that Smith and Wesson was a Military and Police model."

"You think Cairns killed his old man with his own gun and kept it all these years?"

"If he did, and if San Diego County still has the slugs in evidence they took from Sawyer and the Bailey kid, you can wrap up the Sarto killing and three thirty-year-old murders at the same time."

"Then all I'll have to do is find out who murdered Cairns."

"Wait a minute, wait a minute," I said. "Run that by me again."

"The preliminary toxicology report came in this morning. Cairns had enough chloral hydrate and alcohol in him to put out three men. He was unconscious when he strangled."

"If he got his jollies off tying himself up, why would he want to deaden the thrills with a sedative?"

"A good question," he said. "Another couple might be why we didn't find any chloral hydrate at the house, and where he got what was in him. Cairns' doctor says he never gave him a scrip for it."

"What about the lipstick?"

He shook his head. "No lipstick."

"Can the lab identify the brand or the manufacturer from what was on the body?"

"You've been watching too much TV," he scoffed. "You can't I.D. lipstick. You can't even I.D. paint. Too many constituents. The best thing they can do is match it up to a sample, but you'd have to know the brand before you could get a sample."

"Catch-22."

"Right."

"It looks like somebody gave Cairns a dose of his own medicine," I mused, and regretted it as soon as I did. I'd forgotten I wasn't supposed to know about the tapes.

He jumped on it immediately: "What do you mean by that?"

"You told me you found a lot of bondage stuff at the house," I said quickly, hoping he'd buy it.

He didn't. "What do you know, Asch?"

He had reverted to "Asch." The cop had possession of him again. That was the trouble with exorcists; they were never around when you needed one.

"I've told you what I know."

"Bullshit. Where was your client Thursday night?"

"You have to be kidding."

"Do I sound like I'm kidding?"

"Why don't you ask her?"

"I intend to."

"Look, somebody wants this phone booth. I'll call you later." I hung up over his protestations and immediately the phone started ringing. After fifteen rings, it stopped, and I called Lori Norris and arranged to meet her at Fiasco in the Marina at five-fifteen.

Since I had a little time to kill, I stopped at the library and let my fingers do the walking through phone directories from Orange County to Simi Valley. Of course, the guy couldn't have been named Mahatma Kane Jeeves, and by the time I'd finished, I had numbers for seventeen Carls, three Carltons, and ten C. Greens.

The happy-hour crowd hadn't struck Fiasco yet, and I got a table on the glassed-in patio. The setting sun glinted off the water, backlighting the sailboats and schooners that glided in and out of the Marina channel, and I fantasized I was on one of them, heading out to some South Sea paradise. Maybe I'd open a bar there—the Black Cat—with a white sand floor and a tin roof that would sound like a steel drum when the rain banged on it and where all the drinks were served in coconut shells. The only music allowed would be pre-1960. The business hours: whenever I got there until whenever I decided to leave.

I was conjuring up an image of my Sadie Thompson when Lori Norris appeared. Her white cotton dress was open at the throat, accenting her long, Nefertiti-like neck, and clung to her slim body as she wended her way gracefully between tables.

"Hi," she said, smiling, and sat down.

She was prettier than I remembered, maybe because of the smile. No, it was something else, I decided. There was something vulnerably appealing about her, as if the smile would break at the slightest wrong word, something that made you want to protect her. She ordered a vodka-tonic and the smile turned into a worried frown. "I just got a call at work from a Detective McDonald. He says he wants to talk to me about Bill. He's supposed to come to my condo at six-thirty."

"It's just routine, don't worry about it. How are you and Herb Edelstein getting along?"

"Fine. Thank you for recommending him. I have complete faith in him." She paused, and added meaningfully: "And you."

She was staring at me intently, a thin smile on her lips. I broke eye contact and watched a small boat sail by.

"Have you seen Lawrence of Hollywood's column today?"

"No." In all the hurly-burly of the day, I'd forgotten Larry was going to break the story today.

"It's all about Cairns really being Bill. It doesn't mention my name, thankfully, although I guess it'll just be a matter of time before that comes out."

I nodded. "Cairns really wasn't McVey."

Her brow furrowed. "What are you talking about? You proved he was."

"Oh, he was the man you married, all right, but he wasn't Bill McVey. McVey was an identity he created, just like he created Cairns."

I told her everything I'd found during the day, and she said in an astonished voice: "This is fantastic. You're trying to tell me that I lived for four years with a murderer?"

"It hasn't been proven positively, but that's my guess."

She slumped back in her chair, dumbfounded. "That's hard to accept. Bill was strange in a lot of ways—he frightened me sometimes—but it never entered my mind he could be capable of something like that."

I looked back at her. "Frightened you how?"

She looked down at the table. "He was always trying to talk me into letting him tie me up. I let him, once. It seemed to excite him, but it scared me, and I wouldn't let him do it again. Not that I thought he'd hurt me or anything. I just couldn't stand being helpless like that." When she looked up, her cheeks were pink with embarrassment. "I always thought that was one reason he left—our sex life. After a while, I started to think *I* was the abnormal one." She hesitated. "It's weird to think of living with someone that long, and not knowing anything about him."

"Nobody ever knows the totality of anyone, just parts."

Her eyes widened suddenly, like a startled animal's. "My God, does that mean I was next?"

"He had to kill Sarto, but there was no reason for him to kill you. You didn't know he was a murderer. All he would've had to do was disappear. When Sarto contacted him, he started laying the groundwork for a new life. But this time, he wanted to go better financed. He tried to stall Sarto, hoping he could string him along until he could finish up his movie and collect the money due him on completion, but he had problems with one of his stars and fell behind schedule. When Sarto came to Palm Springs, Cairns knew it was too dangerous to leave him alive. Once he killed him, it became too dicey for him to stick around, movie or no movie. Only he got murdered before he could split."

"Murdered?"

"That's what it looks like." I paused and looked into her eyes. "Where were you that night?"

"Me? You can't think I had anything to do with it?"

"Of course not, but McDonald is going to ask you that question at six-thirty. And until Cairns' murder is solved, or until we can offer irrefutable proof that you couldn't have done it, the courts will probably put a hold on any claim you have to his estate. Nobody can benefit from the commission of a felony."

She glanced away. "I went to dinner and a movie."

"With someone?"

"No, alone."

"How long were you out?"

"A few hours. From about seven to midnight."

"Any witnesses to that?"

She shifted in her chair. "No. My daughter was asleep when I got home. How would I have benefited?"

"Alive, you could have taken half of what Cairns had. Dead, you and your daughter have a good claim to all of it, if no more legal heirs are found." It bothered me when I said it. It bothered me because it made sense. I stared at her lipstick, trying to remember the shade on Cairns' body.

"That's ridiculous," she snapped.

"Sure," I said, trying to sound convincing. "And as soon as we prove you were a hundred miles away, it'll sound even more ridiculous. Where did you eat?"

"The Blue Whale."

"Did you have a reservation? Did anyone you know see you there?"

She shook her head and looked worried.

"McDonald is a good man," I assured her. "Just tell him the truth. Whatever you do, don't try to embellish your story or make it sound any better. And don't worry. I know of at least a dozen people with more motive and opportunity to kill Cairns than you, and by now I'd bet McDonald has a dozen more I don't know about. By the way, do you have a prescription for any sleeping pills?"

"Sleeping pills? No, why?"

"It's not important."

She hesitated, then asked: "What are you going to do?"

"Find out who killed Cairns."

"If anybody can do it, you can." She smiled strangely and put her hand on top of mine and squeezed. There was something disconcertingly intimate in the gesture. "You've been wonderful. I don't know what I would have done without you. I really don't."

The look in her eyes was familiar, and I pulled my hand out from under hers and signaled for the check. I'd gone through this before, and it was something I tried to avoid. I've had female clients offer to take my fee out in trade, I've had them send me naked Polaroids in the mail, but it wasn't me they wanted. It was a kind of transference, like a patient for a psychiatrist. I'd succumbed to it once or twice, but that sort of thing never worked out. I'd rather have the money.

The check came and I picked it up, but kept the receipt to put on her bill.

17

I picked up a paper on the way back to the apartment.

Larry had changed his title to "Death, Hollywood Style," and he suggested that Cairns' death resembled an X-rated version of one of his own early movies. Although he only hinted strongly about Cairns' secret sex life, he was explicit about his former identity as Bill McVey, specifically naming McVey and Dynotran. The truth, he went on to say, had been ferreted out by a "prominent private detective in the employ of McVey's abandoned ex-wife," and, as per our agreement, he hadn't named names. I hated to pass up the free publicity—I could have used the business—but I didn't want to be hampered by the media, who would swarm like locusts and try to pick me clean. There would be time for publicity later.

I pulled a Chun-King frozen cashew-chicken dinner out of the freezer and while it got nuked in the microwave, I started calling my list of Greens. Nine turned out to be my lucky number. That Carl Green was a pool contractor in Whittier and when I told him I was a dear friend of Marty Resnick's and was considering having a similar job done as the one he'd done for Marty, he told me all about the beautiful Gunite spa he'd put in at Resnick's house in Bel Air. I told him I might want different tile for mine and I'd get back to him in a day or so.

The cashew chicken tasted as if it had been buried for a while before being frozen. After feeding most of it to the garbage disposal, I threw some fresh clothes into a suitcase and hit the road. Two hours later, I was being greeted by the committee of lighted palm trees, welcoming me back to Paradise.

Someone had painted a sliver of a moon on the star-dotted tapestry. On the horizon, the mountains stood black against the sky, like chunks of night that had condensed and sunk to the land. It was beautiful, almost too beautiful to be real, so that the artificiality of the lighted palm trees and the pastel-colored spotlights of the string of small motels on the way into town seemed somehow natural. I rolled down the window of the car and let in the crisp, cool air, and to my amazement realized I was glad to be back in the clean dryness of the desert and away from the rotting moisture of the beach. Maybe I was finally beginning to make my peace with the place. Who knew? The next step might be a flash of that cosmic consciousness Marla had been talking about.

Traffic on Palm Canyon was sparse until the middle of town, when it suddenly slowed to a crawl. I could see the reason a few blocks up on the left—the blinding-white glare of klieg lights.

Fascinated gawkers were twenty deep on each side of the roped-off sidewalks flanking an open-air plaza, and curious heads stuck out of the windows of the creeping cars, trying to get a look at the action, which consisted of a lot of extras standing around in tuxes and furs and jewels, gabbing among themselves and looking bored. Most of the action was being performed by the uniformed cops who stood in the street, waving angrily at the drivers, trying to get them to move.

As I drove by, I spotted Adrianne Covert standing at the curb by a red Ferrari, listening to Sam Fields as he instructed her as to how he wanted her to get out of the car. It looked like he'd decided not to fire her, after all.

I drove to the International and stopped at the front desk. I gave the clerk an empty envelope with Fields' name on it and watched him stick it in the slot for 216, then went up to my room. I dropped off my suitcase, pocketed half a dozen sheets of hotel stationery, and walked down to the second floor, thinking I'd start with Adrianne's room. The hallway was just the way hallways should be while you're picking a lock—silent and empty—and it stayed that way until I was inside.

The room was an externalization of the girl's state of mind. Dresses, blue jeans, and fashion magazines lay over the chairs and on top of the bed; shoes, by themselves and by the pair, were scattered across the floor; lingerie and sweater tops hung over the open dresser drawers like decorative vines.

The sink sideboard in the bathroom was a disaster area of hair dryers, curling irons, hairbrushes clogged with red hair, a capless, half-squeezed-out tube of Crest, and makeup and prescription bottles of every shape and size.

The woman had pills for every contingency—Talwin for sleep, Dexedrine to get up, Percodan for pain, Robaxin for tense muscles, Librium to relax, Elavil for anxiety—but no chloral hydrate. All the prescriptions had been filled at Sav-Rite Pharmacy on Sunset, in Hollywood, and all had been written by a Dr. R. L. Blatty. I made a note of that and rounded up all the lipsticks I could find.

At the top of one piece of stationery, I wrote "A.C.," then smeared a line of each lipstick horizontally on the right side of the page, writing the brand name and shade alongside it on the left. When I'd finished, I had eight shades representing three brands—Lancôme, Raphael, and Max Factor. That done, I gave the room a quick toss.

A small hand mirror lay carelessly on top of the dresser, its surface covered with a white powder residue. It didn't take much imagination to guess what the residue was, and it didn't take much more to locate the four gram bindles taped behind the Sears print of a Portuguese harbor on the wall. The girl's poor body must have been very confused. I left the coke in place and checked out the rest of the room, and after turning up nothing else to alert Jerry Falwell and the Moral Majority about, I slipped out and went down to Fields' room.

It was rather spartan, and devoid of drugs except for a bottle of aspirin. It looked like his soporific was I. W. Harper; there was a half-empty fifth on the table by the bed. Out of force of habit more than anything, I went through the half-dozen shirts and pairs of slacks hanging in the closet and the shaving kit on the sink without a major discovery.

I felt a twinge of guilt picking Marla's lock. I liked the lady and we had shared a bed, but that had never stopped me before, which was probably why I chuckled by myself so many nights at Letterman's stupid pet tricks. Maybe I'd get a stupid pet and teach it some tricks. At least that would give me something to do at one-thirty when *Late Night* went off and I still couldn't sleep; Cal Worthington was beginning to wear on me.

The room was about like I'd remembered it. I found myself staring at the bed, remembering, then snapped myself out of it and turned on the bathroom light. There were two prescription bottles in the cosmetic case on the sink—one for 5 mg. Valium, and one for Tylenol with codeine. Both prescriptions had been written by a Dr. Goldberg. My heart sunk when I opened the drawer and saw it. A tube of Acyclovir. I could sure pick my fantasies—a sex symbol with herpes. That was all I needed. I slammed the drawer, afraid of what else I'd find, and gathered up all the lipsticks on the sink. There were five shades, all Erno Laszlo, and I took samples and got out.

There was a DO NOT DISTURB sign on Dart's doorknob, and nobody answered my knock. Maybe he was asleep, or passed out. I knocked louder and got the same response. Maybe he'd gone out and forgotten to take the sign off the door. I went to work on the lock.

The lights were off in the room, but it wasn't dark. Light from the pool area outside filtered through the curtains which had been pulled across the windows, throwing uneven shadows across the unmade and empty bed. I shut the door and hit the switch.

"Dart?"

The silence sung ballads to me. The room was still a mess. A zippered canvas suitcase stood open on the jack in the corner, clothes hanging out of it like the guts from a carcass of a disemboweled animal. A Scotch bottle, too full to be the one from the other day, sat next to a typewriter on the table by the window, along with a brown prescription pill bottle. The bottle whistled and waved for me to come over and take a look.

It was unlabeled and contained half a dozen capsules. I removed the white plastic top and shook a couple into my palm. They were red and had writing on them—MR 967. Chloral hydrate.

A couple of lines had been typed on the piece of paper rolled up in the typewriter.

Walter Cairns was killed for murdering my work. I thought I could live with it. I was wrong. Good-bye, everybody.

MATTHEW DART

Somebody had turned down the air-conditioning and the room suddenly felt chill. I stood, stupidly scanning the room, but nothing changed. Knowing it was not likely to, I walked around the bathroom partition.

The door to the toilet was closed. It would be. On the half-mile underwater trek to it, my eyes picked out an open pack of razor blades among the clutter by the sink. I stopped and shook one out. They were the kind used for scraping paint off walls, neatly individually encased in cardboard so that the user would not inadvertently cut himself taking them out of the box. That was thoughtful.

I went the rest of the way to the door and knocked. Maybe

Dart was on the can. If he was, he must not have wanted anyone to know it, because he didn't respond to my knocking. He wouldn't be on the can, not if *I* found him. My hand froze on the knob. I was getting very tired of this. I took a deep breath and pushed open the door.

He was attired in a pair of dirty Bermuda shorts and a soiled white T-shirt, lying on the floor, half in, half out of the open door of the tiny shower stall. The shower floor was red-black, thickly caked with dried blood that had emptied from the cut that gaped obscenely from ear to ear. A blood-crusted razor blade lay next to the drain, beside his outstretched right hand.

I bent down and touched his jaw. The skin was cold and hard, his arms and legs were stiff as tree branches. Allowing eight to twelve hours for the onset of rigor, plus another eight for complete development, put the time of his death sometime between midnight and four last night. Those dark-night-of-the-soul hours again. Maybe Cal Worthington had gotten to him, too. One thing he could be comforted by, wherever he was: No matter how many people died and no matter what else they changed in Dart's screenplay, they wouldn't have to change his title. But they probably would.

I pulled some toilet paper off the roll and wiped off the door handle, and pulled the door closed. I wiped off the pill bottle and did a quick survey of the room to determine what else I might have touched, and then went to the hallway door and cracked it. It was still silent and empty. On my way out, I hung the DO NOT DISTURB sign on the inside doorknob to make sure the room would be cleaned in the morning. I felt a pang of guilt about passing the unpleasant job of discovering Dart's corpse to an unsuspecting maid, but the experience would be a hell of a lot more unpleasant in a couple of days when the writer started to ripen.

I'd somehow lost my taste for the Great Lipstick Hunt, and instead of going through Fields' room, like the truly intrepid sleuth I was supposed to be, I got in my car and drove. I drove aimlessly, or not so aimlessly, because I found myself on the desert road where Marla and I had parked. I killed my engine and sat there, listening to the quiet and peering out into the darkness, trying to carve out shapes with my eyes.

The snakes were out there again, the snakes and the Gila monsters and the tarantulas. Just when you thought it was safe to go back to the desert.

Dart had hated Cairns, had made threatening statements in front of witnesses, and had even been caught lurking around the man's house the night before the murder. He'd flunked on the lie box. It all fit. Like a size-three dress fit Kate Smith.

Disagreement over a script was a thin motive for murder, no matter from what camera angle you looked at it. Dart had been a little ditsy, sure, and I'd seen what he could do to a video game when he was drunk. But a video game isn't a person. Besides, knowing Dart's state of mind, Cairns would hardly have been likely to invite the man into his home at midnight for a little social toddy and allow himself to be drugged.

There was a park near my apartment I jogged by on those rare mornings when the ambition struck me, and on those mornings, no matter what the weather, the old blind man would always be there with his seeing-eye dog. He would be on the same bench, dressed in the same dirty black trenchcoat, throwing his white walking stick, which the dog would joyously retrieve and return to its master. I felt like a blind man now, except I didn't have a dog to fetch for me. To hell with it. The only thing I could do was throw out my stick and hope someone pitied me enough to bring it back.

18

The plaza was still lit up like a football field, but traffic had thinned and the cops that waved me past had lost that frantic glint in their eyes. I parked a block up and walked back.

The open-air plaza was a remnant of the thirties, two

stories of old, Spanish-style storefront that faced each other across the wide parking lot, which right now was clogged with production trucks and trailers.

As I went across the lot toward the lights, I was distracted by a white Le Baron parked behind one of the trailers. The convertible top was down and I went over to it and tried the glove box. It was unlocked and among an assortment of Kleenex and miscellaneous papers was a registration slip.

> Adrianne Covert
> 786 San Rafael
> Brentwood, CA.

I put the slip back and walked over to the small crowd gathered beneath an archway bridging two sections of storefront. There was only a smattering of diehard gawkers, everyone else apparently having discovered that watching a movie being made was about as thrilling as watching slow-motion replays of snail races.

I stopped a curly-headed prop girl as she headed into the crowd and asked her if she could get a message to Marla that I was there. She promised she would and I jockeyed for a view over shoulders and heads while I waited.

The scene was set up in a grassy courtyard at the end of a brick path that ran under the archway. The lights and two Arriflexes on dollies were trained on the back wall, which was covered with vines and punctuated by a series of archways, like the exterior corridor of a mission. Fields was up on the dolly, looking through the camera lens. He shouted to the lighting man: "I'm still getting a little light in the hallway. Close down the barn door on the key a little."

The lighting man nodded and adjusted the bottom flap on one of the big arcs and Fields held up a thumb.

Somebody pinched my ass and I jumped a foot or so. When I whirled around, Marla was smiling at me impishly. "When did you get back?"

"About an hour ago."

"I never got a chance to thank you for the other evening. You slipped out like a thief in the night."

"Stealth is my middle name." I looked down at her faded

blue jeans and yellow V-necked sweater. "You're not working?"

"Not tonight. I'm only a spectator. Adrianne and I have a big scene tomorrow and I wanted to see how she handles the scene with Tommy."

"Fields didn't fire her, then?"

"No. I guess she went to him and Marty and asked for another chance. She promised to straighten up and so far, she has. She's like a different person. Since we resumed shooting, she hasn't been late for a call once, and she even has her lines down."

"What's the cause of the big change?"

"A lot of it is Sam," she said enthusiastically. "He's doing a brilliant job with her. The girl is scared to death, it's there in every line she delivers. Walter tried to bully the fear out of her, but Sam is trying to bring it out in her, to make it work for her. He thinks her appeal is in her insecurity, her vulnerability. So far, it's working."

"Aren't you afraid she'll upstage you?"

"I just want to get this picture finished," she said. "Besides, I feel sorry for her. I was that scared and confused once. Come on."

As we jostled through the crowd, I asked her if she'd seen Larry Bigelow around. "He was here earlier," she said, ducking under the tape being held for her by a uniformed cop, "but he left. I'm supposed to do an interview with him tomorrow. You a friend of Larry's?"

"Long-time."

"He's sweet. He's always been very kind to me in his column."

Just don't let him go through your bathroom drawers, I thought.

In the courtyard, they were setting up for a shot. A lighting man was busy fixing stands, on which cardboard squares with holes cut in them were mounted, in front of the arc lights. The light shone through the holes, casting large patches of shadow on the back wall. Fields was on the camera dolly, surveying the wall through one of the lenses strapped around his neck. "Perfect," he decided. He stood up on the dolly and shouted: "Ready everybody? Let's do it!"

There was a flurry of activity as the mustachioed A.D. shouted for quiet through his bullhorn. I spotted Adrianne Covert standing next to the sound cart, nervously chewing on a fingernail. She had on a lot of makeup and was dressed in a gold lamé jumpsuit that glistened in the lights.

A virile-looking, dark-haired hunk, who looked like he would have a name like Brick Mason or Chuck Roast or Noel Talent or one of those other stupid names they dream up for types like that, moved to a tape-marked spot in front of one of the archways and stood there, looking handsome and bored.

"We're on the bell!" the A.D. shouted, and a school bell rang loudly.

A man stepped up to the camera Fields was on and snapped a marker in front of the lens. "Scene 21, take four. Camera one, mark!"

He repeated the procedure for camera two, and Fields shouted like a baseball umpire calling out a slider: "Ac-*SHUN!*"

The hunk started pacing like a caged wolf, then looked up in anticipation as Adrianne came into the scene, walking hurriedly toward him. "Darling," she said breathlessly, throwing herself at him. They embraced and began a long and passionate kiss. The hunk was definitely getting into his role; he pressed Adrianne hard against him and seemed to be trying to put his tongue through the back of her head.

It had always amazed me how actors could stand around for hour after boring hour, then conjure up the emotional intensity for a scene that lasted forty seconds. Maybe that was why all actors were crazy—the waiting drove them nuts. Or maybe they were only capable of waiting because they were *already* crazy. If I was getting the $120 per forty minutes they were paying their shrinks, I might have given it more thought and come up with an answer, but since I heard no offers, I stood back and watched the show.

Adrianne broke away from him and caught her breath.

"Did you get it?" the hunk asked.

She nodded and pulled a nickel-plated .32 automatic from her gold handbag.

"You're sure you want to go through with it?"

She bit her lip. "I have to. I can't live like this anymore. I hate him. My flesh crawls every time he touches me—" She shuddered violently and rubbed her arms.

I wondered if these were Dart's lines or the ones he'd complained to Cairns about. Whichever, at least whoever was responsible for them was dead now. But despite their triteness, somehow the lines worked coming from her. Maybe it was that fear Marla had talked about; it was in the girl's face, in her trembling lips, and no amount of makeup could hide it. She had the face and body of a sexy woman, but there was something lost and little-girlish about her that made you want to protect her and believe what she was saying.

The hunk grabbed her chin and tilted her head upward. "Let's hear it again. I want to make sure you have it down—"

"Yes," a hoarse voice whispered from the darkness of the corridor behind them, "let's hear it again."

Adrianne gasped and the hunk whirled around as a match flared in the darkness, then suddenly dropped to the ground. "Shit!" A tall, gaunt man dressed in black stepped through the archway, shaking his head.

"*Cut!*" Fields yelled.

"Fucking matches," the gaunt man said angrily, sucking on his fingers. "That's the second one of those goddamn cheap matches that's done that. I want some different matches."

"We need matches that flare up," Fields tried to explain. "That's the surprise of the scene."

"You also need someone with fingers left to strike the fucking things," the man retorted.

"Get some different matches," Fields barked at the A.D., who scurried off like a man on a mission from God.

Adrianne looked up at Fields and asked eagerly: "Was I all right, Sam?"

The older man looked down on her with a paternal smile. "Fine, honey. Just great. Do it just like that, next take."

She smiled gratefully, and drifted back over to the sound man seated at his recorder truck, her tight little butt making muscular ripplings in the gold lamé. The hunk watched her, his square jaw clenched and his eyes hungry.

"Is it true what Hitchcock said, that all love scenes started on the set are finished in the dressing room?" I said.

"Not that one," Marla said, nodding toward Adrianne. "Not since the first week of shooting, anyway."

"What happened the first week of shooting?"

"Susanne Capasco, Adrianne's agent, came down and caught Tommy and Adrianne in one of the trailers getting it on. She threw a shit fit the whole set could hear, screamed at Tommy to get out, that he was the reason Adrianne wasn't concentrating on her lines, and if he didn't stay away from her, she would go to Marty Resnick about it. After that, Adrianne has given Tommy the big chill."

"Do agents usually interfere in their clients' lives like that?"

"Susanne watches over that girl like a mother hen. In fact, it's more like a mother-daughter relationship than agent-client. Susanne discovered her when she was only sixteen and has been bringing her along ever since. Adrianne doesn't do anything Susanne doesn't tell her to."

"Except take drugs."

"Yeah, except that."

She looked at me out of the corner of her eye. "You're awfully interested in Adrianne all of a sudden. Should I be jealous?"

"Only if you want to be," I said, flashing a grin. "Do me a favor. Introduce me."

Her eyes grew thoughtful. "Maybe I should take this upstaging business more seriously."

"Don't worry," I assured her, "I just want to ask her a few questions."

"I've heard that one before," she said scoffingly.

"Detective-type questions."

She gave me a dubious look, then sighed in resignation. "Come on. If my throat is going to get cut, I might as well get it over with."

We walked past the cameras where Tommy the Hunk was complaining to Fields: "The lighting is wrong, Sam—"

"What's wrong with it?" Fields asked, as if he sincerely wanted to know.

"It's exactly like the lighting we had in the first scene in *The Big Rumble*."

"So?"

The actor threw out his hands imploringly and whined: "The picture *bombed*, Sam. Bad. I mean, it didn't even *open*."

That shocking news failed to panic Fields. His expression remained cool and unruffled. "So?"

"It's *unlucky*," Tommy said, not believing the director had missed the point.

"Ah," Fields said, finally grasping what the man was telling him. Then, with barely a moment's deliberation, he decided bravely: "I'll risk it."

Unlucky lighting. "Actors," I muttered, shaking my head. They were more superstitious than Gypsies, and less trustworthy.

Marla's head turned. "Huh?"

"Nothing."

Adrianne and the sound man were bent over behind the recording cart with their backs to us and must not have heard us come up, because when Marla called her name, both of them jumped like animals startled at a water hole. Adrianne quickly wiped a hand across her nose and sniffed, but there was still white on it when she turned around. The sound man, a skinny kid with an acne-scarred face, reconnected the cable to the recorder with lightning speed and tried to look casual. He looked as casual as an aborigine in a tuxedo.

Now I knew why Adrianne liked it over here so much. I wondered who else the kid supplied from his coke stash in the cable connector and whether he was making a little money on the side or marching powder was considered a necessary operating expense and written into the budget as "sound equipment."

I surmised from the dirty look Marla gave the kid that she, for one, hadn't known about the man's sideline. "Adrianne, this is a friend of mine, Jacob Asch. He wanted to meet you."

She smiled uncertainly and held out her hand, which I took.

"Jake is a private detective," Marla went on, and then, as if it needed clarification: "A *real* one."

"A fan first," I said, flashing her my most charming smile, "a detective second."

The sound man, looking suddenly uncomfortable, excused himself and walked away.

"Actually, we almost met the other night under less favorable circumstances," I said.

"Really?" Adrianne said through the smile frozen on her face. She seemed to be having trouble standing still, shifting her weight nervously from foot to foot. Before she tap-danced away, I said: "You were coming out of the International parking lot in your Le Baron and I was coming in. You nearly took off the front end of my car."

"I'm sorry," she said. "I don't seem to remember."

"You probably didn't even see me. You were driving pretty fast." I turned to Marla. "Would you excuse us a moment, Marla?"

Adrianne threw Marla a confused look, but Marla just said: "Now I *really* should be jealous," and walked away.

The confused look was still on Adrianne Covert's face when I said: "Thursday."

"Pardon me?"

"It was Thursday night. The night you nearly hit me. About eleven. Just about the time Walter Cairns was being murdered."

"Murdered?" she gasped. "I thought it was an accident—"

I shook my head. "Somebody slipped him a mickey before he—or she—slipped a noose around his neck."

Her face was a kaleidoscope of emotions now, constantly shifting and changing. I gave it a twist, just to see what pretty patterns came up next. "You don't happen to have a prescription for chloral hydrate, do you?"

The jagged pieces tumbled and locked on fear. She tried to hide it, but she wasn't that good an actress. "Chloral hydrate? No, why? You can't think I had anything to do with Walter's death—"

"Where were you going that night?"

"For a drive," she barked defensively. "I like to drive around at night. It relaxes me."

"That fits. You were driving as if you were upset about

something." I gave another twist. "What was it? Cairns tell you about the tape?"

Her body twitched. She looked as if she were on the verge of an epileptic seizure. White showed all the way around the blue of her irises. "What tape?"

"The videotape Cairns made of the two of you."

"I don't know what you're talking about!" she shrieked. "Leave me alone!"

She turned and bolted down the path into the darkness.

Heads turned and Fields rushed over, lenses dangling around his neck like gaudy necklaces. The pants looked like the same rumpled pair he'd been wearing the other day, but he'd changed his shirt. This one had salmon fishermen and ketchup stains on it. "What the hell is going on here?" he demanded.

I proffered a friendly smile. "Hi, Mr. Fields. Remember me?"

"I remember you," he snapped. "What went on with Adrianne?"

I shrugged innocently. "I don't know. All I did was mention that Cairns' death is now officially a homicide, and she wigged out."

That affected him about as much as the news that his lighting was unlucky. "How did you get past security?"

Marla stepped up. "He's with me."

Fields' head snapped toward her, then toward the A.D., who had returned from his quest for a flareless match and had moved up behind Marla. "Go find Adrianne. Make sure she's all right."

The man jogged off and I said: "I'm really sorry, Mr. Fields. I had no idea she'd get so upset."

He scratched his beard, like an agitated cat grooming itself. "It's taken me a lot of hard work to build that girl's confidence enough so she can function, and you come around and tear it all down in five minutes. I can't have it. I'm going to have to ask you to leave."

"Sure. But before I go, maybe you'd answer a few questions for me."

He glanced around furtively at the crew members who were starting to drift over. I would have preferred to gauge his reactions in private, but I had no choice but to plunge ahead. Once he gave the order to keep me off the set, I might not get access to him again.

"Where did you go after you left Cairns' place Thursday night?"

"Back to the hotel."

"Did you stay there?"

"Yes. Why?"

"Can anybody confirm that?"

A fire stoked up in his cheeks. "I don't have to confirm shit to you."

"You're right," I said, shrugging. "I just thought you might want to rehearse your story for the cops."

"I've already told the police what I know."

"They're going to want to talk to you again. It's a new ballgame now. They're going to want to talk to anyone who had a motive for murdering Cairns."

"What in the hell are you talking about?" he asked angrily. "What possible motive could I have had to kill Walter?"

I pointed at the lenses resting on his chest. "Those."

"You're nuts," he sneered.

"Maybe," I conceded. "But you're a liar. You weren't the vice-president of the Walter Cairns booster club you tried to come off as the other day. You weren't even a charter member. The man treated you like a gofer. The day before he died, in fact, he called you down in front of everybody here, threatening to have you sent back to Movie Purgatory if you ever criticized his directorial style again. That must have been hard for a man of your accomplishments to take."

His eyes grew crafty. "You'd be surprised what a man like me can take for three grand a week."

"Still, it seems strange that Cairns would do something like that, then turn around and recommend you to take over for him."

More of the crew had gathered. His watery eyes darted around nervously. "Whatever you heard about my differences with Walter, I'm sure was blown all out of proportion. This is a business of egos. It's natural that those egos clash once in a while. But the differences do get reconciled. If they didn't, there wouldn't be a person left alive in Hollywood."

"You reconciled your differences with Cairns?"

"Yes."

"The night you were at his house?"

"That's right."

"Then he didn't call you over there to fire you?"

"Of course not," he said, his eyes flaring. "And that's all I'm going to take from you, Buster."

I held up my hands. "Don't bother to call Marv. I'm going." I took a step toward Marla, then turned back. All conversation among the crew had ceased, no mouths were working, only ears. "You know, Walter Cairns dying was the best thing that could have happened to this picture. Maybe the only thing that could save it. It won't even make any difference if it turns out any good; the publicity about the murder will guarantee big bucks at the box office. But if you can pull a rabbit out of the hat, and somehow make it good, you're going to be canonized as a saint in Hollywood, Fields. You'll be able to write your own ticket."

Conversation erupted as I walked away and I felt everyone's eyes on me as I pushed my way through the crowd. I was halfway across the lot when Marla caught up with me. "Was Walter really murdered?" she asked breathlessly as we walked.

"Yes."

"You can't really think Sam did it?"

"I don't know. He had a motive, but then so did half a dozen people I can think of. Including you."

She tried to smile. "You're joking."

When I didn't answer, she stopped and stared at me with her mouth open a little. "You're not, are you?"

I looked back at her silently. There didn't seem to be anything to say.

"Do you trust *anyone*?"

"Not since I caught my father cheating me at gin rummy."

She shook her head sadly. "It must be a lonely life."

"I've gotten used to it."

Thoughts stirred behind her eyes and one corner of her mouth rose into a lopsided, mischievous grin. "Does it excite you to think you might have shared a bed with a murderess?"

"Not particularly," I said.

"Some people get off on the element of danger," she said coyly. "I do."

I thought about that tape. Maybe she hadn't been as doped-up as she claimed. "I'm strictly a hearth-and-slippers man myself."

"Funny, but you didn't strike me that way at all the other night." She put a hand on her hip and struck an insolent pose. "I'll be in my room in half an hour. Why don't you stop by?"

She looked very, very good, and the temptation was stirring in my groin, but then I remembered that tube of Acyclovir in her drawer and said: "I'm all in tonight, but I'll take a rain check."

"Okay," she said casually. "But in case you haven't noticed, we are in the middle of a desert. It might be quite a while until the next rain."

I watched her hips sway saucily away, and beat it to the car before I changed my mind.

19

I could have slept another hour, except the knuckles on my door wouldn't let me. The light outside the curtains looked weak, and when I squinted at my watch on the night table, I could see why. Six-fifty.

The rapping increased in volume and insistence and I shouted to whoever was responsible for it to hold on, I was coming, and got up swearing. I staggered into a pair of pants and went to the door. Whoever owned those goddamned knuckles was going to pay.

I yanked open the door and started to say something appropriately snide, but was stopped by the sight of Marv, the black volcanic island. He was accompanied by a freckle-faced redhead as big as he, and neither of them looked in a particularly jovial mood. I tried to shut the door, but Marv put out his hand and it stopped. "Mr. Resnick wants to see you," he growled.

"Fine. Tell him I'll be up and around in about an hour—"

"Now," he corrected me.

I didn't like being ordered around like a raw recruit at reveille, but I didn't know how far he was prepared to carry out his orders and I didn't feel like testing the strength of the walls with my face. I wanted to talk to Resnick, anyway, so I said: "I'll be right with you," and started to shut the door again. Again, the hand blocked it.

"I said I'd be right with you," I snapped at him. "You want to watch men get dressed, go to the Y."

He ogled me with a malevolent yellow-eyed stare, but dropped his arm, and I closed the door. Four minutes later, I joined them in the hallway, looking spiffy in a yellow sports shirt and pressed brown slacks.

"Where are we going?" I asked as we walked outside.

"Mr. Resnick's house." Marv pointed at a white Buick LeSabre parked in a nearby space. "You can ride with us."

The birds were singing and the morning light was clear and hard, casting the kind of sharp, knife-edged shadows you only see in the desert.

"I'll follow," I said.

Marv shrugged and got into the passenger side of the Buick and the redhead drove. I backed the BMW out and caught up with them at the driveway where they were waiting for me, and we started down Sunrise.

A couple of miles down, they signaled and made a left onto a street called Tamarisk. We passed some joggers out for an early-morning run, then a grassy, palm-lined park where rainbirds whispered softly, across Palm Canyon, into a residential section nestled at the foot of the mountain that looked like old money.

The streets were lined with rambling walled estates and well-seasoned Spanish-style homes with red-tile roofs baking quietly in the sun, the kind of neighborhood where, if you listened closely, you could almost hear the pock-pock of early morning tennis games going on behind the tall, pungent hedges of white-blossoming oleander. After a confusing series of lefts and rights, they signaled and turned into a gated driveway.

The house the driveway belonged to blended in with the neighborhood like a drag queen at a Moral Majority rally. It was a series of stark-white rectangular blocks haphazardly stacked on top of one another in an effort to look modern. A gray stretch Lincoln limo was parked beneath the wide carport out front, and the redhead pulled up behind it. I parked alongside the Buick, boxing them in, just in case I wanted to get out of there fast.

Marv and Red got out of the car and led the way up wide concrete steps flanked by terraced, trickling fountains to the twelve-foot-high double front doors.

No gong crashed when the uniformed Mexican maid opened the door, but it wouldn't have surprised me if one had; the whole scene, from the summoning to the setting, was overstaged.

The maid said that Mr. Resnick was out by the pool, and Marv tapped me on the shoulder and pointed. We went around a glass-brick partition and through a living room that looked like some designer's conscious mockery of conspicuous consumption. The place was a riot of textures and colors, with black-leather chairs, aggregate flooring covered with suede throw rugs that looked like wood shavings, onyx tables, and a redwood-strip ceiling that opened into a skylight bordered with green copper. Cubist art hung on the walls, and in the center of the room, on a marble pedestal, was a large circle of metal tubing I guessed was supposed to be sculpture.

We went through a set of louvered doors out to a spacious courtyard, the center of which was taken up by a meandering indigo-tile pool. Surrounding the pool were boulders and fat saguaro cacti, and in the middle of that, looking incongruous, Marty Resnick sat at a stone table shaded by a white patio umbrella, talking on the phone. He waved me into a chair. I sat and Marv and Red formed a wall of flesh behind me.

Resnick wore a maroon silk bathrobe over a crisp white shirt, beige slacks, and gray leather slippers. On the table in front of him were spread the remnants of breakfast—half a grapefruit, half of a half of an English muffin, an almost empty cup of black coffee, and a sterling-silver pot I assumed contained more of the same. "Who do you think you're talking to, some fucking redneck who just stepped off the bus from Fargo?" he spoke hotly into the phone. "Your client *signed*, Joel. If he wanted more, he should have told you. You're his agent. He's unhappy, let him talk to his shrink."

He paused and his eyes glittered fiercely behind the glasses. "I don't make pictures, Joel. Directors make pictures. I make deals. And the deal we have is for three-fifty plus eight points off the back end—*back*, not front—plus one thousand a week location expenses. You think that putz should have more than that, fine, give it to him out of your commission. All I know is that he'd better be on that fucking plane tonight or I'll have his house, his wife, and kids put up for fucking auction. Right. Love you, too, Joel. Bye."

He hung up and shook his head. "Agents."

"I hear you were one once," I said.

"That's why I can deal with them. I understand them. I started out booking cake-poppers at Moose conventions for fifty bucks a shot. It's been a long time since those days." He looked at me strangely, then said: "You were at Cairns' place."

"That's right."

"I thought you were a cop."

"No."

He nodded and picked up the pot and refilled his cup. "Coffee?"

I shook my head. "I'm trying to give it up. I found it keeps me awake while I'm working."

His smile was as thin and transparent as Saran Wrap. "It's your work I want to talk to you about, Mr. Asch."

"I don't do Moose conventions," I warned him.

"A kidder," he mused, still smiling. His eyes studied me from behind the glasses, adding and subtracting and constantly coming up with minuses. "You have something against me personally, Mr. Asch?"

I tried to look as if I was thinking about that. "Not that I'm aware of."

"Then why are you trying to sabotage my movie?"

"I'm not."

He raised an eyebrow. "Really? Then what were you trying to accomplish with that scene last night?"

I smiled. "I was testing out a theory."

"What theory?"

"The one in the song. You know, that any young mechanic can start a panic?"

He glowered at me; any pretense of friendliness had died and gone to friendliness heaven. "You did that, all right. After you talked to her, she took off, just jumped into her car and disappeared. We had to shut down shooting. I had to call Susanne Capasco to come down and join the search. Adrianne finally came stumbling in at five this morning, looking like shit and coked to the eyeballs. Susanne sedated her and put her to bed. Sam Fields is having to shoot around her today."

"I'm sorry."

"Fifty thousand dollars worth of sorry? Because that's what it's going to cost me. That's *if* she can work tomorrow."

"All I did was ask her a couple of questions," I said innocently.

"Malicious, slanderous questions."

I didn't say anything.

"The girl is high-strung."

"Obviously."

He sat back and sighed, then took off his glasses and pinched the bridge of his nose. "It may sound callous to you, Asch, but I don't care if Walter Cairns was murdered, or who did it if he was. That's a matter for the police. I make pictures and my concern is to get this one finished."

"I thought directors make pictures and you make deals."

He leaned forward aggressively. "That's right. And I'm going to make one with you."

"One I can't refuse, I'll bet."

That didn't ruffle him, but then I didn't expect it to. For any man who handled agents and actors and directors all day long, one smart-mouthed P.I. would be a piece of cake. I decided to see what was on his mind before I gave him a nostalgic glimpse of the good old days and popped out. "I want you to stay away from my movie," he said calmly. "I don't want you to attempt to talk to anyone remotely connected with it, even a prop girl. In fact, until *Death in the Desert* is in the can, I think it would be the best thing all around if you stayed away from Palm Springs. You get what I'm saying?"

"This town isn't big enough for the two of us?"

He showed some teeth. "Something like that."

"Do I have until sundown?" I asked, trying to put a quiver in my voice.

He scowled. "I think it would be better if you went directly back to your hotel from here and packed."

"And what if I don't like my part?" I asked. "You should know actors never like to play scared or flawed. Don't tell me. Pokey and Gumby here get dressed up in Godzilla suits and pretend I'm Tokyo—"

"I think you've been watching too much late-night TV," he commented.

I couldn't argue with that, so I didn't try.

"If you persist in your meddling, you'll wind up in an alley, all right," he went on, "but not from any beating administered by Marv or Serge. You will be living in one, Mr. Asch, eating your dinner out of a trashcan and using yesterday's newspapers for blankets. I talked with my lawyers this morning and they assure me we have grounds for one hell of a lawsuit. Against you and your client. Is that what you, or she, wants?"

"I'm not worried about any lawsuits, Mr. Resnick," I assured him. "Once a jury heard all the facts, I don't think you'd get one red cent in damages. All I've been doing is protecting my client's interest in *Death in the Desert*—"

His brow furrowed. "What interest? What in the hell are you talking about?"

"I'm assuming Cairns had points in the picture."

"What's that to you?" he snapped.

"So far, no will has been found. If one isn't, and no other legitimate heir is found, my client and her daughter have sole legal claim to Cairns' estate."

He looked confused. "So?"

"So, if Cairns had points in *Death in the Desert*, those points would belong to my client. And considering what happened with *Black Thursday*, I think any jury would be able to see how she would be naturally concerned about her interest in this film. Are you using equipment from Canyon Camera on this movie, too, by the way?"

The color left his face and he looked up at Marv and said: "You two wait outside for a moment. I'll call you if I need you."

He watched them leave, then asked: "What was that crack about Canyon Camera?" He was trying to sound confident, but his face had the scared, pinched look of a man no longer in control. He'd hired a stripper to pop out of the cake, but had gotten *The Creature from the Black Lagoon*.

I leaned toward him. "Walter Cairns got hold of a computer printout of the budget of *Black Thursday*. I don't know how, but I don't guess that matters much right now. What matters is that that printout is proof that you've been stealing from your own pictures by submitting dummy invoices from Canyon Camera, a straw company owned—on paper at least—by your wife Shirley. Does she know it exists, by the way? No matter. There are some other interesting entries on the printout, like an eight-thousand-dollar Jacuzzi you had put into your Bel Air home and billed to 'set construction.' Cairns threatened to go public with your indiscretions unless you signed him to a three-picture deal."

He tried out a shaky smile. "You have a good imagination. You should write screenplays."

"It didn't take much imagination to come up with this plot," I said. "See, I have the printout."

He stared at me silently.

"You had to deal with Cairns," I continued. "If he would've gone public, it would have opened the floodgates. Once your investors and the IRS started digging, who knows how many other Jacuzzis they'd find? So you made the deal with Cairns. You probably didn't even mind. He'd made some hits for you and there was always the chance he could do it again. Even if he didn't, you weren't using your own money and indies like you always steal enough to stay ahead of the game. But when Cairns got behind schedule, then called you up and told you he was quitting, he put you in a position where you could lose a lot of money. That must have upset you. Especially when he demanded the rest of the money on his contract."

"That's it?" he asked, raising an eyebrow. "It's not a bad yarn, but it kind of fizzles out at the end."

"Wait. There's a real socko finish. Alive, Cairns was a problem. Dead, he was a solution. You could collect the insurance money and hire another director."

"Now you're accusing me of murder?" he asked in disbelief.

I shrugged. "It makes sense."

"To you, maybe."

"I'm sure it'll make sense to the cops and Larry Bigelow, and the insurance investigators too."

He tilted his head down and scowled. "What do you want, Asch?"

"Straight answers. Cairns told you he was quitting, didn't he?"

"No." He thought for a moment, then said resignedly: "He wanted the hundred and twenty-five thou left on his contract, all right—he said he had an emergency and needed the money—but he never said anything about quitting. He would've had to be nuts to think he could cost me the two point one mil I've already got in *Death in the Desert*, then ask me for money."

"Did you agree to pay him?"

"No way," he said, wagging his head. "I told him I'd come down and we'd discuss it. I figured I could negotiate some sort of deal, depending how big of a bind he was in. I would have been willing to pay him off, but it would've had to be tied to completion of principal photography. And I wanted a release from the other two pictures on his contract."

"What did he say to that?"

"I didn't get a chance to talk to him. I got down late, just like I told the police, and I decided to wait until morning." He paused. "There was no reason for me to kill Walter. Pay him off, yes. Kill him, no. That printout couldn't have seriously hurt me. It shows Canyon Camera was paid, sure, but Cairns would have had to prove that Canyon Camera *hadn't* supplied equipment for that money. As far as the IRS is concerned, Canyon Camera has always paid its taxes, so they wouldn't have given a shit."

"It wouldn't have done your professional reputation much good if word got out that you were a thief—"

He laughed mockingly. "You've got to be kidding. *Everybody* steals in this business, Asch. It's built into the system. Everybody is getting a piece of the pie, so everybody cheats to make sure his own doesn't get gobbled up. Directors get short-counted by producers who get short-counted by distributors who get short-counted by exhibitors. You really think my colleagues are going to start wagging fingers at me because I built a Jacuzzi with art-department money? Eighty percent of the Jacuzzis in Hollywood were built with art-department money. The true artists in this business aren't the directors or the actors, Asch, they are the accountants."

I wasn't sure I believed him about the IRS, but the rest of it made sense. We were talking about a business where a guy like David Begelman could get caught red-handed forging checks for thousands and get immediately hired as head of another studio. If Vegas had perfected the Big Skim, Hollywood was an avid pupil.

"What do you intend to do with that printout?" Resnick asked.

"I don't know yet."

"I could throw a lot of business your way."

"I'll bet you could. The people in your business seem to have a lot of problems."

"It won't be helping your client if you go public with it. It will only hurt *Death in the Desert*." He thought, then said quickly: "Maybe we can work out something. A percentage of the gross instead of the net for your client, and a piece of the action for you, of course."

I didn't say anything. That seemed to make him uncomfortable. He squirmed in his chair and said: "Look, Asch, you might not approve of me or the way I do things, but my job isn't easy. I have responsibilities—to the studio, to my investors, to everyone involved in the making of my movies, right down to the lowest grip. I deal in people's dreams. That's an awesome burden. I can see where I might strike you as a crook, but I'm not really. I'm not a bad man. It's the way things are done."

I felt as if I'd heard this speech before, then I remembered where. Richard Nixon, 1974. Resnick must have been encouraged by my silence, because he went on: "A movie is like a lifeboat, Asch, a lifeboat that holds twenty people. For every twenty I let on board, I have to leave a hundred in the water. Young, talented people who have come to me hoping I'll make their lifelong dreams come true. You think it's easy turning them down? This job is a heartbreaker."

I leaned across the table and examined his hands. His expression turned puzzled. "What are you doing?"

"Checking for stigmata."

His face reddened angrily, but the phone rang before he had a chance to put words to the color. He snatched it up. "Yeah? *What!* When? How?"

I waited for "who" and "where" to complete the set of interrogatories, but he fooled me and said: "Call Bernie. Tell him to get on top of this before it gets out of hand. Tell him to find out what the fuck happened and find out the best angle for the press. They aren't going to like this at Universal. I'm going to call Charlie right now and try to keep them from pulling the plug on us. Right."

He hung up and I asked as if I didn't already know: "Bad news?"

"Dart's dead," he said, with a thoughtfully troubled expression. "A maid found him in his room a little while ago."

"How?" Now I was doing it.

"I don't know. The cops aren't saying."

I stood up.

"Where are you going?"

"To find out how."

"What about my offer?"

"I'll talk it over with my client," I said.

"Will you let me know about Dart?" he asked urgently.

"Call me at the hotel," I said. "And I wouldn't worry about Universal. Just tell them they have a built-in sequel here—a murder mystery about the making of *Death in the Desert.*"

He latched onto that and unleashed a smile that looked genuine. "Yeah. I like the way you think, Asch."

"I thought you would," I said, and left him.

20

On the way to the International, I thought about who should play me in the sequel. Newman was too old, Eric Roberts was too young, Beatty was not masculine enough. Then it hit me. The obvious choice was . . . *me*. I could play myself. Why not? I knew myself better than anyone and I could be as temperamental as any star. I could demand limos and perks and location expenses with the best of them. I was wondering how I would handle being a matinee idol, if all that fortune and fame would change me, when whirling blue and red lights jarred me back to reality.

The lights were on top of the two squad cars blocking off the back of the hotel parking lot. A brown-shirted patrolman standing in front of them waved me toward the front of the hotel, and I conjured up a parking space near the entrance and went inside. I stopped at my room to pick up the lipstick smears, then went downstairs to Dart's floor.

The hallway outside Dart's room was clogged with people and the crackling buzz of excited conversation. The media was well represented, the faces of the men and women holding microphones and minicams looked hungry, but happy. Why shouldn't they be? They'd lucked out. They'd converged for one death and they'd gotten two. Such a deal.

"Make way, make way," I ordered them, and shoved my way to the front. I must have looked enough like a cop that nobody tried to stop me, and a couple of the reporters even asked me whether it was true the dead man was Matthew Dart, the screenwriter. I told them gruffly a statement would be issued later, and fought through to the phalanx of police guarding the door of Dart's room.

One of the cops was the blond patrolman from Cairns' condo, and I reminded him who I was and asked him if McDonald was inside. He said he was and sent one of his buddies inside to fetch him. A moment later, McDonald stuck his head out of the door and told me to come in. Immediately, the crowd surged forward and the hallway was filled with the brilliant glare of minicam lights and the confused cacophony of shouted questions. McDonald ignored them and pulled me inside as the police tried to push back the human wave.

The cast in the room was the same as at the condo. "Return of the Palm Springs Five." I could hear Jaime in the bathroom whistling "Singin' in the Rain."

"Dart?" I asked.

McDonald nodded. He didn't look cold anymore, just tired. The gray bags under his eyes looked as if they were made of Samsonite. "His throat was cut, probably with a razor blade. Looks like suicide."

"That's what you said about Cairns," I reminded him.

"This time there was a suicide note," he said in a vexed tone. "He confessed to killing Cairns in it. And next to it was a bottle of chloral hydrate."

"Was the note handwritten?"

"Typed."

"Signed?"

He made a face. "No."

"How about the chloral hydrate? Did Dart have a scrip for it?"

"I don't know. The bottle was unmarked."

"I'll bet you find it in his bloodstream too," I said.

He frowned. "What are you getting at?"

"It's too pat."

"There's no such thing as 'too pat,' except on *Mike Hammer*," he said scoffingly. "*A*, Dart threatened Cairns. He hated his guts. *B*, he was caught hanging around Cairns' place the night of the murder. *C*, he had no legitimate alibi for the time of the murder. *D*, he flunked on the lie box. He had motive, opportunity, and means. What more do you want?"

I held off on that. "What about the scar?"

"Right instep."

"Then Cairns was Sawyer," I said.

"That's what it looks like," he said. "The gun was registered to Willard Sawyer. Unfortunately, the ballistics evidence from the Sawyer case is gone, so we'll never know for sure whether that was the gun that did in the Sawyers and the Bailey kid. Or even if that was the Bailey kid in the house."

"Has L.A. picked up the gun yet?"

"They're sending somebody down this morning."

I watched the I.D. tech dust the typewriter table and asked casually: "You find any video cassettes at Cairns' place in Malibu?"

His tone turned sharp: "What do you know about video cassettes?"

I looked at him and shrugged. "Just what I hear around, that Cairns was into taping SM scenes there."

He stroked his mustache nervously, like an agitated cat grooming itself. "Where did you hear that?"

I shook my head. "I promised my sources I wouldn't divulge their names, Ron."

He didn't look pleased, but he knew he wouldn't get anywhere trying to press me on that issue. He said: "Whoever they are, they're right. We found a dozen VHS tapes at the beach place. You've heard of couch casting? Cairns was into pillory casting. He interviewed prospective stars for his movies by getting them to submit to his whims. Some of them he drugged, some of them he didn't have to. But none of them knew he was secretly recording them for posterity. Until last week, that is."

"Blackmail?"

He nodded. "Cairns started calling them three days before he got croaked, trying to hit them up for 'loans.' The amount varied as to how much each one could afford, but the average was between five and ten grand somewhere. He made sure each one of them knew about the tapes, of course."

"Did any of them pay?"

"No. Cairns conveniently died first."

"You've checked their alibis for the night of Cairns' death?"

He nodded. "All but two of them are airtight."

"That should simplify things," I said. "Besides everybody here, that only leaves those two to check out for the time Dart died."

He gave me a searching look. "And why would I want to do that?"

"Try to follow me on this," I said. "What if, just for speculation, Dart didn't kill Cairns, but knew who did. What if, while he was sitting outside Cairns' condo, trying to work up the nerve to confront the man, he saw someone come and go—the murderer. That would explain why he didn't have an alibi for the time of the killing and why he flunked on the lie box."

"Why didn't he say anything about it before?"

"Why should he? There wasn't a murder before. Until the autopsy report came in, the only person who knew Cairns' death was not an accident was the person who slipped him the mickey. But once it came out that Cairns was murdered, it would be a different ballgame, and Dart would be sure to start talking. That made him too dangerous to leave alive."

"So the murderer came up here, slit Dart's throat, and planted evidence to make it look like Dart had killed Cairns, then himself?" He smiled scoffingly.

He walked away and I followed. "Did you question Adrianne Covert about her whereabouts on the night of Cairns' murder?"

He stopped at the bathroom partition and looked at me. "What do you think?"

"Where did she say she was?"

"In her room."

"All night?"

"Yeah. Why?"

I thought about it. Adrianne was already teetering on the brink of hysteria; a good grilling by McDonald might send her screaming over the edge, which could wind up costing *Death in the Desert*—and perhaps my client—a chunk of change, or even succeed in getting the picture scrapped by the studio. I didn't want to be responsible for that, at least until I had something more substantial than the fact that the girl was a liar. Besides, he was starting to irritate me. I'd given him something major—the Sawyer connection—and here he was treating me like some sort of an asshole.

"Just curious." Before he could pursue it, I pulled the sheets of stationery out of my pocket and handed them to him. He unfolded them and took a look. "What's this?"

"The Great Kiss-Off of 1986," I said. "Samples of Adrianne Covert's and Marla McKinnon's lipsticks. You said the lab would need samples to compare against the swabs they took from Cairns' body—"

"Where did you get these?"

"What difference does it make?"

He pursed his lips and nodded. "You're right. Even if we got a spectrograph match on one of them, it wouldn't mean a fucking thing. How many women use these lipsticks?"

"I just thought it might be a starting point—"

"We have a starting *and* a finishing point, right in that bathroom," he said gruffly.

Now he was *really* starting to irritate me. I put the papers back in my pocket. That had been an exercise in futility, well, not totally. At least I found out I might have herpes. "Never mind," I said, and started out.

"Where are you going?"

I walked out the door without turning around.

21

I went to my room and got Dr. Blatty's office number from Beverly Hills information. The receptionist who answered told me Dr. Blatty was busy and could not possibly come to the phone, but I told her in a bitchy tone that this was an emergency, that I was calling for Ms. Adrianne Covert, and that unless the doctor wanted her blood on his hands, he'd better get on the horn pronto. She told me to wait, and after a minute or two Blatty got on the line.

I explained that I was Ms. Covert's personal secretary and that I was calling from Palm Springs because Ms. Covert was in very bad shape due to the fact that she had not been able to sleep in the past three nights and desperately needed a refill of her chloral hydrate prescription. After quickly checking the chart, Dr. Blatty informed me gruffly that he had given Adrianne a prescription for fifty 500 mg. chloral hydrate capsules only three weeks ago, and she couldn't have possibly taken them all, and I told him that she'd accidentally dropped the bottle down the toilet four days ago, and she'd been trying to get by without them, but the situation was now critical and if she didn't get some sleep soon, the poor girl would simply die. He grudgingly agreed to call the prescription to the pharmacy whose name I picked out of the Yellow Pages, and I told him gratefully that he had just saved Adrianne and the picture, and hung up.

I didn't have time to think about the conversation; the receiver wasn't on its cradle three seconds before the phone rang.

"What is this I hear about Dart?" Larry Bigelow asked shrilly.

I filled him in briefly and he asked: "You think he killed Walter?"

"I don't know."

"This whole thing is turning very strange."

"You haven't heard the half of it," I assured him.

"I will, though. Over lunch. The Palm Court at Maxim's. Half an hour."

Maxim's Hotel epitomized the metamorphosis Palm Springs had been undergoing over the past ten years. Since the 1930s, the city planners had strictly prohibited any building on Palm Canyon to be over two stories, to maintain the town's "village" feel and ensure downtown strollers an uninterrupted view of the mountains, but now the mountains were gone, blotted out by Maxim's six-story sloping trapezoid of so-called luxury suites.

And the changes weren't all on the outside. The interior was joltingly slick and urbane, with twin glass elevators that slid up and down one wall toward the skylighted ceiling, taking guests to their rooms, all of which overlooked the open and vast marble-floored lobby. The tiered railings in front of the rooms dripped philodendrons, and at the far end of the room a huge, impressionistic brass sculpture of the sun floated ethereally, suspended between the floors by brass rays. The place was impressive, but somehow disturbingly out-of-sync, something that belonged more in New York or San Francisco than in a small town in the middle of the Mojave Desert, even if the town *was* Palm Springs. The elegance and formality of the place didn't seem to bother the patrons milling about the lobby, however, dressed in tennis togs, T-shirts, and Bermuda shorts, their thongs making slapping sounds on the marble floor. That, at least, was one thing they could never change about the town; informality was too deeply embedded in the Palm Springs mystique. No matter how chic the place, the clientele would always look as if it were going to a barbecue. People came here to relax and hang loose, and any restaurant that had ever opened with a jacket-and-tie dress code had dropped it in short order or folded within a season.

Larry was sitting at a table in front of a fountained wall in the lobby restaurant, sipping a glass of white wine and scribbling notes on a legal-sized pad. I dropped into a chair opposite and he looked up and beamed. "Jacob, dear boy, good to see you." His beaming turned to concern and he asked: "Are you all right?"

That kind of question, coming from a friend, in that tone, always got to me. I fought down the urge to take my own pulse and said: "As far as I know. Why?"

"You look a little peaked."

"Detectives are supposed to look peaked," I said, relieved. "It's part of the image."

Larry never looked peaked. He was always nut-brown, the result of working on his column in his backyard surrounded by reflectors. He was tall and thin, and his long, narrow face, into which were set dark, thoughtful eyes, combined with his premature-gray hair and black mustache, had always reminded me of Dashiell Hammett. I somehow doubted Hammett would have liked the Rex Reed voice that had been dubbed in over his own, though, or the pink, long-sleeved shirt and cream-colored slacks and white canvas loafers he was wearing or the socks that he wasn't. Or the thick gold chain around his neck or the gaudy diamond ring on each hand or the black leather zipper pouch he carried. But that would have been Hammett's hang-up.

"You are a very unpopular fellow in certain moviemaking circles this morning," he chided me.

I tried to look heartbroken. "You mean, I'll never work in this town again?"

I hailed down a passing waitress and ordered a double Bloody Mary and a menu. I was wired from the morning and needed to mellow out.

"What's this I hear about you practically accusing Sam Fields of murdering Cairns?"

"See how important it is to triple-check your sources? All I said was that he had a motive. So did a lot of other people."

"Like Matthew Dart?"

"Like anybody who knew him. He wasn't a nice man."

"Then you don't think Dart did it?"

"I don't know."

The waitress brought my drink and I ordered a house salad and the salmon. Larry ordered a petite New York, and when the waitress was out of hearing range, asked: "What did you say to Adrianne Covert last night that set her off?"

"I told her she was a shitty driver."

His eyes twinkled craftily. "I talked to Susanne Capasco this morning. She's really hot about you upsetting her client. She says that if Adrianne gets bounced from this movie, she's going to sue you."

I took a good swallow of the Bloody Mary. "She'd wind up with a lot. She'd be better off not bothering."

He chuckled. "That's what I told her."

"Thanks."

He shrugged his narrow shoulders. "You know me, Jake. I can't help telling the truth."

"What's her story, anyway?"

"Susanne? She used to be with CMA, but broke out on her own four or five years ago. She handles a few bit players, and not many of them, because Adrianne Covert takes up most of her time."

"You'd think she'd dump her if she was that much trouble."

"She says she's convinced the girl is going to be a big star. She picked her out of a talent show at Hollywood High when Adrianne was only sixteen, and she's been grooming her for the past four years, getting her ready for the big time."

"Looks to me like she's got a tiger by the tail," I said. "Could there be more to the relationship than business?"

His eyes looked interested. "Like what?"

"The day after Cairns died, I passed by Adrianne's room and saw the two of them sitting on the bed. If I hadn't known, I wouldn't have guessed they were agent-client. Mother-daughter, maybe, or lovers, but not agent-client."

"Half the time, agents end up as mother-confessors, you know—"

"I also heard that when they first started shooting *Death in the Desert*, this Capasco broad caught Adrianne and her leading man *in flagrante* and went totally bat-shit."

He tugged thoughtfully on his lower lip. "If you want to know if Susanne Capasco is gay, I don't know. I've never asked her, and there's never been a reason to try to find out." He paused. "Is there one now?"

"You can't always look for meaning and purpose in things," I admonished him as our lunches arrived. "Any dirty little fact is worth knowing for itself."

He looked at me admiringly and said: "You would have made a great columnist."

By the time lunch arrived, the vodka had lubricated my tongue and he had to write furiously to keep up with its wagging. When I finished the saga of Cairns/McVey/Sawyer and the killing of Sarto, Larry's face was flushed with excitement. "I can't print this," he said breathlessly.

"Why not?"

"It's too good. You know what we have here? The movie

rights alone would be worth millions, never mind book sales and TV rights. We *have* to write this, Jake. You and I."

"I'm game," I said, infected by his excitement.

"A vice-president at Simon and Schuster is a good friend of mine. I'll call him this afternoon."

I wondered if it would make more sense from a business standpoint to buy the BMW outright and take the depreciation, or lease with an option to buy. I'd have to talk to Sol, my accountant.

"Of course, we have to have an ending," he said.

"Of course."

"So the sooner you wind it up, the sooner we can sell the story and get an advance."

"I'll get right on it," I said, taking one last forkful of salmon.

His face turned suddenly terribly serious. "I certainly hope you're right about Dart not being the one. The whole thing sort of craps out, if he was."

I drained my Bloody Mary, suddenly wishing I had another full one. "I see your point."

He made a grandiose limp-wristed gesture. "I mean, it would be much better for us if we could finish *big*, you know what I mean? Like a chase, or something exciting like that. It'd be like money in the bank."

"I'll keep that in mind." I was beginning to think he'd been hanging around those people too long; whatever they had was definitely contagious. I left him with the check and got the hell out of there before I caught it, too, and wound up hang-gliding from the top of Mt. San Jacinto in pursuit of Cairns' killer.

22

There were two call-back messages waiting for me when I got back to my room, one from Resnick, the other from Marla. I tried Marla, got no answer, and called McDonald's extension at the P.D. "Detectives, McDonald," he grumbled sourly.

"You ever want to quit the force, you could always get a receptionist job at Santa Claus Lane."

"Bah, humbug." There was a pause, then a sigh. "Look, Jake, I'm sorry I spouted off at you like that—"

"Forget it."

"It's just that I have everybody from the chief to the fucking TV reporters steaming up the back of my neck—"

"I said forget it. I know how PMS affects you. Take a couple of Midol and do me a favor." I rattled off a list of names. "Find out if any of those people are licensed to carry Mace."

"Mace? Why?"

"Favors don't come with strings," I reminded him. "Don't worry, I'll explain it all later."

He agreed to do it, but said it might take a while, as he had some other things to do that wouldn't wait.

I told him whenever, and hung up. I pulled the pint bottle of Gordon's vodka from my suitcase that I'd packed for an emergency, stripped off my shirt, and went out onto the lanai. There was no wind and the afternoon sun was warm. I sat in one of the deck chairs, soaking up the rays and sipping vodka, trying to let my thoughts about the case disentangle themselves, but after half an hour, they were more jumbled up than ever, so I went back inside and turned on the afternoon news. The Russians were bombing the shit out of a village of yak-herders in Afghanistan who had thrown rocks at one of their tanks, and Khaddafi was starting to talk about a new "line of death." Little did he know, we already had one here—the Palm Springs city limits. There was a faint, uncertain knock at the door.

Adrianne Covert stood in the hallway with a finger in her mouth. She was barefoot and wore a high-necked white gauze dress and an expression that was somewhere between shy and scared. Her strawberry hair was mussed and some strands of it had fallen over one eye. Veronica Lake style. The blue eye that showed burned with a wild and strange light. "You have to help me," she said in a tremulous voice.

"I do?"

"Please," she pleaded. "I have to talk to you."

I stepped back and told her to come in. She walked past me and looked around uncertainly before sitting on the edge of the bed. She dropped her gaze to her knees, which were locked together, and began picking nervously at her dress. "Who have you told about seeing me the night Walter died?"

"Nobody. Yet." I remained standing.

She tucked the loose strands of hair neatly behind one ear and looked up. "I'm gambling that I can trust you, Mr. Asch. You seem like a nice man. I thought if I explained things, you might understand." She took a deep breath, trying to screw up her courage. "I've been seeing a man."

"Congratulations."

"A *married* man," she amended. "We've been having an affair for a month now. I was going to meet him when you saw me. We love each other very much, and he intends to get a divorce, but for the time being, we have to keep things secret. He's socially very prominent, and if it got out, not only would his wife try to take him for everything he has— she's a very vindictive woman—the publicity would hurt both of us."

She bit her lip. She seemed to be having a hard time with this. I looked into her eyes, trying to determine whether she was on something. She didn't seem to be; the fire in them was being stoked from an internal source that was barely under control. She went on: "When you came up to me last night, I thought you were working for his wife and had been following me. That's why I flipped out."

"This guy live down here?"

She nodded, and her hair fell back over one eye, making her look like a frightened little girl. There was nothing little-girlish about her breasts, though; they were firm and perfectly sculpted and the nipples were plainly visible through the fabric. I found myself staring at them and looked away, but not before she caught me. "Does he have a name?"

Her eyes grew wide. "I couldn't tell you that. I promised him I would never tell anyone."

"You might have to tell the police—"

"No, no, I *can't*," she said, her features working desperately. "If the police go to see him, it'll ruin everything."

"The police are usually pretty discreet about things like that—"

She rocked back and forth on the bed. "You don't understand. He'll freak out."

"If he's any kind of guy worth having, he'll understand—"

Her head wagged violently from side to side. "No, he won't," she whined. "You don't know him."

If he was *that* uptight, I didn't *want* to know him. If he existed. "So what do you want from me?"

"Please don't tell the police." She reached out and grabbed my hand. I tried to pull it away gently, but she held onto it firmly and looked up at me imploringly, like a peasant woman beseeching some icon in the Shrine of Guadalupe. "I'm begging you—"

I shook my head implacably. "This is a murder investigation now. I could get into trouble for withholding evidence."

"I'll pay you."

"No."

"What do you want?" she asked, her voice quavering. "I'll do anything—"

I'd never had so many women offer me their bodies on a case. I guess in the movie business, they're a normal means of exchange—like cowrie shells, and about as valuable. She was young and very sexy, but the offer didn't tempt me. I'd already fucked one movie star and look what it had gotten me. The next one, my cock would probably fall off and my head swell up like a watermelon. I looked down at her and asked: "What did you do for Cairns?"

She let go of my hand as if she had just gotten a shock from it. "What do you mean?"

"How did you get the part in this movie?"

"I read for it," she said defensively.

"Where?"

"At the production office at Warner Hollywood."

"He didn't ask you to come out to his Malibu house?"

"No," she said and looked away. She began rubbing her right wrist.

"Tell me about the tape," I said.

Her face went blank. "What tape? I don't know what you're talking about."

"You seemed to last night."

"I told you what I was reacting to last night," she argued. I smiled. "Okay."

"What are you going to do? Are you going to tell?"

"I don't know. I want to think about it." I sat down on the bed next to her. "Did you always want to be an actress, Adrianne?"

She shook her head. "No."

"What did you want to be?"

"I didn't really think about it much. Until Susanne came along." She gave me a searching look. "Do you ever feel as if your life isn't your own, that it's running totally out of control?"

"All the time," I said.

She nodded and her face grew melancholy. "Sometimes I feel like a puppet, and all these people are pulling the strings—"

Her thought was interrupted by the phone.

"Mr. Asch?" a female voice asked. "This is Susanne Capasco. I think we need to have a talk."

"Any time," I told her.

"Five minutes? The bar downstairs?"

"Fine," I said, and hung up. I looked down at Adrianne and said: "I'll make you a deal. You give me the name of your mystery man and I'll approach him very discreetly. If he verifies what you've said, I won't tell the cops."

She shook her head vehemently. "I can't—"

I shrugged. "Then I'm going to have to tell them about seeing you. By the way, how many chloral hydrate capsules do you have left out of the fifty Dr. Blatty gave you a scrip for? They'll want to know that too."

That one split the cooling tanks wide open, and her face immediately went into meltdown. Her eyes were the size of silver dollars and she did a repeat performance of the choked-sob, fleeing-in-terror scene of last night. There went another fifty grand. That would cost me a good ten points tomorrow in the Production Popularity Polls.

I put on a clean shirt and went downstairs.

Except for Susanne Capasco, nursing a drink at a cocktail table by the iron railing overlooking the pool table, and the bartender, the bar was empty. The Trivia game had been replaced and the new one was busy flashing its colored categories at nothing. "Miss Capasco? I'm Jacob Asch."

She smiled stiffly and offered her hand. She had on a lightweight, smartly tailored beige skirt with matching jacket, and a high-collared white shirt with ruffles down the front. Her platinum hair was pulled back and fixed in a bun. Her eyes were not so heavily made up today, but the strain of the past few days showed in them.

I sat down and the bartender came over, grumbling unhappily that he had to move for his tip, instead of having the money thrown at him. I ordered a vodka-soda and he went away.

"Larry Bigelow says you're an all-right guy," she began.

"That was nice of him."

"That's why I thought we should talk," she said, taking out a cigarette. "I thought maybe if I explained a few things, I could make you understand, and we could reach some sort of agreement. I have problems enough handling Adrianne as it is, without adding more."

She took a pack of matches from her purse and I took them out of her hand and lit her cigarette. There was nothing the least bit masculine about the way she lightly cupped my hand as she bent over the flame or the way she held her cigarette.

There wasn't anything butch about her I could see, in fact. I was beginning to think I'd read the scene in Adrianne's room wrong.

"You don't have to explain that the girl has problems, Miss Capasco. I know. She just left my room."

"*Your* room?" she asked. Her reaction was not angry, and only mildly surprised. "Goddamn her, she's supposed to be sleeping. What was she doing in your room?"

"She dropped by to ask me to forget I'd seen her leaving the hotel the night Cairns was murdered."

She exhaled smoke away from me, and dropped her eyes to the matchbook, which she turned over and over on the table. "She told you about her secret rendezvous?"

I nodded. "Who is the guy?"

She shrugged. "She won't even tell me."

"She lied to the cops."

The bartender came with my drink and I gave him a five. He went away and Susanne Capasco looked into my eyes and said earnestly: "Look, Mr. Asch, Adrianne is a very emotional girl. That's what makes her a good actress, and when she learns to harness it, is going to make her a great actress. It's also what makes her hard to handle. I've lost a lot of clients because of her. She's very demanding and takes up most of my time. She has to be watched, constantly. As you probably have surmised, she has a drug problem and when she takes drugs, she not only becomes unreliable, she also becomes, shall we say, indiscreet? I've had to pull her out of a couple of situations that could have turned into major problems if they hadn't been nipped in the bud. What I'm trying to say is that I wouldn't have invested my time and energies and money if I didn't believe in her. She is going to be a star. A big star."

"Are you sure that's what she wants?"

She stiffened. "Of course that's what she wants. What do you think we've been working for all these years. It's her dream—"

"Hers or yours?"

Her eyes narrowed. "Just what is that supposed to mean?"

"The girl doesn't seem to think she's had a chance to

dream a dream of her own," I said. "She seems to think her life is a runaway."

She made a scoffing face. "That's ridiculous."

"Is it? If the dream is hers, why is she constantly trying to fuck it up? People take drugs to escape, Miss Capasco. From themselves or the world around them. Have you ever sat down and asked her if this is what she really wants to do with her life?"

"I've never had to," she said harshly. "I *know* what she wants, what she's destined for." She sat back and regarded me thoughtfully, as if trying to decide what type she could best market me as. "Adrianne's dreams and aspirations aren't your concern, Mr. Asch, and that isn't what I asked you here to discuss. I'm trying to prevent us from tangling, which is what we are going to do if you insist on interfering in Adrianne's life. Selling a client is only part of an agent's job. The other part is making sure the client is protected, from him or herself, as well as other people."

"People like me," I said, always clever to catch a point.

"Adrianne was very upset by Walter's death. Not only did your accusations last night distress her to the point where she couldn't work and thereby put her future employment on this picture in jeopardy, they were the kind of malicious gossip that, if picked up and repeated by the media, could ruin a career. To the fans, every star is guilty even *after* he or she is proven innocent."

"It isn't gossip that I saw her leaving the hotel, Miss Capasco."

"She explained that," she said, her voice growing emotional. "That's why she came to see you. Is she going to have to explain it now to the police and the media too? Do you know what that would do to her?"

I had an idea. The girl had a helping wheel missing, but I didn't see the need to belabor that now. As her agent, the woman had to know already. I hit her with something else.

"It isn't gossip that Walter Cairns was given a dose of chloral hydrate before he was trussed up and hung, Miss Capasco. And it isn't gossip that Adrianne has a prescription for chloral hydrate."

Thoughts darted quickly behind her eyes. She tried to

corner them as she picked up her drink and took a sip. She asked coolly: "How do you know that?"

I took a swallow of my own drink. He'd floated the vodka and it burned my throat. "I talked to her doctor."

"Plenty of people must have prescriptions for chloral hydrate. That doesn't mean Adrianne is guilty of murder."

"No, it doesn't," I agreed. "But it doesn't particularly look good for her, either." I paused and watched her mash out her cigarette in the ashtray. "How did she land this part, anyway?"

"I saw Walter's ad in *Variety* and called him up. She read for him and he hired her immediately. He could see she was perfect for Gabrielle."

"Where did she read?"

Her eyebrows knitted. "Warner Hollywood."

"Not at Cairns' house?"

"No. Warner Hollywood. Why?"

"Cairns liked to interview actresses at his Malibu house," I said. "He had a hidden video setup there. You knew he was into SM?"

Her face remained calm. "No, I didn't."

"Adrianne never went there?"

"She would have told me if he'd suggested anything like that," she said definitely.

"How can you be sure? She won't even tell you the name of her mystery man."

"That is personal," she said. "When it comes to business, she keeps no secrets from me."

I nodded. "How long have you handled her?"

"Six years. Ever since she was sixteen. They were looking for a new teen-age face for a supporting role in a TV series called *The Jensens*. I saw Adrianne sing in a talent show at Hollywood High and I knew she was it. I went backstage and signed her up on the spot. That was the beginning."

"You must have grown very attached to her in all that time," I said.

"She's like a daughter to me," she said. Her eyes turned hard. "What do you intend to do?"

"That's what everybody seems to want to know," I said,

standing. "When I come up with the answer, I'll let you know."

"Just remember, Mr. Asch, you have Adrianne's career in your hands. If she gets bounced from this picture because of more shooting delays, the reality or nonreality of her dreams of stardom will be a totally moot point. I won't be able to sell her for a McDonald's commercial. If I have been creating false dreams for Adrianne for my own selfish motives, you would be destroying those dreams for your own selfish motives. Adrianne will be an innocent victim."

I wondered if this meant I had to share in the "awesome responsibility" Resnick had talked about. I was beginning to feel like Tyrone Power in *Abandon Ship*, picking those passengers who would be expelled from the lifeboat and fed to the sharks. Except in this case there might be more sharks in the lifeboat than in the water.

On the way out, I stopped by the bar, where the bartender was absorbed in the sports page. I disturbed him to ask if he'd had any word from my change.

He snapped his fingers as if he knew there was something he'd forgotten, and took three ones out of the register. I pocketed all three. "That's how I got the money," I told him and walked out, his grumbling trailing behind me.

23

The phone was ringing when I got back to my room. It was Marla. "Have you been avoiding me for some reason?"

"I called your room, but you weren't in," I hedged.

"You should have called the production office. I was shooting all day."

"How did it go?"

"All right," she said noncommittally. "You heard about Adrianne?"

"Yeah."

"See the effect you have on women?"

"It helps if they're crazy."

"I must be crazy, then, because you have an effect on me. You want to observe it over dinner?"

It had to be faced sooner or later; it might as well be sooner. "Sure," I said.

"I have a five o'clock wake-up tomorrow, so we'll have to make it early. Are you hungry? I'm famished."

She got too hungry for dinner at eight; maybe that was why the lady was a tramp. "It's five now," I said, checking my watch. "I'll be by in an hour."

We went to a charming little French restaurant that was a converted house at the very foot of the mountain, and we sat out back on the patio, covered by a protective canopy of branches of the big, old oak trees surrounding it, and warmed by electric heaters.

Probably because it was so early, there were only three other tables occupied, and our waiter was very attentive. We each had a couple glasses of white wine and watched the sky turn purple, then indigo, and the waiter translated the menu, which was written on a wheeled chalkboard. It was all very romantic, only I wasn't exactly in a romantic mood.

She had a whitefish *dijonaise*, and I had lamb *noisettes*, and both were very good. Unfortunately, my conscience couldn't justify putting it on my expense sheet, and the prices prevented me from wholeheartedly enjoying the meal.

Over coffee, she commented: "You're awfully quiet tonight. Something the matter?"

"It's just the case," I hedged. I seemed to be having trouble making decisions lately. I should have turned in the BMW this afternoon, but I hadn't. I wondered why I was procrastinating about that. Could it be that I was becoming tainted by the values of these people, that I was beginning to aspire to the same superficial dreams and yearnings? Would I become an avid watcher of *Lives of the Rich and Famous*? At that point, I would follow Peg Entwistle's lead and settle for whatever letter was available.

"I still can't believe it about Matthew," she said, shaking her dark head. She looked beautiful in the candlelight. Too goddamn beautiful. I hesitated, wondering what approach to use, and decided on the old reliable frontal assault. If it was good enough for Pickett at Gettysburg, it was good enough for me. "I have to ask you a question, Marla."

She smiled. "Go ahead."

"Do you have herpes?"

Her smile fell. "Why do you ask that?" I didn't know how to answer that without getting into trouble. It turned out I didn't have to; she beat me to it. "You sonofabitch," she said, as the realization hit her, throwing her napkin on the table angrily. "You went through my drawers."

And wished I hadn't, I thought.

"What's the matter, you don't get in enough snooping during working hours? What is it, a compulsion with you? You can't help yourself?"

There was some truth in what she said, enough to make me feel slightly uncomfortable. It was a kind of compulsion which was one reason most of my relationships wound up shish kabob on a flaming sword. Either they found out about that compulsion, or I, because of it, found out too much about them.

She leaned across the table, her face a hard mask. She kept her voice low. "For your information, Mr. Snoop, I do have herpes, but not the kind you have to worry about. I have shingles, and it isn't contagious, so you can rest easy." She stood up and her chair scraped loudly on the cement.

"You want to open my mail while you're at it?" She was no longer bothering to keep her voice down, and the other patrons were starting to stare.

"I think you're overreacting—"

"Yeah? You do, huh? Well, it may be something people in your noble profession don't think is important, but I value my privacy. And I don't like it invaded by keyhole-peeping detectives." She picked up her purse. "I'll wait in the car."

All eyes on the patio watched her go, including mine. I smiled around embarrassedly and signaled the waiter for the check. I'd forgotten in my haste that Pickett had been killed during his famous charge at Gettysburg; I was sure I'd just joined his ranks, at least with Marla. I'd found out long ago that too many questions can kick the shit out of any romance, but that had never stopped me from asking them. What the hell, I told myself. At least now I knew and wouldn't be checking my genitalia in a panic every morning for the next three months, searching for the first sign of a blister.

The waiter came with the check, which I managed to pay without wincing, and went out to the car.

She stayed mad all the way back to the hotel and slammed the car door so hard when she got out that the compression of the air inside the cabin nearly blew out my eardrums. She might simmer down later, she might not, but there didn't seem to be any use trying to smooth anything over tonight, so I checked with the front desk, found out Larry had called, and went up to my room.

"You were right about Capasco," he said when I called him at Maxim's. "I talked to an ex-client of hers, Betty Frazer. You'd know her if you saw her, she does a lot of guest shots on TV sitcoms. Anyway, Susanne used to be her agent when she was younger and struggling. She said after a while she began to get very domineering, to the point of telling Betty who she could go out with and who she couldn't. She found out what the deal was when Susanne cornered her one day and tried to put the make on her. She fired her and got another agent."

"Good work, Larry, thanks."

"How does that fit in?"

"I'm not sure yet, but I have an idea."

"Just think *big ending*," he said.

"*The Wild Bunch*," I told him.

"I like it," he said excitedly. "I like it *a lot*."

I polished off the pint of vodka, but that didn't help me sleep. It wasn't until halfway through the late-night movie, *Target Earth*, a sci-fi epic about an invasion of Venusian robots, complete with blinking lights in their cardboard helmets and presumably powered by the long extension cords brilliantly photographed trailing behind them, that I finally dozed off, wondering if Venusian current was 110 or 220.

The robots were gone when I woke up, lost in a blizzard of snow and static. I sat up and tried to clear my head, then picked up my watch from the table. Three-ten. I'd gotten a whole hour's sleep. I got up and turned off the set and started to go back to bed, but was stopped by the sound of soft but insistent knocking. That must have been what had awakened me. Who in the hell would come visiting at three o'clock in the morning? I went to the door and called out: "Who is it?"

The rapping answered, but no voice. The knocking was too delicate for Marv's hand; he wouldn't be able to touch a door that softly.

"Marla?"

Again, no answer. I opened the door a crack and peeked groggily. All I caught was a glimpse of a gray trenchcoat and the horribly withered, toothless old man's face under the brim of a gray fedora, but that was enough to know that this was not someone I wanted to entertain in my black bikini Jockey shorts at three in the morning. I didn't see the gun before I slammed the door, but then I didn't have to see it, I heard it just fine as it pop-pop-popped in rapid succession and three holes splintered through the wood near the knob.

As I yanked my hand back and dropped to the floor, I kept thinking how amazingly quiet the gun sounded, more like a popgun than a real gun (it was funny the details the mind fixes on at times like that) and then three more bullets ripped through the door over my head, sending a shower of plywood and sawdust raining down around me. I hunkered down and waited for more, muttering silent curses about cheap fucking motel room doors and silent prayers that it would hold, but no more came.

Footsteps pounded heavily down the hallway, and then for a long time there was no sound except my heart. After lying there a while enjoying the sound of its rhythmic beating, I crawled to the phone on the night table and dialed 911. That was when I noticed the trail of blood. There was a hole in my left side, through the love handle that had been steadily growing over the past three or four years. I knew it would get in the way of something sooner or later. I told the man who answered the phone that I'd been shot and gave him my room number, then pulled the bedspread off the bed and tried to stanch the blood which was flowing freely onto the carpet.

Larry had come close to getting his "Wild Bunch" finale,

too damned close. Maybe . . . no, no, he wouldn't go that far to sell a few books.

My would-be assassin was more than likely long gone, but there was no sense taking any chances, so I crawled into the bathroom and stood up and took a look in the mirror. There was another hole in the back of the love handle where the bullet had exited.

I suddenly felt dizzy and nauseated and barely made it to the toilet. It seemed a shame to waste all that expensive French food, but there was nothing I could do about it.

I walked back into the room, keeping to the wall like a roach, and lay down on the bed. I was bathed in a cold, clammy sweat. My side hurt more with each minute that passed, and with the pain came the sudden realization of how close I'd come to biting the big weenie. I felt a combination of emotions—fear-rage, a feeling of profound violation and helplessness. I read in an essay by some biologist once that every mammal, no matter what its life span, has approximately 200,000,000 breaths. I wanted all of mine.

24

The emergency-room doctor was named Kmetko and didn't look old enough to have graduated medical school, and after determining that the bullet hadn't hit anything vital and cleaning and dressing the wounds, he charged me $110.00 and told me to take it easy for a few days.

McDonald was waiting for me outside the ER when I came out. "You all right?"

"I've felt better."

"You were goddamned lucky—"

I nodded. "I've been trying to get rid of that roll for a

couple of years. Now all I have to do is find someone to shoot off the other side and all my old pants will fit again."

"Did you get a look at the shooter?"

"Whoever it was had on a Halloween mask."

"Man? Woman?"

I shook my head. "Trenchcoat and fedora."

"How about the hands?"

"It happened too fast. I didn't even see the gun."

"It was a .32-caliber automatic," he said. "We found the shell casings."

A .32 automatic. I knew she was annoyed, but I didn't think she was *that* annoyed. "Marla McKinnon owns a .32 automatic."

"Why in the hell would she want to kill you?"

"Let's go ask her," I said, then glanced at my watch. "She should be getting up right about now. Did you find out about the Mace?"

He nodded. "Susanne Capasco has a Mace license. What's this about Mace, anyway?"

I told him about the incident in Malibu, and he started yelling, which didn't surprise me. "Shit! I should call the D.A. and have charges filed on you just on general principles! What did you take from the house?"

"Nothing, I swear." A sudden pain shot through my side and I grimaced and sucked in some air.

He looked at me, concerned. "You okay?"

"Yeah." I resumed walking and talking:

"I made copies of the birth certificates and that budget printout for *Black Thursday*, but I put them back. You figure out what that printout is yet?"

"No," he mumbled.

When I told him, he quieted down and stroked his mustache thoughtfully. "Looks like everybody had a motive to kill that guy." He paused and said grudgingly: "You were right about Dart, by the way. He had chloral hydrate in his blood."

We walked outside. The air was cool and the dawn was breaking yellow over the mountains, like scrambled eggs spreading over a purple Formica countertop. The birds were chirping cheerfully, heralding the start of another shitty day in paradise.

"Call a meeting for this morning," I told McDonald. "Resnick, Fields, Marla, Adrianne, and Capasco. Tell them you want them at Marla's trailer at ten, but don't tell them why."

He stopped walking. "How about me? Do I get to know why?"

"Don't you watch movies?" I asked him. "The cop or the detective gets everybody together in a room and the guilty one always breaks down and confesses or grabs a gun and tries to get away."

The look on his face was one of utter disbelief. "You kidding me, or what? That never happens in real life."

"But these people don't *know* that," I tried to explain. "They're *movie people*. That's the only reality they know. They think it's supposed to happen that way."

He waved a hand at me. "You're out of your fucking mind."

I gave him a knowing smile and winked. "Trust me."

25

They were all unhappily assembled in Marla's dresing-room trailer when I came in.

"What is this crap about, Asch? This is costing me fourteen grand an hour," said Resnick.

He was sitting on the couch next to Fields and Marla. Adrianne and Susanne Capasco sat in two chairs nearby. McDonald was strategically placed in the doorway, smoking a cigarette and watching everyone closely.

"It's about two murders," I said. "Three if you count a guy by the name of Harold Sarto. Cairns killed him."

"Harold Sarto?" Resnick blustered. "Who in the hell is Harold Sarto?"

I paced in front of the couch. "Let's start at the beginning. It might be easier to understand that way. Walter Cairns' real name was Ed Sawyer and he lived in Fallbrook, California. Thirty-two years ago, Ed Sawyer killed his father and mother and a town bully named Terence Bailey and burned his house to the ground.

"Everyone thought that Sawyer had been the one who had died in the fire and Bailey had been the culprit, which was just what Sawyer wanted them to think. In the meantime, Sawyer, being an unusually precocious kid, assumed the identity of one Bill McVey. He must have gotten an education somewhere, because he wound up in Atlanta as an engineer for an outfit named Dynotran. Am I going too fast for you?"

"Go on," Resnick muttered.

"He got married and settled down, but for one reason or another—boredom with married life or his yearnings to be a writer, it isn't really important—he split on his wife and came back to California. He wrote a script, sold it, and the rest we know. Cairns was always aware that his past might catch up with him if anyone recognized him, so he was always careful never to be photographed. But at a party, he was unwittingly snapped by a photographer from *People*. That led to his downfall. His wife, or ex-wife by now, saw the picture and so did Ed Sawyer's best friend in Fallbrook, Harold Sarto. When Sarto showed up in Palm Springs wanting money to keep his mouth shut, Cairns knew the game was over. He made plans to set up a new identity and tried to stall Sarto while he converted what assets he had into cash, but Sarto got impatient, so Cairns killed him. That gave him some days, or weeks—he really couldn't tell how long it would take the police to link up him and Sarto, or even if they would at all—but he couldn't take chances. He had to leave right away, which meant he couldn't finish *Death in the Desert*, which bothered him, for more reasons than one.

"He wanted to see it finished because his ego was wrapped up in it. It would be his last directorial effort, and he wanted to see it completed in his image. He had had his differences with Fields, even demeaned the man publicly, but he must have had a real respect for his talents; besides, there was nobody else he could turn to. He went over in detail how he wanted the film to turn out, how the problems they had encountered could be solved, then he dropped the bombshell. He told Fields he was quitting and that he wanted Fields to take over as his successor. He thought he could get Resnick to approve it, but he asked Fields to keep it under his hat until he gave him the word. He wanted to keep it quiet not only because of the panic at the studio the news would cause if it leaked out, but because he wanted the pleasure of performing one last act as director. He wanted to fire Adrianne Covert, the one person who was almost singlehandedly responsible for screwing up his movie."

"That's a lie!" Susanne Capasco blurted out.

"Let him finish," Fields said quietly.

Adrianne said nothing, but chewed on a nail nervously. She wouldn't look at me.

I went on: "To get the picture in proper perspective, I'm going to have to do a flashback. Cairns was a devious master of the casting couch, and over the years he had played on the hopes of many an aspiring actress by doling out parts in exchange for their participation in certain kinky scenes he set up. They had no way of knowing at the time that he was taping these scenes with a secret video setup at his house. More than likely, Cairns had never intended to use the tapes for anything more than his own amusement on lonely nights, but desperate men resort to desperate measures. In Cairns' case, blackmail."

Marla McKinnon squirmed uncomfortably and gave me the Evil Eye. I ignored it and panned the rest of the faces in the room. None of them gave away anything and nobody jumped up and screamed, "I did it!" "Tell you what," I said. "To save all of this long narration, I'll give whoever confesses a Ride-and-Dine Special on the Palm Springs Aerial Tramway. No takers? The offer will cease to be valid if I have to go through this whole megillah."

Nobody said anything.

"Okay," I said, shrugging. "Blackmail was not new to

Cairns. His last two pictures had been bombs at the box office and until *Death in the Desert*, he couldn't buy a job. He bought that job essentially by threatening to expose Marty Resnick as a thief. He got hold of a computer printout of the budget for *Black Thursday*, Cairns' last epic for Triad, and found out that Resnick had been stealing from his own pictures, not exactly shocking news in Hollywood, but news that might have caused Resnick some problems if it got out. So he signed Cairns to a three-picture deal.''

Everyone was looking at Resnick, who seemed unfazed by the revelation. There was no need for him to be; everyone in the room was at his mercy. I resumed pacing.

"Cairns' deal for *Death in the Desert* was a standard step deal, and Cairns was due a good chunk of change at the completion of principal photography. But since he wouldn't be around for that, he asked Resnick to advance him the money, in exchange for the printout. He didn't intend to inform Resnick he was walking until he got the money in his hands, knowing full well Resnick wouldn't give it to him. In the meantime, he was calling all the actresses whose finest moments he had captured on videotape and informed them of the existence of the tapes. He asked them for 'loans,' promising to repay them in full, but that was just an attempt to sugar-coat what it really was—blackmail. The amounts varied according to the victim's ability to pay. Some actresses had made the big time and were able to pay more. Only Cairns never had a chance to pass the collection plate. He was killed first.''

Adrianne Covert twisted the hem of her skirt. She looked as if she might start to scream at any time. I whirled around and tossed a fastball at Marla: "Where is your gun?"

She blinked. "I don't know."

"What do you mean, you don't know?"

"I can't find it," she said. "It was right here yesterday in my purse, but it was missing last night."

"You didn't say anything about it at dinner."

"I might have," she said venomously, "but if you remember, you wanted to talk about other things."

I let that go and turned back to Adrianne. "Cairns called you up that night and told you he wanted to see you. You went over there and he told you he was firing you. But not only that, he also told you about the audition tape he'd made of you. Only he didn't ask you for money. He had bigger plans for that tape. You'd made his life hell for weeks, and in repayment, he was going to ruin your career permanently. He wanted to tell you that personally, to see the reaction on your face. His sexual tastes weren't the only sadistic thing about the man. He never anticipated that you would get the last laugh by slipping him a mickey and tying him up on the bed."

Adrianne's face contorted spasmodically and tears welled up in her eyes. "I didn't mean to *kill* him," she wailed. "Really I didn't. All I wanted to do was get back at him. When he didn't show up on the set the next morning, I knew the production office would send someone over to his house to find out what the trouble was. I just wanted them to find him like that, for him to look stupid. I didn't know he would roll off the bed and kill himself."

I looked over at McDonald and smiled smugly. "Oh ye of little faith."

He grunted and asked skeptically: "Cairns must have weighed at least one-eighty. How did you manage to lug his body all the way into the bedroom and onto the bed?"

Susanne Capasco jumped up before Adrianne could answer. "Don't say anything until I get a lawyer here."

McDonald nodded tiredly. He began reciting Adrianne her rights, but the girl cut him off: "I don't want a lawyer! I want this over with. I can't go on like this anymore." She sniffled and said: "I didn't have to lug him anywhere. He went himself. He thought I was going to ball him. I made him think that, that I was begging him not to fire me. He liked that, the bastard."

"So then you dressed him in women's lingerie and used his own bondage equipment to tie him to the bed," I offered.

She nodded like a marionette. "Yes."

"And handcuffed him—"

She turned her wild, teary eyes on me and shouted: "Yes! Yes! I told you! How many times do I have to say it? I did it!"

"How?" I asked. "In front or in back?"

Her crazed look turned to one of incomprehension. "Huh?"

"Did you cuff his hands in front of him or behind him?"

She searched her memory for a moment, and said: "Behind, I think. Yeah, I'm sure it was behind because I remember I didn't want there to be any chance he'd be able to get loose."

I glanced at McDonald. "Those were the impressions the coroner found on Cairns' back. He'd been lying on the cuffs."

"What are you saying," McDonald asked derisively, "that while he was knocked out, Cairns unlocked the cuffs and switched them around to the front?"

"No. I'm saying somebody else did."

"But why?" Marla piped up. Resnick and Fields were very quiet, staring at Adrianne with open mouths.

"To make it look as if Cairns died accidentally," I explained, as if it were elementary, and she was my Watson. "Suicides don't hang themselves from their bedposts. They do it so their feet don't touch the ground. And nobody into autoerotic asphyxia would cuff his hands behind his back. It would be too dangerous, in case something went wrong. The object of the whole experience, after all, is to live through it." I turned back to Adrianne, who had stopped crying. "That night, when you got back to the hotel, did you tell anybody what you'd done?"

"Don't say anything," Susanne Capasco said, tight-lipped. Her head whirled around like Linda Blair's in *The Exorcist*, and stopped on McDonald. She growled like Linda Blair too: "I *demand* to have a lawyer present."

McDonald shrugged helplessly. "The girl has waived her right to a lawyer, Miss Capasco—"

The agent bit her lip and looked away.

"You went back to the hotel and told Susanne Capasco," I said. "And what did she do?"

"She went over there," Adrianne said listlessly.

"In your car," I led her.

She nodded.

"What is all this supposed to prove?" Susanne Capasco demanded.

I faced her. "It was you I saw leaving the hotel that night."

"So what if it was?" she asked belligerently. "Cairns was dead when I got there."

"Not according to the coroner," I said. "According to him, those marks on his back were made when the man was still alive."

That tripped her up a bit. "So? Ten people could have gone in that house before I got there—"

"But ten people didn't," I said. "Just you. Maybe Adrianne was willing to let Cairns flush all those years of sweat and sacrifice down the toilet, but not you. You wanted the success and stardom—even if it was vicarious—more than she did. So when you saw Walter Cairns lying on the bed passed out, just like Adrianne said, you switched the cuffs and rolled him off the bed. It was easy. Then you went back and told Adrianne the terrible news, that Cairns was dead and she was responsible. That gave you something you've been needing, a hold over her, something you could use to make her straighten up and perform—in the movie and other ways."

Adrianne looked up, bewildered. "Susanne, is that true?"

"Of course not, honey," the woman assured her, patting her arm with a leather-gloved hand.

"You two have been lovers since the girl was sixteen, isn't that true, Adrianne? She probably broke you into that act, too, didn't she?"

The girl began to cry again, and buried her head in her hands. Susanne Capasco's eyes glowed like hot, hateful coals, but they didn't slow me up; I was on a roll. "But lately, Susanne's grip began to slip. Adrianne had started to find men interesting—"

"I don't have to listen to this crap," the agent snarled, and took a step toward the door, but McDonald moved in her way and did some snarling of his own: "You're not going anywhere, sister. Nobody is. Sit down."

She sat and I addressed the coup de grâce to her: "The next morning, you rented a car, drove to Malibu, and got the tape. It was all neat and tidy until Dart told you he'd seen you at Cairns' place that night. At the time, of course, he didn't know Cairns had been murdered, but when he found out, it might get sticky, so he had to go too. You killed him and set it up to make it look like he'd killed Cairns, then committed suicide, a bill of goods you would later sell Adrianne to alleviate her conscience. That was one thing that tipped me. Only an agent could cut a man's throat like that."

Adrianne was staring at her in wide-eyed astonishment, as was everyone else in the room. "Susanne, how could you—"

The agent waved a gloved hand in the air. "This is absurd—"

"Is it?" I asked Adrianne: "She sent you to see me yesterday afternoon, didn't she? She wanted you to find out how much I knew and to feed me that cock-and-bull story about a mystery boyfriend, to try to get me to keep my mouth shut."

The girl nodded, dully, still seeming to have trouble grasping the significance of what was going on.

"When she found out I knew too much, she knew she had to get rid of me too. She knew Marla carried a gun, and yesterday afternoon, while she was shooting a scene, Susanne snuck in here and stole it from her purse. She came trick-or-treating to my room last night and nearly succeeded in canceling all my future Halloweens, but botched it." I held out my hand to Susanne Capasco. "May I have your purse, please?"

The woman grinned, but she was breathing heavily, her nostrils flaring with each breath like those of a laboring horse. She kept her hate-filled eyes on me while she handed me her Louis Vuitton bag. I passed it over to McDonald, who unzipped it and began to go through it.

"Would you stand up, please?" I asked her.

She shrugged and stood up, and I pulled the seat cushion off the chair. There was a collective gasp from the room as all eyes came to rest on the shiny nickel-plated .32. "Gee, golly-willikens," I said, "I wonder how that got there?" I took a pen from my inside pocket, picked it up by the barrel and sniffed. "And recently fired too."

McDonald began his recitation again, and again he was cut off, this time by Susanne Capasco, who sneered. "Try and prove I put it there. Try and prove anything."

"I noticed you were wearing gloves," I said. "I imagine

you wiped all the prints off before you put it in your purse.
But proving anything is the D.A.'s job, not mine. One thing
is for sure, though, no matter what they prove or don't—"

"Yeah?" she challenged. "What's that, Mr. Hotshot
Detective?"

I smiled at her. "You'll never work in this town again.
Right, Marty baby?"

26

I checked out of the International the next morning, turned in
the BMW with a twinge of sadness, and drove my Plymouth
through a flawless day, past the toll gate where Marla had first
taken me, out the rutted concrete ribbon that wound up
through the hills that belonged to the richest Indian tribe in
the world.

They were set up by a trading post that sold soft drinks and
postcards overlooking the canyon. I parked and spotted
Marla among the bustle of the crew, standing by the railing
that ran along the edge of the steep side of the canyon, and
walked over. The canyon was packed with Washington palms
that extended as far as the eye could see, which was pretty
far.

"Hi," I said.

She looked up and smiled. "Hi. How is your side?"

"All right. How is your privacy?"

"Almost back to normal." She hesitated. "I'm sorry I lost
my temper—"

"Forget it. You were entitled."

"What's happening with Susanne?"

"They found the Halloween mask in her room and they've

charged her with attempted murder, but they don't know if they'll be able to make the murder charges stick."

She looked dumbfounded. "You mean she's going to get off?"

I shrugged. "There isn't a lot of solid evidence tying her to either Cairns' or Dart's death. If the D.A. doesn't think he can get a conviction, he might not bother with it. How is Adrianne doing?"

"Fine, now that she knows she didn't kill anybody. So well, in fact, that it looks like we'll get a wrap early next week."

"What are you going to do then?"

"My agent just got an offer for a feature that starts shooting in Barbados in two weeks. I told her to take it. It's another T and A flick, but I can use the money."

I wondered if they would ever let her make the transition she wanted—to actress—or would keep her in T and A roles until the Ts and the A sagged a little too much, then discard her, leaving her to become a plump, mottle-faced entry in one of those "Where Are They Now?" books that the public finds so fascinating. "Well, good luck. I just dropped by to say good-bye. I'm going back to L.A."

She nodded and bit her lip, uncertainly. "Does McDonald know about the tape I burned?"

"No."

She nodded and smiled and held out her hand. "Thanks."

We shook hands, a rather unintimate gesture, it struck me, considering the intimacy we had shared, or was it intimacy at all? Strangely enough, she seemed as distant and remote to me now as before I had met her, when she had been just an image on a screen. I didn't know her, but then she didn't know me, either. Pieces, that was all anyone ever knew.

About a mile down the road, I pulled over and got out of the car. The sky was bright blue, the visibility was fifty miles, the light-dappled landscape seared clean by the sun and unspoiled by the aluminum cans and Twinkie wrappers of civilization. This must have been what it looked like before the Hollywood crowd had come seeking sanctuary from the lights and the star-crazed fans, the Gables and the Flynns and the Crosbys and the Crawfords, who had come to swim and bake and ride horses through the desert and stare at the stars around open campfires. The ones who had made it and survived. The Peg Entwistles had stayed back in L.A.

A roadrunner darted out from behind a creosote bush and paused, long enough to give me a circumspect stare, before taking off across the road in his comic, Groucho Marx way. A lizard skittered from underneath a clump of cholla, did a couple of pushups, and disappeared into a hole a few feet away. I looked around at the cacti, the stubborn sagebrush, inhaled the smells of the desert flowers, listened to the birds and the humming of the insects, and suddenly—for the first time, really—I felt comfortable here, as if I understood its essence. The desert was a survival school, where only the tough, the cunning, and the quick lived to graduate.

I took my mortarboard and went home.

MORE MYSTERIOUS PLEASURES

JAMES M. CAIN
THE ENCHANTED ISLE
A beautiful runaway is involved in a deadly bank robbery in this posthumously published novel.   #415 $3.95

CLOUD NINE
Two brothers—one good, one evil—battle over a million-dollar land deal and a luscious 16-year-old in this posthumously published novel.
#507 $3.95

ROBERT CAMPBELL
IN LA-LA LAND WE TRUST
Child porn, snuff films, and drunken TV stars in fast cars—that's what makes the L.A. world go 'round. Whistler, a luckless P.I., finds that it's not good to know too much about the porn trade in the City of Angels.
#508 $3.95

GEORGE C. CHESBRO
VEIL
Clairvoyant artist Veil Kendry volunteers to be tested at the Institute for Human Studies and finds that his life is in deadly peril; is he threatened by the Institute, the Army, or the CIA?   #509 $3.95

WILLIAM L. DeANDREA
THE LUNATIC FRINGE
Police Commissioner Teddy Roosevelt and Officer Dennis Muldoon comb 1896 New York for a missing exotic dancer who holds the key to the murder of a prominent political cartoonist.   #306 $3.95

SNARK
Espionage agent Bellman must locate the missing director of British Intelligence—and elude a master terrorist who has sworn to kill him.
#510 $3.50

KILLED IN THE ACT
Brash, witty Matt Cobb, TV network troubleshooter, must contend with bizarre crimes connected with a TV spectacular—one of which is a murder committed before 40 million witnesses.   #511 $3.50

KILLED WITH A PASSION
In seeking to clear an old college friend of murder, Matt Cobb must deal with the Mad Karate Killer and the Organic Hit Man, among other eccentric criminals.   #512 $3.50

KILLED ON THE ICE
When a famous psychiatrist is stabbed in a Manhattan skating rink, Matt Cobb finds it necessary to protect a beautiful Olympic skater who appears to be the next victim.   #513 $3.50

JAMES ELLROY
SUICIDE HILL
Brilliant L.A. Police sergeant Lloyd Hopkins teams up with the FBI to solve a series of inside bank robberies—but is he working with or against them?   #514 $3.95

PAUL ENGLEMAN
CATCH A FALLEN ANGEL
Private eye Mark Renzler becomes involved in publishing mayhem and murder when two slick mens' magazines battle for control of the lucrative market.   #515 $3.50

LOREN D. ESTLEMAN
ROSES ARE DEAD
Someone's put a contract out on freelance hit man Peter Macklin. Is he as good as the killers on his trail?   #516 $3.95

ANY MAN'S DEATH
Hit man Peter Macklin is engaged to keep a famous television evangelist *alive*—quite a switch from his normal line.   #517 $3.95

DICK FRANCIS
THE SPORT OF QUEENS
The autobiography of the celebrated race jockey/crime novelist.
                                                                    #410 $3.95

JOHN GARDNER
THE GARDEN OF WEAPONS
Big Herbie Kruger returns to East Berlin to uncover a double agent. He confronts his own past and life's only certainty—death.
                                                                    #103 $4.50

BRIAN GARFIELD
DEATH WISH
Paul Benjamin is a modern-day New York vigilante, stalking the rapist-killers who victimized his wife and daughter. The basis for the Charles Bronson movie.   #301 $3.95

DEATH SENTENCE
A riveting sequel to *Death Wish*. The action moves to Chicago as Paul Benjamin continues his heroic (or is it psychotic?) mission to make city streets safe.   #302 $3.95

TRIPWIRE
A crime novel set in the American West of the late 1800s. Boag, a black outlaw, seeks revenge on the white cohorts who left him for dead. "One of the most compelling characters in recent fiction."—Robert Ludlum.   #303 $3.95

FEAR IN A HANDFUL OF DUST
Four psychiatrists, three men and a woman, struggle across the blazing Arizona desert—pursued by a fanatic killer they themselves have judged insane. "Unique and disturbing."—Alfred Coppel.   #304 $3.95

JOE GORES
A TIME OF PREDATORS
When Paula Halstead kills herself after witnessing a horrid crime, her husband vows to avenge her death. Winner of the Edgar Allan Poe Award. #215 $3.95

COME MORNING
Two million in diamonds are at stake, and the ex-con who knows their whereabouts may have trouble staying alive if he turns them up at the wrong moment. #518 $3.95

NAT HENTOFF
BLUES FOR CHARLIE DARWIN
Gritty, colorful Greenwich Village sets the scene for Noah Green and Sam McKibbon, two street-wise New York cops who are as at home in jazz clubs as they are at a homicide scene. #208 $3.95

THE MAN FROM INTERNAL AFFAIRS
Detective Noah Green wants to know who's stuffing corpses into East Village garbage cans . . . and who's lying about him to the Internal Affairs Division. #409 $3.95

PATRICIA HIGHSMITH
THE BLUNDERER
An unhappy husband attempts to kill his wife by applying the murderous methods of another man. When things go wrong, he pays a visit to the more successful killer—a dreadful error. #305 $3.95

DOUG HORNIG
THE DARK SIDE
Insurance detective Loren Swift is called to a rural commune to investigate a carbon-monoxide murder. Are the commune inhabitants as gentle as they seem? #519 $3.95

P.D. JAMES/T.A. CRITCHLEY
THE MAUL AND THE PEAR TREE
The noted mystery novelist teams up with a police historian to create a fascinating factual account of the 1811 Ratcliffe Highway murders. #520 $3.95

STUART KAMINSKY'S "TOBY PETERS" SERIES
NEVER CROSS A VAMPIRE
When Bela Lugosi receives a dead bat in the mail, Toby tries to catch the prankster. But Toby's time is at a premium because he's also trying to clear William Faulkner of a murder charge! #107 $3.95

HIGH MIDNIGHT
When Gary Cooper and Ernest Hemingway come to Toby for protection, he tries to save them from vicious blackmailers.   #106 $3.95

HE DONE HER WRONG
Someone has stolen Mae West's autobiography, and when she asks Toby to come up and see her sometime, he doesn't know how deadly a visit it could be.   #105 $3.95

BULLET FOR A STAR
Warner Brothers hires Toby Peters to clear the name of Errol Flynn, a blackmail victim with a penchant for young girls. The first novel in the acclaimed Hollywood-based private eye series.   #308 $3.95

THE FALA FACTOR
Toby comes to the rescue of lady-in-distress Eleanor Roosevelt, and must match wits with a right-wing fanatic who is scheming to overthrow the U.S. Government.   #309 $3.95

JOSEPH KOENIG
FLOATER
Florida Everglades sheriff Buck White matches wits with a Miami murder-and-larceny team who just may have hidden his ex-wife's corpse in a remote bayou.   #521 $3.50

ELMORE LEONARD
THE HUNTED
Long out of print, this 1974 novel by the author of *Glitz* details the attempts of a man to escape killers from his past.   #401 $3.95

MR. MAJESTYK
Sometimes bad guys can push a good man too far, and when that good guy is a Special Forces veteran, everyone had better duck.   #402 $3.95

THE BIG BOUNCE
Suspense and black comedy are cleverly combined in this tale of a dangerous drifter's affair with a beautiful woman out for kicks.   #403 $3.95

ELSA LEWIN
I, ANNA
A recently divorced woman commits murder to avenge her degradation at the hands of a sleazy lothario.   #522 $3.50

THOMAS MAXWELL
KISS ME ONCE
An epic *roman noir* which explores the romantic but seamy underworld of New York during the WWII years. When the good guys are off fighting in Europe, the bad guys run amok in America.
    #523 $3.95

ED McBAIN
ANOTHER PART OF THE CITY
The master of the police procedural moves from the fictional 87th precinct to the gritty reality of Manhattan. "McBain's best in several years."—*San Francisco Chronicle*.   #524 $3.95

SNOW WHITE AND ROSE RED
A beautiful heiress confined to a sanitarium engages Matthew Hope to free her—and her $650,000.   #414 $3.95

CINDERELLA
A dead detective and a hot young hooker lead Matthew Hope into a multi-layered plot among Miami cocaine dealers. "A gem of sting and countersting."—*Time*.   #525 $3.95

PETER O'DONNELL
MODESTY BLAISE
Modesty and Willie Garvin must protect a shipment of diamonds from a gentleman about to murder his lover and an *un*civilized sheik.   #216 $3.95

SABRE TOOTH
Modesty faces Willie's apparent betrayal and a modern-day Genghis Khan who wants her for his mercenary army.   #217 $3.95

A TASTE FOR DEATH
Modesty and Willie are pitted against a giant enemy in the Sahara, where their only hope of escape is a blind girl whose time is running out.   #218 $3.95

I, LUCIFER
Some people carry a nickname too far . . . like the maniac calling himself Lucifer. He's targeted 120 souls, and Modesty and Willie find they have a personal stake in stopping him.   #219 $3.95

THE IMPOSSIBLE VIRGIN
Modesty fights for her soul when she and Willie attempt to rescue an albino girl from the evil Brunel, who lusts after the secret power of an idol called the Impossible Virgin.   #220 $3.95

DEAD MAN'S HANDLE
Modesty Blaise must deal with a brainwashed—and deadly—Willie Garvin as well as with a host of outré religion-crazed villains.
                                    #526 $3.95

ELIZABETH PETERS
CROCODILE ON THE SANDBANK
Amelia Peabody's trip to Egypt brings her face to face with an ancient mystery. With the help of Radcliffe Emerson, she uncovers a tomb and the solution to a deadly threat.   #209 $3.95

THE CURSE OF THE PHAROAHS
Amelia and Radcliffe Emerson head for Egypt to excavate a cursed tomb but must confront the burial ground's evil history before it claims them both.   #210 $3.95

THE SEVENTH SINNER
Murder in an ancient subterranean Roman temple sparks Jacqueline Kirby's first recorded case.   #411 $3.95

THE MURDERS OF RICHARD III
Death by archaic means haunts the costumed weekend get-together of a group of eccentric Ricardians.   #412 $3.95

ANTHONY PRICE
THE LABYRINTH MAKERS
Dr. David Audley does his job too well in his first documented case, embarrassing British Intelligence, the CIA, and the KGB in one swoop.   #404 $3.95

THE ALAMUT AMBUSH
Alamut, in Northern Persia, is considered by many to be the original home of terrorism. Audley moves to the Mideast to put the cap on an explosive threat.   #405 $3.95

COLONEL BUTLER'S WOLF
The Soviets are recruiting spies from among Oxford's best and brightest; it's up to Dr. Audley to identify the Russian wolf in don's clothing.   #527 $3.95

OCTOBER MEN
Dr. Audley's "holiday" in Rome stirs up old Intelligence feuds and echoes of partisan warfare during World War II—and leads him into new danger.   #529 $3.95

OTHER PATHS TO GLORY
What can a World War I battlefield in France have in common with a deadly secret of the present? A modern assault on Bouillet Wood leads to the answers.   #530 $3.95

SION CROSSING
What does the chairman of a new NATO-like committee have to do with the American Civil War? Audley travels to Georgia in this espionage thriller.   #406 $3.95

HERE BE MONSTERS
The assassination of an American veteran forces Dr. David Audley into a confrontation with undercover KGB agents.   #528 $3.95

BILL PRONZINI AND JOHN LUTZ
THE EYE
A lunatic watches over the residents of West 98th Street with a powerful telescope. When his "children" displease him, he is swift to mete out deadly punishment.   #408 $3.95

PATRICK RUELL
RED CHRISTMAS
Murderers and political terrorists come down the chimney during an old-fashioned Dickensian Christmas at a British country inn.

#531 $3.50

DEATH TAKES THE LOW ROAD
William Hazlitt, a universtiy administrator who moonlights as a Soviet mole, is on the run from both Russian and British agents who want him to assassinate an African general.   #532 $3.50

DELL SHANNON
CASE PENDING
In the first novel in the best-selling series, Lt. Luis Mendoza must solve a series of horrifying Los Angeles mutilation murders.   #211 $3.95

THE ACE OF SPADES
When the police find an overdosed junkie, they're ready to write off the case—until the autopsy reveals that this junkie *wasn't* a junkie.   #212 $3.95

EXTRA KILL
In "The Temple of Mystic Truth," Mendoza discovers idol worship, pornography, murder, and the clue to the death of a Los Angeles patrolman.   #213 $3.95

KNAVE OF HEARTS
Mendoza must clear the name of the L.A.P.D. when it's discovered that an innocent man has been executed and the real killer is still on the loose.   #214 $3.95

DEATH OF A BUSYBODY
When the West Coast's most industrious gossip and meddler turns up dead in a freight yard, Mendoza must work without clues to find the killer of a woman who had offended nearly everyone in Los Angeles.   #315 $3.95

DOUBLE BLUFF
Mendoza goes against the evidence to dissect what looks like an air-tight case against suspected wife-killer Francis Ingram—a man the lieutenant insists is too nice to be a murderer.   #316 $3.95

MARK OF MURDER
Mendoza investigates the near-fatal attack on an old friend as well as trying to track down an insane serial killer.   #417 $3.95

ROOT OF ALL EVIL
The murder of a "nice" girl leads Mendoza to team up with the FBI in the search for her not-so-nice boyfriend—a Soviet agent.   #418 $3.95

JULIE SMITH
TRUE-LIFE ADVENTURE
Paul McDonald earned a meager living ghosting reports for a San Francisco private eye until the gumshoe turned up dead . . . now the killers are after him. #407 $3.95

TOURIST TRAP
A lunatic is out to destroy San Francisco's tourism industry; can feisty lawyer/sleuth Rebecca Schwartz stop him while clearing an innocent man of a murder charge? #533 $3.95

ROSS H. SPENCER
THE MISSING BISHOP
Chicago P.I. Buzz Deckard has a missing person to find. Unfortunately his client has disappeared as well, and no one else seems to be who or what they claim. #416 $3.50

MONASTERY NIGHTMARE
Chicago P.I. Luke Lassiter tries his hand at writing novels, and encounters murder in an abandoned monastery. #534 $3.50

REX STOUT
UNDER THE ANDES
A long-lost 1914 fantasy novel from the creator of the immortal Nero Wolfe series. "The most exciting yarn we have read since *Tarzan of the Apes.*"—*All-Story Magazine.* #419 $3.50

ROSS THOMAS
CAST A YELLOW SHADOW
McCorkle's wife is kidnapped by agents of the South African government. The ransom—his cohort Padillo must assassinate their prime minister. #535 $3.95

THE SINGAPORE WINK
Ex-Hollywood stunt man Ed Cauthorne is offered $25,000 to search for colleague Angelo Sacchetti—a man he thought he'd killed in Singapore two years earlier. #536 $3.95

THE FOOLS IN TOWN ARE ON OUR SIDE
Lucifer Dye, just resigned from a top secret U.S. Intelligence post, accepts a princely fee to undertake the corruption of an entire American city. #537 $3.95

JIM THOMPSON
THE KILL-OFF
Luanne Devore was loathed by everyone in her small New England town. Her plots and designs threatened to destroy them—unless they destroyed her first. #538 $3.95

DONALD E. WESTLAKE
THE HOT ROCK
The unlucky master thief John Dortmunder debuts in this spectacular caper novel. How many times do you have to steal an emerald to make sure it *stays* stolen?   #539 $3.95

BANK SHOT
Dortmunder and company return. A bank is temporarily housed in a trailer, so why not just hook it up and make off with the whole shebang? Too bad nothing is ever that simple.   #540 $3.95

THE BUSY BODY
Aloysius Engel is a gangster, the Big Man's right hand. So when he's ordered to dig a suit loaded with drugs out of a fresh grave, how come the corpse it's wrapped around won't lie still?   #541 $3.95

THE SPY IN THE OINTMENT
Pacifist agitator J. Eugene Raxford is mistakenly listed as a terrorist by the FBI, which leads to his enforced recruitment to a group bent on world domination. Will very good Good triumph over absolutely villainous Evil?   #542 $3.95

GOD SAVE THE MARK
Fred Fitch is the sucker's sucker—con men line up to bilk him. But when he inherits $300,000 from a murdered uncle, he finds it necessary to dodge killers as well as hustlers.   #543 $3.95

TERI WHITE
TIGHTROPE
This second novel featuring L.A. cops Blue Maguire and Spaceman Kowalski takes them into the nooks and crannies of the city's Little Saigon.   #544 $3.95

COLLIN WILCOX
VICTIMS
Lt. Frank Hastings investigates the murder of a police colleague in the home of a powerful—and nasty—San Francisco attorney.
                                                    #413 $3.95

NIGHT GAMES
Lt. Frank Hastings of the San Francisco Police returns to investigate the at-home death of an unfaithful husband—whose affairs have led to his murder.   #545 $3.95

DAVID WILLIAMS' "MARK TREASURE" SERIES
UNHOLY WRIT
London financier Mark Treasure helps a friend reacquire some property. He stays to unravel the mystery when a Shakespeare manuscript is discovered and foul murder done.   #112 $3.95

TREASURE BY DEGREES
Mark Treasure discovers there's nothing funny about a board game called "Funny Farms." When he becomes involved in the takeover struggle for a small university, he also finds there's nothing funny about murder.   #113 $3.95